# LYLA DAVIS

## Trusting Her Heart

*Dedicated to all the women who have endured
the pain of verbal, emotional, or physical abuse
at the hand of the person they trusted and loved.
I wrote this book to help those who needed to know
there is sunshine at the end of a storm,
and that they are not alone.*

*My hope is that verbal and emotional abuse will
one day be seen as just as damaging as physical abuse is,
and that there will be help for those who need it.*

*You are stronger than you know!
My love to you all.*

# Chapter One

Luke Benson rubbed his eyes as he sat up to start another day. The bright summer sun was trying to peek through the heavy clouds in the gloomy Seattle sky. It was a typical workday morning in Seattle… one that would start with some sun in the morning, lighting his latest building project, followed by a light rain falling and dark clouds filling the sky by afternoon. As Luke looked around the quaint bedroom, he grunted his concession to the morning and rolled to the side of the bed to get on with his day. He stood slowly, stretching his stiff, aching muscles. Today, it seemed he could feel the weight of his muscular body as he moved, every step making him question his choice of such a physical occupation.

Luke walked into the bathroom and looked at his reflection in the mirror. His sandy-blond hair was kept short in the same military cut his mother had chosen for him as a child, and his tanned skin gave him a rugged appearance. His blue eyes were still full of sleep and his face adorned with a fresh layer of dark stubble. Rubbing his chin with his hand, he decided he'd have to shave it later, as he was running late this morning. He splashed some water on his face to wake himself up a little more before brushing his teeth and heading back to the bedroom to get dressed for the day.

Seattle weather was typically unpredictable at best, so he always settled for a t-shirt with a flannel shirt covering it in case he needed the extra layer. Luke loved flannel shirts… they were practical and made him look sexy, at least it did in *his* mind. This morning was no exception. He reached into his closet and pulled out a light blue fishing tee and one of his favorite flannels- a white and deep blue one that he had bought himself a few years before at his favorite sporting goods store in the city. He also grabbed a pair of jeans that fit him perfectly, sliding over his work boots as if the jeans had been made for them. He carried the clothes over to the bed and sat down to get dressed, still trying to fully wake up and submit to the start of the day. Yawning, he slipped into his jeans and then threw his tee on and tucked it in.

In cooler weather like today, he often wore his flannel shirt with the buttons unbuttoned, providing a glimpse of the tee underneath, sometimes even adding a vest over top that could quickly be removed later after it got warmer. Today he decided against the vest, lacing up his work boots and heading back to the mirror for one more glance. Satisfied with his appearance, he let out a heavy breath, heading out of the bedroom, feeling ready to tackle whatever the day had in store for him. He walked past the living room and turned the small TV on in the corner of the kitchen as he headed over to the small wooden table that sat in the opposite corner. The table sat by a large window looking out over the front yard. Sadie, his wife, was already up and about, as usual. He lazily looked up to see what she was doing, both curious and annoyed by her humming as she worked. He preferred quiet as he enjoyed his morning coffee with breakfast.

Sadie Benson was of average build, standing a little over five and a half feet tall. Her fair skin was sprinkled with freckles, and her shoulder-length brown hair had a slight hint of auburn that got brighter in the sunlight. Her blue eyes had a way of looking right into a person's soul, which really irritated Luke. He wished that she would just do her job and take care of things at home and let him do his own thing. He already had a mother, and he didn't need another one. As she moved around the kitchen, he noticed that she wore her reading glasses, which meant she had probably been reading the newspaper that morning. As much as her singing was bothering him, he did have to admit that she was cute in those glasses. Her teeth peeked out in a hesitant smile as she noticed Luke looking at her. He refocused his gaze out the window and she returned to making his morning coffee.

Sadie was low-maintenance and preferred a simple and comfortable style. Today, she chose a pair of jeans and a comfy top that suited her laid-back demeanor. Her shy face brightened with a smile as she handed Luke his coffee and a plate of steak and eggs. She knew he loved a hearty breakfast before starting his day, and she always made sure to take care of him in this small, affectionate way. She wanted to make him happy… it was so much easier for everyone when he was happy. She went to a nearby seat at the table and sat while he ate. She loved sitting in that spot and watching the birds in the feeders outside the window. They seemed so carefree and oblivious to the worries of the world around them. Today she smiled as a hummingbird flew past, seeming to have somewhere to get to, with too little time to stop and visit the feeder hanging from the beautiful pink flowering crab tree out front.

In their charming Seattle home, the couple's morning routine played out like a well-rehearsed dance. Luke sipped on his coffee, savoring the taste and warmth, while Sadie enjoyed her tea. She exchanged soft smiles and words of encouragement with Hazel, her 4-year-old daughter who was playing on the floor of the room, their connection evident in the simple gestures they shared. Hazel was playing with her favorite tea set near her mother's feet. She pretended to serve tea to her stuffed animals that were spread around the small room.

"More coffee?" Sadie asked Luke who was just finishing his last bites of steak.

"Yeah," he answered, his eyes fixed on the TV in the corner. Sadie grabbed the pot from the counter. As she stepped towards Luke to pour the coffee, she felt a sharp pain under her left foot. She lunged forward and the coffee spilled onto the table. Before she could react, it flowed over the side of the table and landed on Luke's shirt and lap. He yelped with anger and pain as it soaked his work clothes. "Son of a-" he yelled.

"Oh, my goodness! I'm so sorry! Are you okay? Here, let me get that." Sadie Benson was a quick apologizer, fearing the impending temper that would follow. Instinctively so, she grabbed the towel and started to wipe at Luke's shirt.

"You don't seriously think you can get rid of coffee stains with a towel, do you? Are you really that stupid? I was already running late, and now because of *you* I'm probably going to get into trouble! You wouldn't understand that though, would you? I go to work and put in a full day trying to provide for this family, and you just sit here all day doing nothing! Still, the least you could do is stay out of the way and not make things even worse for me!"

"I'm sorry." Sadie looked up at him apologetically, the tears welling in her eyes. She should have been more careful, and now her husband was disappointed in her, and angered by her clumsiness. She hated that she always screwed up and made him so mad. He was happy in the beginning, or it seemed like he had been anyway! She couldn't figure out how she had messed up so badly and made him so unhappy with her. With slouched shoulders, she started to walk toward the kitchen, her hands shaky and her heart pounding loudly in her ears. Silently, she prayed that the hurtful words would be the end of it.

She was wrong.

"Where do you think you're going?" Luke said in a low tone. With apprehension, Sadie turned to face her angry husband.

"To get a soapy cloth and try to clean off the stain." she answered quietly.

Luke glared at her. "I just told you that won't work. Why don't you do something useful for once and go get me a new shirt to wear!" he said in a tone that was all too familiar to her. Sadie glanced over at Hazel who was staring at them, startled and scared. At some point during the confrontation their family dog, Cliff, had come into the room and was sitting next to Hazel with his ears perked in curiosity. The only thing that mattered to her in the moment was avoiding a fight in front of Hazel. She knew he'd blame her for putting Hazel through that, just as he always did. She mustered up a smile and nodded at Luke. She left quickly and came back holding a neatly ironed black and red flannel shirt to replace the white and blue one she'd just spilled coffee on.

"You know, for a full-grown woman, you sure are clumsy. How many times have I told you that those toys and stuffed animals need to be picked up. She can play without having it all out at once, and she'll never learn to clean up after herself if you don't stop babying her! I work hard all day and I shouldn't have to come home and work here too."

"She's just a child, Luke. She likes to play with those things and be close to us too. She doesn't understand why you want to watch TV instead of play with her." Sadie replied quickly. She just wished Luke would see that she meant to make him happy, not upset. Hazel just wanted to play with her things, and she didn't understand why that bothered him so much.

Luke got up swiftly and grabbed her arm, the stench of his coffee breath blowing into her face. "And what is that supposed to mean? You are at fault here! You let her litter toys around the house without ever considering the possibility that someone might trip over them. You spilled coffee on me, and now you want to make it sound like it's my fault? Really?"

The tension had thickened in the room. Hazel had begun to cry, and Cliff had started barking as he sensed something was wrong. Suddenly, it felt like all of Seattle was being pressed into one tiny room.

"Shut that mutt up!" Luke yelled, directing even more anger towards her.

"I'm sorry Luke, that's not what I was trying to say. I know it's my fault. I should have kept the toys picked up, and I should have been more careful. Please stop yelling. I'm sorry." Sadie pleaded, but Luke's grip only got tighter. Wincing from the pain, she pleaded, "You're hurting me, Luke, please, I'm sorry. I promise I'll keep things picked up better, just please stop." Luke let go and backed away. For a second she thought it was over. Then, before she knew what was happening, she felt the back of Luke's hand hit her face with a force that knocked her onto the floor of the kitchen, just missing the counter on her way down. As her head hit the floor, she felt the impact so hard that she could see stars everywhere. She lay there attempting to blink them away, trying to figure out what was happening.

"Next time you should listen to what I say and stop making such dumb mistakes!" he commanded, looking down at her with disgust in his eyes, while she lay on the hard wooden floor still trying to blink away the clouds and the throbbing in her head. His rage was strong, and no matter how hard Hazel cried from the next room where she had gone to hide, she was too tiny to do any good. He firmly told her to "shut up!" and left the room. "I hate when you make me mad like that! Now Hazel is upset because of you." he yelled from the hallway. Sadie tried to get up, but the fog wouldn't lift from her hurting head. She prayed Hazel would stay in the other room and that Luke wouldn't hurt her. Suddenly, Sadie saw the front door burst open and she could swear her father was standing there looking larger than life. She tried to focus but she couldn't make the figure out. Hearing ringing all around her, she closed her eyes and succumbed to her head's screaming, falling into the deep darkness inside her eyelids.

* * *

Sadie's eyes slowly opened, and she felt as though a truck had parked itself directly on her head. Confusion clouded her brain as she tried to figure out where she was and what was happening. She could feel the warmth of the sun shining in the window as the light made it hard for her to make out the room around her. As her eyes began to adjust to the light and the room slowly came into focus, she realized she was in the hospital. She could feel a weight at her hip and gingerly looked down to find Hazel lying there, clinging tightly to her favorite teddy bear. Beside her, sitting ever so quietly, with his head against Hazel's legs, was Cliff. Both looked up at her with such love and worry as they saw her come back to life beside them. Next to both was her mother, gently rubbing Hazel's back to comfort her.

"Mommy?" Hazel's tiny voice echoed in her waking mind. Sadie smiled, wanting to show her little girl that she was okay. Cliff let out a hesitant bark, which meant in his own language that he was happy to see her awake. Moving closer to Sadie, Cliff enjoyed the feel of her hand on his head as she reached down to pet him and assure him everything was okay.

"Hello sweet pea," she said to Hazel, touching her tiny cheek with her hand. "Mommy's okay, I promise."

"Good morning, Sadie." her mother said, smiling with relief at her daughter's awakening. "We were all very worried about you!"

"You were out a while there," a familiar male voice said from a chair in the corner. The fear associated with a masculine voice jerked her up, causing her to flinch from the pain in her head, but she realized quickly that it was her father, not Luke. Henry Archer crossed the room and gave his daughter a warm and familiar hug, making her feel safe and reminiscent of her childhood innocence. "I'm sorry I didn't get to you sooner. I called an ambulance and got you here as quickly as I could. I thought we might lose you there for a minute," he said with a sadness in his voice.

"Oh, daddy," Sadie sighed. "How did you–"

"Hazel called me," Henry said, smiling at Hazel before returning his attention to Sadie. "She sounded scared, and I could hear Luke yelling in the background. As soon as I heard her sweet little voice crying and saying your name, I knew something was wrong and I got there as fast as I could."

Sadie smiled at her daughter, grabbing her and pulling her in for a big hug. "Thank you, sweetheart, you are such a brave little girl… mommy's little hero!"

"I have no idea how she knew how to find my number and call me," he added. "She's never done that before."

"Hazel, how *did* you figure out how to call Grandpa Henry?" she asked her little girl. "I know you know my pass code because we've played little games on it together before, but I've never shown you how to make a phone call with it…"

"It was easy, Mommy… I just looked for that funny picture of Grandpa you have on your phone and pushed the button by it that looks like a phone." Hazel explained, and they all laughed. The purity of her heart and childlikeness was enough to make the pain lessen.

Even though there was no sign of Luke in the hospital room, Sadie still found herself scanning the room for him. He had yelled at her many times before when she messed up, and he had even slapped her before, but he'd never hit her so hard that he had knocked her out before. That was new, and she wasn't sure what to do with that yet.

"He's not here," Henry said, sensing his daughter's worry and knowing what she was probably thinking. He moved closer to her and held her hand in his, giving it a little squeeze. "He won't hurt you again, sweetheart. I just don't understand why you kept all this from me."

Sadie looked up at her father. Henry was a tall, physically fit man, even at his age, who could be very intimidating if he wanted to be. He was retired from the US Army and knew how to command a room, as well as interrogate someone when the need arose. She had been in this position before as a teenager, trying to hide something she had done, knowing full well that he was going to figure it out one way or the other. This time, though, was different. This time, she felt so small and defeated as she tried to figure out how to explain this to him.

"Dad, I'm a grown woman with a family that I am responsible for, and I just didn't–"

"You didn't what? You didn't want me to worry? You didn't want to admit something was wrong? What, Sadie?" he interrupted in a frustrated tone that she was pretty sure stemmed from the fear of knowing he easily could have just lost his daughter.

Sensing the need for some privacy without little ears present, Sadie's mother picked Hazel up and led her from the room. "You know what, Miss Hazel? Grandma is starving! How about you and I go find some breakfast in the cafeteria while Mommy and Grandpa have a little talk. Does that sound good to you?"

"Yes! I'm hungry too! Bye, Mamma!" she said as the two headed for some breakfast. Cliff looked between the little girl and Sadie, not sure what to do.

"Cliff, you stay here and sit. They'll be right back." she said, knowing he was confused.

After they were out of sight, she re-focused her attention on her father. She had to try to find a way to explain all of this to him, but she was having a hard time finding the words.

"I guess I just felt kind of like a failure, Dad. I didn't want to disappoint you and mom. I wanted to prove that I could make my marriage work." she tried to explain.

"We knew you were hiding something from us, we just didn't realize it was this bad. I'm not sure what I expected I guess, but not this." Sadie could see the disappointment on his face, could hear it in his voice. She hated that she was causing him so much inner turmoil, and she hated disappointing him.

"I'm sorry, dad. I just didn't want to cause a bunch of drama or bother you and mom just because I was failing at my marriage. It was my fault, and there was nothing you could have done to prevent it. He doesn't always get that bad, I promise… I just made him mad, and he lost his temper." She looked at her dad and saw him looking down at her with so much sadness in his eyes that she felt like her heart would shatter for causing it.

"You could have *died,* honey," he choked out, a tear falling down his cheek.

"No. I'm *fine*, dad." she said, feeling as though someone had just punched her in the gut, like she had every time she had done something that she knew had disappointed her parents when she was young.

"No, you're not, Sadie! He is a strong man, and he is much larger and stronger than you. If he had hit you just right or you had hit your head on the counter or table or something, it could have been a very different ending. One wrong move that would leave Hazel without a mommy."

"Daddy…"

"Promise me, Sadie," Henry cut in. "Promise me you will *never* hide things from me again. From us, your mother and I.

Promise me, *please*."

Sadie sighed as she turned her gaze to the window. All this seriousness was going on in her room, yet the street seemed busy with people who were oblivious to the cares of others. They were happy and going about their day as if it was any other. For her, though, it was different. For her, life had taken a 180-degree turn, and she wasn't sure what to do with it all. To make matters worse, her actions had affected her family, something she had tried very hard *not* to do. As she thought about what he had said, she suddenly focused in on something he had said in the beginning before asking, "Dad… Earlier, you said that Luke won't hurt me again, what did you mean?"

"That doesn't matter right now. As your father, my responsibility is to protect you, and right now all that matters is that the two of you are safe," he said, avoiding her question and eye contact as he looked around the room. "This morning, the doctor was in and said that once you are fully awake, he will be in to examine you again. Then, if you can hold down some food and use the restroom, and if you promise to take it easy and rest, you can go home very soon." Henry looked at Sadie again, smiling as he held her hand. Sensing something else was coming, she asked, "*and?*"

Laughing softly, he added, "Your mother and I think it would be best if we stay a few days to help out. The doctor won't let you go home unless you are going to truly rest. With us there to take care of Hazel, you'll be able to do just that. Plus, our little granddaughter could use a playmate or two, and you know she loves it when we're around."

Sadie hated being a source of concern or a burden to anyone. She felt like everywhere she turned she was messing up and causing the ones she loved to hurt. But, as usual, her father was right. She was going to need some help for a little bit, and Hazel would love if her grandparents were there. After all, Hazel was the most important person in her life, and as much as she'd rather be left alone to think at this point, she couldn't stop her parents from doing what they thought was best for her. She knew that she would do the same thing for Hazel in a heartbeat. She also knew that it had been a long time since her parents had spent any quality time with her little girl, so she was sure this would be good for everyone involved.

"Okay, Dad," she yielded, looking at Hazel as she and Sadie's mother, Rose, walked back into the room carrying a pear and a bagel. As she watched her daughter hop up onto a chair by her bed, she wondered how much harm may have been done to her by witnessing the unfortunate events that played out between her and Luke. She prayed that she wouldn't have nightmares, or long-term scars from seeing that. She had tried too hard to protect her and make sure she felt safe, and she felt terrible that she hadn't' been able to do that this time.

"Grandpa, will my daddy come back and hurt mommy again?" Hazel's tiny voice interrupted their conversation. Henry patted her hair as she looked up at him with such innocent and worrisome blue eyes.

"No, sweetie pie, he won't," he said reassuringly.

"I don't like when he does that, it scares me. I like when daddy is happy and plays with me," she said in a matter-of-fact tone. Henry sighed. He felt like he had failed them both by not figuring out what was going on sooner. Sadie had been going through this longer than he suspected, he realized.

"Grandpa won't let that happen ever again," he said, feeling defeated and sad deep down in his bones.

***

From the sofa where she lay resting, Sadie looked down at Hazel, who was playing with her dolls and pretending they were at the zoo. Hazel didn't leave her mom's side very often, and she was doing a very good job at keeping her entertained, that was for sure. Sadie laughed, looking up to see her father sauntering into the living room. He had been outside doing something in the yard, although she wasn't sure what since he had mowed the lawn the day before, and the day before that he had cleaned up the flower beds, filled the bird feeders, and swept the sidewalk. She knew he was struggling to find things to do, and her heart felt full, knowing he was sacrificing so much time taking care of them. "What would my little zookeeper like for lunch today?" he asked them.

Hazel giggled. "I want mommy's basketti," she said excitedly.

"And let me guess, some chocolate milk to drink?" he said, laughing.

"Oh, my goodness, I just realized what time it is! Just give me a minute and I'll make her—"

"Sadie, your mother already made it," Henry cut in. "While you were resting." Sadie breathed, relieved. She sat up, gingerly, and pulled the throw blanket off her legs, setting it beside her on the sofa. She got up, feeling every muscle in her body scream at her, and a new throbbing sensation in her head. She took a moment to let everything settle before walking slowly to the bathroom.

As she turned the faucet on to wash her hands, she looked in the mirror. The face that stared back at her was heartbreaking. She could see the bruise on her face near her left eye. It extended down her cheek as well and was a dark purple color with some yellow beginning to creep in as it started to heal. She was still in shock as she thought about the fact that her husband, a man who had promised to love her, had done this to her. Worst of all, he'd done it in front of his own little girl. She hated that Hazel saw this ugly bruise every time she looked at her mommy. It was embarrassing when others saw it, too, but it was different with Hazel. It was a reminder of the fact that she had provoked her husband into hurting her, and that she had allowed it to happen in front of Hazel. She dried her hands and headed back to the sofa to lay down again, willing her head to stop pounding.

"When will Luke be back home, dad?" she asked quietly as her father came in to bring her some lunch on a tray.

She had a right to ask and to have questions, but he wasn't about to give her the truth at this point. She only needed to know that she and Hazel were safe. The rest would be shared when she was feeling better and had gotten on her feet again. "I'm not sure when he'll be back, Sadie. Honestly, I think it would be best if he never showed his face around here again, but I suppose that's not for me to decide. I wouldn't give him any more thought, though. Just eat some grub and get some rest and get your strength back so you can take care yourself and your daughter," he stated in a tone that told her, from experience, that there was no use in arguing with him, because she wouldn't win.

Sadie tried to think of a way to tell her dad that it was okay to tell her, what had happened, that she wanted to know what was going on and that she could handle it, but she knew he wasn't going to listen. She was deep in thought when he broke the silence, speaking as he sat next to her on the sofa.

"What if Hazel hadn't found a way to call me and I hadn't gotten here on time? This is no longer just about you, sweetie, this is about her, too." He nodded towards Hazel who had finished her lunch and was giggling while Cliff danced around playfully in front of her.

"I'm sorry, Dad." Sadie could see both the disappointment and pain in her father's eyes, but she knew it wasn't coming from anger toward her. He knew his daughter was fiercely independent and always wanted to make those around her happy, and he could never fault her for that. No, this was anger toward himself for not knowing just how far Sadie would go to try to keep them out of her troubles, even risking her own life. He knew he had taught her to take ownership of your wrongdoings, and to always work hard to find solutions to any problem that arose, but now he realized that, in doing so, he may have missed teaching her that getting help when you need it is honorable too.

"You're not the one who should be sorry, honey. I guess it makes sense now– you, constantly apologizing. None of this is your fault. This is on Luke, not you."

"Dad." Sadie was apologetic still. She'd caused her father to worry and imagine the worst. "I'm so sorry for making you worry."

Smiling, he stood. "You'll never stop making me worry, sweetheart. As you already know, that comes as part of the package every parent gets when they see their child for the first time. I'll always worry over you."

Sadie forced a smile. She knew exactly what he was talking about, and she was grateful that she had parents who cared for her so deeply. It was their kind of marriage, so beautiful and filled with kindness and love, that she had so desperately wanted for herself.  Unfortunately, something had went terribly wrong with that dream.

# Chapter Two

Luke got done with work, worn down by the day's toils, sick of listening to whining young workers. Even worse, he knew the torture that the next hour or so was going to bring, and he wasn't in the mood for it. He crawled out of his truck, slamming the door shut behind him, and walked up the steps to his own house. Even though this was his damn house, he knew he'd have to ring the doorbell and wait for someone to answer, and he hoped it wasn't his father-in-law. He rang the doorbell and waited, kicking a small rock off the step in frustration. His countenance was dour and his shoulders were stiff as he watched the door open slowly, Sadie standing on the other side of the threshold. He was annoyed by the way she stood there, like a wounded dog, looking at him as if she was waiting for him to hug her or something. Hell if that was going to happen! She looked horrible, with a large, ugly bruise under her left eye, and even though she had been the one beaten, she looked like a child begging their parent to forgive them, and it was pathetic. He needed to grab his things and had really hoped he wouldn't have to deal with his in-laws while he was there. In fact, he had hoped nobody would be home, but he found out quickly that he wasn't that lucky.

As he waited for Sadie to move out of his way so he could go in, he suddenly saw Hazel come running toward the door. "Who is it, Mommy?" As she saw her daddy in the door, she stopped behind Sadie. She stood unsure, not knowing if she should run into his arms or back away. Luke caught her eyes and forced a smile. Hazel smiled back hesitantly, revealing a left-sided dimple, then at her mom's nod, slowly started to walk towards him. "It's Daddy, sweetheart. Go ahead, you can give him a hug." she assured her.

As Luke stood there, an eerie silence permeated the air, magnified by the uncertainty that now enveloped little Hazel's heart. She stood before him, her pudgy little arms and legs revealed through the cute dress she picked out herself, her long curly brown hair and freckles, like her mother's, stared back at Luke. Hazel's bright blue eyes were innocent and torn between the love she had for her daddy and the fear she had after witnessing the hurt he had inflicted upon her mommy.

Luke could tell she was conflicted, and that made him even more upset with Sadie for causing him to do what he had done. He mustered up the strength to smile at his daughter more broadly. "Hello, baby," he said softly, and whether his voice was laden with remorse and genuine affection, there was no way she could tell, so instead, she did what every child would do, and put her arms in the air to be picked up.

"Hi Luke," Sadie finally said, moving out of his way. Luke looked around cautiously. "He's not here," she said, reading his mind. "I was able to convince them that it was okay to leave." It hadn't been easy dissuading her parents from staying any longer, but she had done it anyway. She had needed to pull herself together and start taking care of things herself.

"Come, Hazel, why don't you go play with Cliff for a little bit," she said in a loving tone, taking her from him and setting her down. "Daddy and I have to talk." Hazel looked curiously at both and then ran off to find Cliff.

As Hazel left to meet Cliff, Luke stared down at her disinterestedly. Whoever told her he wanted to talk? The last thing he wanted to do was talk. Sadie was wrong, she spilled hot coffee on his shirt, and told her father on him like a little child. Luke loathed the idea of anyone taking pre-eminence in matters concerning him. He was in charge, this was his home, or at least it used to be. He just wanted to grab his shit and go, without having to talk to Sadie, was that *really* too much to ask?

"I'm just here to grab a few bags of my stuff, so if you'll get out of my way, I can do that. I have no interest in talking to you." Although she felt as though her heart was tearing in two, she recognized his tone and knew that she needed to back off and leave him alone. She wasn't going to risk another episode like earlier that week. She followed Hazel into the kitchen and sat at the table with her to color, while Luke headed into the bedroom to pack.

In a matter of minutes, he was back out and stomping down the hall. He dropped his bags in the doorway and yelled for Hazel to come give him a hug. She looked at her mom for approval and walked to him when she nodded. Sadie followed her, but when she tried to ask Luke when he would be back, he cut her off with a look of hatred, one she had seen so many times. He gave Hazel a hug, picked up his things, and slammed the door behind him. She wasn't sure what was going on, but she found herself letting out a long-held breath after he left. She hadn't even realized she was holding it. Then, after laying Hazel down for a nap, she went into her bedroom and sat alone on the bed for a while, tears flowing freely down her cheeks. She lay down, hugging a pillow close to her chest, trying to calm down so her head wouldn't hurt any worse. What was she going to do now?

* * *

"Sawyer? Oh my God! Sawyer?" Sadie burst into tears. When the doorbell had rung at 2am, she had thought the worst, but she hadn't expected to see Sawyer on the other side of the door. It'd been a couple of years since she had seen her best friend. Sawyer Quinn was the exact opposite of Sadie, and perhaps that was what made their friendship so exciting and such a perfect fit.

She couldn't believe she was looking at her best friend since the 7th grade, a friend she had drifted apart from after she met Luke. She'd missed her. Sawyer had moved to Illinois after her graduation from college, and they had lost touch.

Sawyer held her in her arms as she cried, not sure whether it was because they hadn't seen each other in years or because of the things she'd heard Luke had done to her. Sadie didn't care what her reason was, she was just elated that she was here now.

"Why… How… What are you doing here, Sawyer?" Sadie managed to ask through sniffing and throat clearing.

"Your parents called, Sadie. They told me about the hospital and Luke hurting you. Why didn't you tell me?"

"We haven't really been in touch, so how could I? Calling my best friend because I was in trouble? You know that's not how it should be." Sawyer hugged her, fighting back the urge to cry herself.

"Sadie… That's exactly what friends are for! If you can't call or talk to me when you're in trouble, then what kind of friend would I be? Even so, I'm not sure I believe that you not wanting to worry me is that why you wouldn't call, Sadie. I'm guessing there is more to this story…"

If there was anyone who knew Sadie deep down, Sawyer was that person. She could see the underlying fear, it was in Sadie's hesitation to ask her in. She could tell that Sadie had a story to tell, but she also knew that she couldn't push her. This had to be handled delicately, and the dark bruises on Sadie were evidence of the hell she had been through lately. Sensing her internal struggle, she gently moved past Sadie and stepped in.

"You never wrote me back, you never called me back, and you never texted me back." Sawyer told her. "Why not?

"Wait… I didn't get any letters or calls from you, Sawyer. If I had, I'd *definitely* have responded. I thought you had just gotten so busy that you didn't have time, and I tried *really* hard to let you have your space."

"I'm pretty sure I know how that happened… I'm guessing that Luke kept it all from you." Sawyer shook her head, anger filling her face.

Sadie stared at her, obviously very confused at what she was being told. She'd had no idea Luke was doing that. "I'm sorry, it's my fault. I should have called or texted or written you anyway. I've missed you so much, Sawyer!"

"Wow, you're seriously going to blame yourself for this?" Sawyer looked at her friend and the pain wrapped itself in a tight knot in her stomach. Seeing her best friend like this broke her heart.

"But it *was* my fault. You're my best friend, Sawyer, and I let you go. I should have questioned him, and I should have called or written to you anyway!" Sawyer took her hand and led her to one of two couches in the living room and they sat together.

"Sadie Benson, you are the most wonderful human I have ever known, and you don't deserve this life. You deserve so much more, so much better, and it breaks my heart to watch a man who promised to love you and protect you treat you like this." She brushed her hand against Sadie's fair, freckled face, causing her to flinch slightly from the ache in her cheek. "And I'm sorry I left without checking in. I should have known something was wrong, known that you weren't one to let your loved ones in on troubles. How could I forget that my best friend was so altruistic that in the wrong hands, she could lose herself?"

"No, Sawyer, this isn't on you. I'm the one who didn't call, and for that I'm sorry. I missed you terribly, but what happened a week ago wouldn't have happened if I hadn't been distracted. I ruined his favorite work shirt, and that made him mad."

"Sadie," Sawyer cut in, grabbing both of her arms gently. "There is a threshold for how much you can let a person hurt you. Think about your baby girl! This isn't the kind of home you grew up in, and it isn't one she should either. It won't be healthy for her. Your folks said that Luke is gone for now, so is it okay if I sleep here tonight?"

"Of course, you can! You can just climb in with me, we don't have any extra beds unfortunately." Sadie replied.

"Perfect. I have a full week with you before I go back to IL, and you and Hazel and I are going to have a little fun together if that's okay with you! From the pictures your mom showed me, she's so stinking adorable, Sadie!  I can't wait to get to know her. We'll do some crying, some catching up, and some dreaming of what's to come." Sadie yielded, there was no use fighting it, Sawyer would never take *no* for an answer.

"Oh, and one more thing, Sadie," Sawyer added, "If you're thinking of waking up early to make me breakfast, think again. You know I can be both a night owl and an early bird. Being friends with you taught me that. And thank you, by the way, it helps me immensely now! Running a business isn't for the sleepy headed. Besides, I'm here to help you out for a bit, not be waited on by you."

"I've missed you so much, Sawyer." Sadie said, hugging her best friend tightly.

"Me too, Sadie. Now, let's go get some sleep. I'm exhausted."

* * *

The morning sun was peeking through the curtains as Hazel's tiny feet found their way to her parents' bedroom. Pushing the door open, she saw her mom in bed still, and she noticed that someone was next to her. Assuming it was her Dad, she hesitantly climbed up on her mom's side of the bed, sliding under the covers and into her mom's arms.  Sadie moaned softly, her body feeling the impact of Luke's attack on her more with each day that passed. "Mommy, can we get up now?" she asked, trying not to wake her father.

"Let your mommy sleep, honey," Hazel heard, peeking over her mom's shoulder when she realized it wasn't her daddy. Sawyer smiled at the sweet little girl, realizing she probably had no idea who she even was. She tried to wake up by rubbing her hands against her eyes. "Good morning, Hazel!" she said as cheerfully as she could for 7 o'clock in the morning, especially after such a late night. "Come on, you and I have a lot of catching up to do," she said, smiling ever so broadly and lifting Hazel off her mom. "I'm your mommy's best friend!"

Hazel looked curiously at Sawyer. She didn't know this woman, but she remembered her mamma telling her stories about her, and she knew her mommy loved her, so she figured she could trust her. Sawyer, being the ball of energy that she was, knew how to get people to like her, even her best friend's never-before-seen-or-spoken-to daughter. With a smile, she carried the little girl out of the room so Sadie could get some much-needed rest.

"I know you don't know me, but I'm here to take care of the both of you," she explained. "So, let's go brush your teeth first, then we can make you something to eat while we chat about whatever you want to talk about. We'll even keep our jammies on and have a PJ Day! How does that sound?"

As she popped her up on the counter in the bathroom to brush her teeth, Hazel giggled, her beautiful trusting smile warming Sawyer's heart. "Yes!" She said excitedly, reaching up and running her tiny fingers through Sawyer's hair. She had a look of sadness in her eyes that tugged at Sawyer's heart.

"What honey?" She asked.

Hazel spat into the sink and said, "I *kinda* know you. You're in all of mommy's pictures from when she was in school… you're my Aunt Soya!" Hazel's examining eyes grew even larger, and Sawyer felt her heart melting. The joy of having a little one, to her, was priceless, and she couldn't wait to spend some time with Hazel.

"Darn right I am!" She replied with the same energy. "Now that you're all brushed up, what would you like for breakfast?"

"Basketti and chocolate milk!" She said excitedly as Sawyer grabbed her hand and headed to the kitchen. She couldn't believe how this little girl, with the weight of her hand so light and delicate, had already found a place in her heart.

"Just like your mommy, aren't you?" Sawyer laughed.

"Yes! My mommy makes the best basketti!" Hazel easily giggled, and that was exactly what she kept doing.

"Has anyone told you just how adorable you are? Beautiful like your mommy." Sawyer took a calm tone, one that made kids easily respond. "I'll beat you to the kitchen!"

Hazel giggled and turned to run to the kitchen. She couldn't wait to help Sawyer make breakfast for her mommy.

*For one morning,* Sawyer thought, *this sweet little girl is going to be happy and forget the awful things she's witnessed recently.* She knew she wasn't magic and that she couldn't make it better forever for her, but she was here to make it better for a little while, and when she put her mind to something, she followed through!

# Chapter Three

"Luke, I can't believe you would do this to Hazel and me! I might not be perfect, but it can't be so bad that you'd really throw away 5 years of marriage… There *must* be something I can do to make you want to stay. Please call me back so we can at least talk about this," she urged as she clicked the button on her phone to end the message she was leaving.

Ever since he left the other day, Sadie had been trying to figure out what was going on.  An hour before, she had answered a knock on the door to find a man in a suit who had served her divorce papers.  She had been stunned. After looking them over, she was even more bewildered and confused.  Not only was Luke filing for divorce, but he was also giving her full custody of Hazel. She knew he was mad at her, but she never saw this one coming!  She sat on the edge of her bed, tears flowing, trying to figure out what had happened. As she stared at the blue walls of her bedroom, her mood matching the gloomy, depressing color, she wondered what she was going to do now.

Sawyer and Hazel sat just outside the bedroom door in the living room watching cartoons. Sadie had needed a few minutes to think, or that is what she had told Sawyer, anyway. She wasn't ready to tell her about the divorce papers yet. She wondered what Sawyer would think when she showed her what she had received. She knew Sawyer hated Luke and would probably think this was for the best, and she knew that if Sawyer knew she was trying to get in touch with him, she'd be disappointed. Sadie just knew that she needed to at least try to fix what she had worked so hard to keep afloat for the last few years. She wasn't the type of person to just hang up the towel on things without knowing she'd done her best.

Suddenly, her phone alerted her to a text message. She hesitantly looked at it, already knowing, somehow, who it was from.

*You will never be able to fix this. I'm not happy and I deserve someone who makes me happy! Stop calling me. It's over.*

She read the words three times before her brain could really process what they were saying. She was right, it was her fault.

*I'm sorry I made you so mad. I love you and I want you to be happy. If you don't want to be married to me anymore, I understand, but why Hazel?*

She still couldn't wrap her mind around the fact that he had chosen to never see his daughter again. He *had* to love *her* at least, right? She had seen him interact with Hazel many times in a loving way, and she just couldn't accept that he'd be okay with giving her up like this. It just didn't' make any sense.

*I don't have to explain myself to you. Don't call or text me again.*

Sadie sat her phone down by her on the bed. She felt like the walls of her room were closing in on her. How could it be over, just like that? What was she going to tell Hazel? She'd be devastated. She loved her daddy, even if she was a little hesitant around him after seeing what happened the other day. Sadie had hoped that, with time, Hazel would be able to trust him again and things could be the way they were before that horrible morning.

With that thought, she lay down on the bed and let the tears flow. She was obviously not *wife* material. She made the man she loved hate her so much that he'd hurt her, physically *and* emotionally. What was wrong with her? Nobody was ever going to want to be with her, and Hazel was never going to have a daddy to love her and do all the things little girls loved to do with their dads. She had ruined everything.

"Sadie?" Sawyer walked through the door carefully. "Are you okay?" She had come to check on her and could hear her soft sobs at the doorway.

"This was not how this was supposed to go. We are supposed to work at our marriage, to fix what is broken, not throw it out! My marriage is over, Sawyer, and it's all because of–"

"Don't you dare say it, Sadie!" Sawyer closed the door quietly and walked over to the bed. She held her best friend wrapped within her arms as she sobbed. This broken person was not the friend she remembered, and it broke her heart. Why had she been so selfish and left to live out their dream without her best friend?

"He filed for divorce, Sawyer, and worse yet, he gave up any connection to Hazel! Why would he do that to us?" Sawyer knew what the right answer was, but she knew she couldn't say the words yet. She knew that Sadie had fallen victim to an abusive husband, and that even though he had done an excellent job of making her feel that it was all her fault, it wasn't. She had heard so many stories of victims blaming themselves. She just couldn't believe it had happened to someone she loved.

"Maybe this is for the better, Sadie. I think that you need to take some time to find yourself again… if not for you, then for that little girl out there." she said, pointing towards the living room.

"He said he doesn't love me, that he is done and doesn't want me to contact him ever again."

Sadie began to cry again, but mindful that Hazel was right in the other room.

"I know it hurts right now, Sadie, and I'm so sorry that you are going through all of this. I can't even imagine how you are feeling. The thing is, I think you are giving that man *way* too much credit here. A man that would do what Luke did to you is *not* a man! As far as I'm concerned, he's incapable of loving you the way you deserve to be loved because he has no idea what that even is. *No man* that truly loves a woman with his whole heart would *ever* hurt her. That's not love, and Luke is not a man in my book."

"Sawyer, I know you think this is Luke's fault, but it's not, not completely anyway. I wasn't a good wife." Sadie said.

Sawyer gently held her, rubbing a hand slowly on her back to calm and comfort her. "Sadie, I know this is incredibly difficult for you, but you have to understand that none of this is your fault. Luke's actions were his own, and he is responsible for them, not you."

Amidst her tears, Sadie choked out, "But maybe if I had been a better wife, he wouldn't have treated me this way. I must have done something to make him stop loving me."

Sawyer looked into her eyes with empathy and replied, "Sadie, you are not responsible for Luke's behavior. He's an adult and he made the decision to treat you like that. You deserve love, respect, and kindness, and it's not your job to fix what's wrong with him."

Still feeling burdened with guilt, Sadie questioned, "I still feel like I should have seen the signs earlier. Maybe I could have stopped it before it got this bad."

Sawyer shook her head gently and said, "Just like most abusers, Luke knew how to hide his ugly side from you until he wanted to show it. You can't blame yourself for not knowing. The important thing now is to focus on *your* healing and well-being."

Sadie sighed, wiping her tears away, "I just wish I could have saved our marriage somehow."

Sawyer reassured her, "Sometimes, marriages are not meant to be saved, especially when they involve abuse. Your priority should be you and Hazel's safety and happiness. You have the strength to overcome this, and I'll be here every step of the way to support you."

Sadie clung to Sawyer and cried a little longer, all the while, Hazel sat in the living room watching cartoons with Cliff, oblivious to the conversation that was unfolding in the other room.

"What do you say we spend a few days running around Seattle like we used to do when we were teenagers? I'd love another shot at catching some fish down by the market… I bet Hazel would love that! And there's the gum wall too… have you and Hazel stuck some gum to it yet?" Sawyer asked, getting excited and trying to change the mood of the room.

"Actually, we haven't." Sadie replied, once again realizing how sheltered her life had been over the last few years.

"Well, if you're feeling up to it, I'd really love to spend some time with you girls. I have to head back to the winery in a few days, unfortunately, because it's coming up on our busy season, but I've carved out 3 days of fun in the time being."

"Hazel and I would love that!" Sadie said, smiling as she wiped the last few tears from her cheeks. "I think it would be good for both of us to spend some time with you... you always did know how to have a fun time more than I did!"

"Okie dokie... it's a date!" Sawyer said, earning her a curious look from Sadie. "Yeah, that's one of those interesting Midwesterner things to say... I guess I've picked quite a few of those up since I moved there." she laughed.

Sadie knew this would be good for both Hazel and herself. She could put off thinking about what they were going to do next until after Sawyer left. For now, they were going to take a breath and have some fun.

* * *

Seattle was beginning to feel a little less like home every day. Less familiar and more tormenting. Nothing felt right anymore, and nothing seemed to make sense. Luke hadn't allowed her to work because he wanted her to take care of everything at home, so he didn't have to help when he got done with work each day, so she didn't have that to keep her busy. She also realized now that she didn't have any friends or a life beyond her own home and her parents. She was so thankful that Sawyer had been there for a few days, as Sawyer had given her a sense of purpose and belonging again, one that she hadn't even realized she had missed. Now, after a couple weeks of her not being around, she was feeling out of place and lost. She wasn't sure she could have handled all of this without her. As she drove down the road, she felt a sense of loneliness she had never felt before.

She needed some fresh air to clear her mind… a way to figure out what she should do next to help Hazel and herself find their footing again. She headed towards the mountain- the winding road leading her to open skies and the natural Washington beauty she hadn't seen for so long. The grass was a stunning shade of green, sparkling with the morning's dew. Wildflowers adorned the sides of the roads, signs that summer was in full bloom. A trickling stream flowed opposite her direction as she slowly climbed the mountainside, directing her on a path towards the hillside that lie ahead. She rolled her window down, allowing the fresh mountain air to blow into her car, loving the way it felt against her skin and hair. She wasn't sure what she was looking for here, but she had hoped to at least find some clarity, and maybe even some peace in her troubled heart.

The sun bore down on the distant ocean as it moved farther and farther away in her rear-view mirror. The sun hadn't shown through the clouds for what felt like forever, although it had probably only been a few days. The rainy nature of Seattle was beginning to affect her mood, exacerbating her headache. Gripping the steering wheel tightly, she maintained a slightly higher speed than allowed, cautiously monitoring the speedometer. Drawing attention and getting pulled over was the last thing she needed right now, and she also was well aware of the dangers of driving too quickly on the winding mountain roads.

Life used to be so different. Her last visit to Lake Washington was with her family, her parents, Luke, herself, and Hazel. Luke had been the one who drove them to the Lake, and during the drive, he couldn't resist criticizing Sadie's family. He always complained about her family, although never in front of them, of course. She hated when he did that, but Sadie could never say anything, knowing that any confrontation would only lead to more trouble.

Though her drive was brief, the pain of listening to her husband talk badly about her father lingered in her mind, as did the memory of Luke slapping her face during their ride home from the groceries a few nights after their trip to the lake. They had just gotten in the car after grocery shopping, and he had gotten angry with her when she told him she wanted to take Hazel to her parents for a visit the next day. They had gotten into it about him not wanting them around her, and he had backhanded her when she had argued. She flinched at the memory, feeling the sting on her cheek again, the hurtful words echoing in her mind. She shook her head slightly as if to push the memories away, focusing on the road ahead. If only she had been quiet. She had known better than to argue with him.

As she pulled into a parking spot, she felt a heaviness in her heart. How had everything gone so wrong? It was her fault, had to be. She should have seen the signs back when she had first met Luke, but instead she had been so excited about all his promises that she had missed all the warnings. The way he acted around her parents, the pangs of fear she felt occasionally when he got mad, the way he pulled her from her best friend and made her feel guilty for wanting to hang out with her sometimes. It was all there, so how had she missed it all?

She got out of her car, stepping onto a narrow walking path that led to the water. The path was paved, and there were beautiful trees surrounding it, forming a canopy over the top. Ahead of her, a young couple were taking photos together. She carefully passed them so she would not accidentally end up in their photos. As she continued along the path, the trees opened, and she was able to look out over the lake. With sadness, her thoughts moved to her little girl. It wasn't fair that she'd have to grow up wondering about her father and missing him in her life. How could she explain to *Hazel* why he had left them when she didn't even know *herself*? She felt a shiver roll down her spine, and pulled her sweater closed as if to feel the warmth of it somehow take the pain away. Suddenly, she felt very much alone. She looked around, finding nobody on the water or the walking path. She got an uneasy feeling in her stomach and decided to head back to her car. The couple taking photos were gone now as well, leaving her all alone in the parking area.

Even though her walk had been short, Sadie felt the need to leave this area, one that had once carried so many wonderful feelings and memories, quickly. She had little desire to stay back and take in the scenery as it brought back feelings that she wanted to remain in the past. When she was last at the lake with Luke, her parents, and Hazel, she had wanted to find a way to tell her parents about her unhappiness, but she hadn't been able to bring herself to do it, and Luke hadn't let her out of his sight anyway. While her parents and Hazel had played and laughed together, she could remember wondering why she felt so sad and alone. Her parents had known nothing about her married life, and she had dreaded the thought of what they'd think of her if they had found out.

Getting back in her car, Sadie pulled out from her parking spot and left the beautiful area without looking back. As she drove down through the hills, back to Seattle, she suddenly realized something… she had to leave here. She needed to start over somehow and somewhere. She and Hazel needed to figure out what was next for them and how to function as a family of 2, without Luke in the picture. Sawyer had been right, she needed to put Hazel first, and it was time she started looking forward and not backward. It was time to find herself again and build a life with Hazel that would give her the childhood she deserved. For the first time since Luke left, Sadie felt a pang of hope. A smile made its way into the light through her tear-stained cheeks. She could do this… now she just had to figure out how.

* * *

"I hope you had some time to clear your head at the lake, sweetheart," Henry said, sitting next to Sadie on the sofa. Looking at her now, he couldn't believe how quickly her life had taken a turn away from the ambitious and happy young woman she had been only a handful of years prior. He was her father; it was his job to protect his little girl and he felt as though he had failed miserably at doing so. "I always go there myself, when I need to think about things or make tough decisions."

"Yeah, me too. I did a lot of thinking on the way there, too, and I realized something today, Dad."

"Oh, you did, did you? And what is that?" Henry asked.

"Hazel and I have been through so much, and we have a lot of healing to do ahead of us. The more I think about it, the more I realize that we need a new start. We need to figure out how to move past everything that has happened and move forward, or I'm afraid we never will find happiness and security, and I can't allow that to happen to Hazel. She deserves every opportunity I can find her to be happy. I can't keep being so sad all the time, it's not good for her, and I'm her mamma so I need to put her first." Sadie looked at her dad with worry as she spoke those last words... worry that he would be upset with her or that he would think she was making a mistake.

Henry thought for a moment before a great big smile took over his aging face. "Honey, I think that it's a great idea. And the only thing I'd add to your revelation is that you *both* deserve every happiness, not just the munchkin."

"Really, dad? You don't think I'm making a mistake?" she asked with so much apprehension it made his heart ache for her.

"Absolutely!" he said, happy that she was finally moving in the right direction.

"I appreciate the fact that you are being so understanding. Now, we just have to figure out where we are going to go for our fresh start." she said, thinking out loud.

"You know what? I think I might know the perfect place! Just this morning, I had a thought that maybe you should consider going to stay with Sawyer for a little while. She reminded me when she was here about you two and your dreams of owning a business together all those years ago. I'm honestly not sure why I didn't think of it sooner!"

"Yes, that's true," she replied. "But I don't want to just invite

Hazel and I there and cause any trouble… They're super busy, especially with the busy season coming so soon."

"Nonsense. Sadie, that girl loves you and wants what's best for you just as much as your mom and I do. She'd be thrilled to have the two of you come stay for a while… guarantee it!" Sensing her hesitation, he added, "It doesn't have to be forever, you know. Take it one day at a time and see where the road leads."

Sadie sat for a while chewing on everything her father had said to her. She really did miss Sawyer like crazy, and she'd love to see her home and the life she'd built for herself there. Maybe it *would* be the perfect place to figure out what was next for Hazel and herself.

"But, what about you and mom? Hazel and I would miss you both so much!" she said as tears began to well up in her already puffy eyes.

Henry turned her shoulders towards his and put his hand softly on her cheek. As she leaned into his loving embrace, he softly said "Love doesn't know distances, Sadie. We are always here and will be here when you return. Plus… I've never been to Illinois before! We will head that way and visit… you know how much your mother loves wine!" he chuckled.

"I heard that!" her mother shouted from the kitchen, her father forgetting to lower his voice when he talked about his wife's 'wine habit' as he called it.

She leaned over and hugged her father with so much sadness that his heart felt like it would melt into a puddle on the floor. This girl always could do that to him. She felt so child-like in his arms, so frail and damaged, as though the energy had completed exited her body over the last few weeks. He wanted nothing more than to wave a wand and fix everything that hurt inside her. Since he couldn't do that, encouraging her to go find her happiness seemed like a close second.

"Go ahead and give Sawyer a call when you get home. See what she says and then let us know your plans. We are here for you… whatever you need."

Sadie gathered Hazel up in her arms and headed to the car. As she drove home with Hazel singing away in the back seat, she felt a smile creeping in. She couldn't wait to get home and call Sawyer, but she was also trying to prepare herself in case Sawyer's answer was no. After all, taking on a woman who was going through a divorce, and a little girl who had been through so much hurt, would be a lot for Sawyer, especially in the busy season.  Maybe she wouldn't be up for it.  Oh, how she hoped she'd say yes, though. When she got into the house and got Hazel settled playing with her toys, she picked up her phone and dialed the number Sawyer had given her. Even though every instinct she had learned over the last 5 years had told her to be cautious, she was hopeful. She'd held back for so long when it came to thinking about what was best for her… always putting her daughter first for fear of what might happen if she didn't.  This wasn't the time for baby steps, though, and she had realized that today. Nope, she wasn't going to back away from a challenge this time because now it was time to leap!

# Chapter Four

Sadie, her 4-year-old mini-me Hazel, and their dog, Cliff, headed to the train station to hop on a train from Seattle to Chicago. The decision to travel by train promised an adventure, and Sadie, though still shaken by her divorce from Luke, was excited to share this experience with her little girl. Her mom had suggested riding the train would be fun for Hazel, and Sadie had agreed instantly. As they boarded the train, Hazel's eyes sparkled with wonder, eager to begin the journey. She had a million-and-one questions, and Sadie did her best to answer them all.

She had flinched when the train attendant raised his hand to show her where to put her luggage. He didn't know why, but she could see the sympathy in his eyes toward her. She wondered just how obvious it was that she was a broken woman.

As they entered the passenger car, Sadie's eyes widened. It was even better than she had imagined it to be. The windows extended from the floor to the ceiling, curving as they reached the top, the beautiful blue sky visible all around them. The seats were puffy, with large blue cushions padding them, and they faced the windows, allowing the passengers to see the world around them in a way that only a train could show it to them. There was a small aisle between the backs of the chairs for them to walk down to find their seats. She could barely wait for the beauty they were about to see on their journey. Moving forward, she and Hazel found their seats, about halfway down the car. Sitting down, Sadie looked out the big window in front of her and smiled at her parents. She pointed them out to Hazel who began waving excitedly. Cliff sat at their feet, happy to look out, tail wagging as he settled his head on her knee. Her parents had stood with them while they boarded, and now were waiting for the train to take off. As it did, Hazel's pudgy little hands kept on waving until they were out of sight.

Although she was trying to be brave and happy for Hazel's sake, Sadie's mood instantly sank, and tears feel down her cheeks. She wiped them away quickly as she looked down at Cliff, now looking at her with sad eyes as the train slowly chugged out of the station. She pet him softly as she felt the train gradually picking up speed, venturing into the heart of the countryside. As the cityscape of Seattle faded into the distance, the landscape transformed into a mesmerizing tapestry of nature's beauty. Hazel clung tightly to her brown teddy bear. Sadie watched her, thinking about how sorry she was that she was the reason Hazel may never see her father again. She touched her curly brown hair, a much longer version of her own and ran a curl through her fingers. The last thing she ever wanted to do was cause any sadness for Hazel.

"Mommy, why isn't daddy coming too?" Hazel asked, innocence shining in her eyes.

Sadie took a deep breath, snuggling Hazel to her side tenderly. She knew she had to give an answer to her, but what should she say? This was not what she wanted for her, a life away from her father. She knew the joy and wholeness her dad had brought her during her childhood, and even now, and she wanted that for her daughter too. She loved Hazel more than anyone in the whole world, and she hated that she hadn't been able to fix their marriage so that Hazel could have had both of her parents with her.

"Daddy is not feeling very well, honey. He had to go somewhere to help him feel better, okay?"

"Will daddy be okay? He is all alone. Who will take care of him?"

"Oh, honey, daddy has Grandpa Charles and Grandma Linda to look after him, just like Grandpa Henry and Grandma Rose looked after me when I wasn't feeling well. Don't worry, okay? I'm sure daddy will be okay." Sadie knew she had to tell her whatever she needed to hear for now. She had to give herself time to figure out what to tell her about what had happened.

Hazel stopped asking questions and slowly fell asleep, leaving Sadie awake with her own thoughts. Even after everything, she wondered what Luke was up to right now. It was not like him to give up things without a fight, especially not his daughter. It all made her wonder whether she and Hazel had truly meant anything to him, or if they had just been people he lived with and tolerated. As she pondered that though, she looked out the window to the scenery that flew past as the train chugged along.

The vast green fields rolled out like an endless carpet, stretching as far as the eye could see. Gentle hills adorned with wildflowers and grazing livestock added charm to the countryside. Every now and then, they passed by quaint little towns. She wondered if life was simpler in those towns. As they traveled along, every new and different scene brought with it a different kind of emotion and thoughts.

As the train meandered through the countryside, it carved a path through dense forests. Towering trees adorned with vibrant foliage formed a natural tunnel, casting dancing shadows on the passing carriages. Rays of sunlight filtered through the leaves, creating a picturesque play of light and shadow inside the train.

They crossed over crystal-clear streams and rivers, their waters glistening under the golden rays of the sun. Birds soared gracefully overhead, their melodious songs serenading the travelers, as if welcoming them to this enchanting landscape.

Each changing season painted the scenery with a diverse palette of colors. Spring brought blossoms of pink and white, a delicate floral spectacle. Summer bathed the countryside in rich shades of green. Autumn, Sadie's favorite season, was next, bringing its breathtaking symphony of red, orange, and gold as the leaves fell like confetti from the trees. Even winter, with its snowy blanket covering the earth, added a magical touch to the already charming vista. Sadie was amazed at the beauty she saw before her, the lush and picturesque landscapes of the Pacific Northwest. Over the hours that passed she saw dense forests of evergreen trees, majestic mountains, and sparkling rivers and lakes. The scenery was often characterized by vibrant greenery and misty surroundings. As the train ventured eastward into Montana, it entered the

Rocky Mountains. The landscape became more rugged and mountainous, with snow-capped peaks, deep valleys, and winding rivers.

Through the Rockies, the ride offered breathtaking scenery. After crossing the Rockies, they entered valleys stretched as far as the eye could see, and she loved the ranches and majestic cattle she saw filling them. The train chugged alone through the vast Great Plains, where the landscape was flatter and more expansive, with wide-open grasslands stretching as far as the eye could see. They enjoyed supper as it was served, followed by a walk to a special train car that was just for the four-legged friends on the train, allowing Cliff some time to go to the bathroom and sniff around for other dogs. After some time, they cleaned up and stopped at the bathrooms on their way back to their seats. Sadie opened a little yellow case, removing their toothbrushes and toothpaste. They steadied themselves as the train heaved each direction on the bumpy tracks, giggling as they tried to brush their teeth, struggling to keep their balance. She helped Hazel into her jammies, and they headed back to their seats.

Settling back in, Sadie read an adorable little train book to Hazel, secretly laughing as she imagined her mother placing that in the bag for them. She was always thinking ahead! She pulled a snack out for Hazel to munch on while she read to her. After the story ended, she snuggled them up under the quilt her mother had sent with them, and they all lay back in the seat, watching the sleeping world pass by.

Sadie loved staring at the fields of crops, grazing livestock, and wild animals running free through the valley. It wasn't long until she could hear Hazel's breath become rhythmic as she fell asleep. As she held her sleeping daughter, she allowed her thoughts to continue falling back on her marriage to Luke. She thought about who she was before she had met Luke… a smart and gentle young woman, with such big dreams for her life. When she saw something she had wanted, she'd went for it with no regard for fear or worry. Now, she barely even recognized the woman that was staring back at her in the glass. As the evening sun fell below the trees, she closed her eyes and joined Hazel and Cliff in sleeping.

* * *

Sadie woke up early and gently slid Hazel off her lap and onto the seat next to them. She stretched her cramped legs, wishing for her soft bed instead of the padded train seats. She looked out the window as the train continued eastward. After a little bit, she realized they were already passing between Minnesota and Wisconsin, the agricultural heartland of America. She'd never been here before, but she had always dreamed of it, and she was excited to finally be seeing it up close.

The Midwest was known for its golden fields of corn and wheat, especially during the summer months. Sadie looked at the vast farmlands with neatly arranged rows of crops, barns, and farmhouses, amazed at the way it all seemed to be divided out, as if by a cookie cutter. Each field was filled with fresh green leaves as the newly planted crops began to rise above the soil. As she watched it all fly by, the dream to own a winery became fresh in her mind. Before they got married, Luke seemed to be on board with her working towards her dream, but not long after their wedding things had changed. Luke had told her he wanted her to stay home, and that was exactly what she had done. He said that their dream was childish, and that their life was in Seattle. At first, she had been horribly sad about the thought of leaving that dream behind, but slowly, it became less and less of a dream and more of an afterthought.

Their train would eventually pass through several cities and urban areas as it approached Chicago. It was likely that they would catch glimpses of iconic landmarks and bustling cityscapes, offering a contrast to the serene countryside they had seen for most of the trip. Sadie looked forward to each sight. It had been almost 24 hours since they had gotten on the train, and every stop it made had her feeling a little more antsy about their arrival in Illinois. Still, she was not in a hurry, and she reminded herself that the amazing countryside they were getting to see from this fabulous viewpoint was worth the wait. The train journey was meant to be a perfect blend of meditation, reflection, relaxation and admiration, with ample opportunities to take in the breathtaking scenery along the way. The rhythmic clacking of the train's wheels against the tracks, coupled with the gentle sway of the carriage, created a soothing ambiance that lulled Hazel back to sleep each time a bump or stop of the train woke her. She was once again cradled in her mother's arms.

As the time passed, she often glanced across the aisle at a couple near them on the train. They sat close to one another, their hands intertwined in a tender embrace, often laughing together as they watched the countryside fly by. Their affectionate gazes and frequent smiles showcased a deep connection between them. Observing their happiness stirred mixed emotions within her. When they smiled at each other, it was contagious. Her own face couldn't help but mirror their joy, it made a smile force its way through her own worry. Yet, when they laughed together, a bittersweet pang tugged at her heart as she realized it was hard to remember a time when she had *actually* been happy with Luke, a time when she had laughed like that– genuinely, heartfelt. It made her question herself and the choices she had made in her life, reminding her of the hollowness she felt inside. It had been so long since she genuinely laughed from the depths of her soul, and witnessing their happiness made her question how she possibly could have allowed things to get so out of hand. It also made her long to feel that feeling too.

As she was getting lost in her thoughts, she heard Hazel giggle sweetly in her sleep. Sadie smiled down at her as she wondered what the little girl could be dreaming about. Cliff sat up, excited to hear Hazel's laughter, licking her face before Sadie gently told him to lay back down, hoping that he wouldn't wake her up again. As she looked at Hazel's sweet little face, she realized she was wrong in thinking she was all alone: She had Hazel, and she was the light in her life, the one thing that made sense. She was the one thing Sadie and Luke had done right in their marriage. Still, there was a void that she realized could only come from the connection a husband and wife were supposed to feel with one another. Safety and love. She hadn't had either of those with Luke.

In the quiet moments, her mind wandered, reminiscing about the past. She genuinely tried to recall a time when laughter came effortlessly, when happiness seemed abundant. Yet, the memories felt distant, as if obscured by a thick fog of sadness and discontent.

Watching the couple on the train made her realize how much she longed for that kind of happiness, the kind that fills the heart and soul, and it made her question why she hadn't realized that she had been missing that. She reflected on the choices she had made, the paths she had taken, and how far astray they had led her from true contentment. Her own parents were happy together, and she had wanted that too, but it seemed to suddenly feel like she could never have had that with Luke. The problem was, she wasn't sure that she could make any man happy, or that she would ever feel that connection with someone.

As the train continued the final leg of its rhythmic journey, she wrestled with these feelings, unsure of what lie ahead. The couple's laughter and affection became a beacon of hope, yet also a reminder of her own failures and fears. And so, she sat there, lost in thought, silently wondering what was next for her and Hazel, praying they would find happiness and love.

As she shifted in her seat to slide Hazel onto her side to sleep again, she felt something poking at her side. She reached in her pocket and pulled out the envelope her parents had handed her before she got on the train, realizing she had forgotten about it until now. They had told her to wait until later to open it, so she gently tore open the seal. She recognized her mother's beautiful handwriting instantly.

*My Dearest Sadie~*

*You and Hazel are the greatest gifts God has ever given your father and me. You have brought, and continue to bring, us so much joy and happiness. As you go on this journey together, we hope you find everything you're looking for. Your dad and I want you to always remember this: Happiness is not something you can force. Happiness is something that comes from within you. You have been through so much, but you have come out an even*

*stronger woman than before and we couldn't be prouder of you.
Now, you need to find yourself again, and in so doing, you will
find that happiness has been locked within you all along.
We love you, always and forever.
Mom and Dad*

She closed the letter gently and carefully placed it back in the envelope, Sadie wiped a tear from her eye. When it came to the parent department, she had the best. They were so understanding and loving, and she knew they were standing behind her for anything life was going to throw at her. She laid her head back on the seat and rested while Hazel slept.

No sooner than she had closed her eyes, she heard Hazel wake up, laughing as Cliff licked at her face.

"Good morning, cutie pie!" she said, giving her daughter a hug.

"Good morning, Mommy!" Hazel returned.

"How about we take Cliff for a little walk before we eat our breakfast… Does that sound good?" she asked, laughing as Hazel jumped off the seat, ready to get up and go.

They made the same route as the night before, allowing Cliff to relieve himself and to get some steps in before having to sit down for the final couple of hours of their journey. They ate breakfast together, and as they ate, they made a game of naming the trees and flowers they saw. They also tried counting the cows in the pastures as they flew by, laughing as they lost track. Sadie found solace in her daughter's presence and unending questions. Hazel and Cliff entertained her, as well as the couple down the aisle. Sadie also found comfort in Cliff's continued emotional support. Ever since she had gotten him as a puppy, it had seemed as if he knew when she needed him, and he attempted to cheer her up with a shake of the paw or his goofy antics.

As Chicago moved closer and closer to them, the anticipation of reaching their destination, and being with her friend became more and more exciting. The train continued its voyage through the captivating countryside, amazing Sadie with its beauty. Sadie couldn't help but wonder what this chapter of her life would bring.

Living apart from her husband was not something she had ever envisioned, let alone traveling away from where she had always called home. Still, this had to be good, had to be the right decision and the right place to go to figure out what came next for them. After all, this was her dream back then, back before she had fallen in love with Luke.

# Chapter Five

Sadie, Hazel, and Cliff arrived at the train depot in Chicago, exhausted but excited nonetheless, and they were eagerly greeted by Sawyer. Standing a bit taller than Sadie, Sawyer had a walk that exuded a sense of confidence and professionalism, even amid her excitement at seeing her best friend and her adorable little travel mates. Her long blond curls cascaded gracefully down her shoulders, adding a touch of playfulness to her overall demeanor.

Sawyer's beauty was undeniable, with a radiant complexion that seemed to glow under the soft natural light. Her makeup, though tastefully applied, accentuated her features, enhancing her already stunning appearance. Her bright and warm smile was infectious, immediately putting both Sawyer and Hazel at ease.

"Auntie Sawyer!" Hazel jumped into her arms, and Sawyer threw her into the air laughing and calling her sweet names. Hazel's giggling softened as she clung to Sawyer in a loving hug.

Sawyer's sense of style was both fashionable and comfortable. She often donned tight-fitting jeans that showcased her athletic figure while still allowing her to move with ease. A flowy blouse completed her ensemble, adding a touch of femininity and grace to her look.

As she walked to Sadie to hug her, delicate hoop earrings swayed gently, catching the light and emphasizing her lively persona. While Sadie had always preferred to dress comfortably and with little extra added to her ensemble, Sawyer loved to add some sparkle. It had never bothered either one of them that they shared that difference in style. Sadie noticed, for the first time, the glimmer of a modest-sized diamond ring on Sawyer's finger. She knew it hinted at the special connection she had with her husband, one that she held close to her heart. A connection that Sadie had only recently realized she had never had with Luke. A pang of sadness filled her heart, but she did her best to hide it with a smile at her best friend.

Sawyer's presence was captivating, and her genuine warmth made those around her feel valued and cherished. Her confidence and cheerfulness were a perfect blend, leaving a lasting impression on anyone fortunate enough to meet her. With her magnetic personality and radiant beauty, Sawyer embodied a wonderful balance of grace and strength that resonated deeply with Sadie, making her feel truly fortunate to have her as a friend.

After the long train journey from Seattle to Chicago, the trio felt relieved to finally reach their destination, but it was Sawyer's warm smile and enthusiastic hugs that immediately made them feel at home. "Well, should we head home? You three must be tuckered from that long train ride," she motioned towards the exit. "My car is right out front."

When they got to Sawyer's car, Sadie got Hazel settled into her car seat in the back, handing her a little container filled with her favorite crackers and some fruit snacks for the ride. She buckled herself into the front seat and sighed deeply. She hadn't realized she'd been so stressed, but it felt like a weight had just been lifted. Sawyer gave her a knowing look as she squeezed her hand and started the car. Hazel ate from her box as they embarked on the drive to Sawyer's house in Stone Creek, Illinois, the picturesque countryside unfolding before them. Rolling hills adorned with emerald green fields stretched out as far as the eye could see, similar to their home in Washington, only the hills were much smaller. The landscape was dotted with charming farmhouses and quaint barns, adding to the rural charm of the area. It was just how she had imagined it would be all those years ago.

As they drove, she and Sawyer talked often, catching up on missed moments and talking about the quaint beauty of Illinois, a state that Sawyer was obviously in love with. Sadie was entranced by the way the road wound its way through enchanting woodlands, where the lush canopy of trees filtered the golden rays of the setting sun. Shafts of light penetrated through the foliage, creating a mesmerizing interplay of light and shadow on the forest floor. Seattle, with its constant dancing lights, noise, and busy bodies was exciting and never dull, but she much preferred the natural silence and muted beauty she was seeing out her window here.

Approaching Stone Creek, the scenery shifted to a tranquil small-town ambiance. The streets were lined with old-fashioned lamp posts, casting a warm glow as the evening began to settle in. Vintage storefronts with charming facades adorned the sidewalks, exuding a sense of timeless nostalgia.

Nostalgia, a feeling Sadie had come to experience the most, and at every turn, with every sound, all the way from Seattle to Stone Creek. Sadie felt it in nearly everything. It yearned to creep in and dwell every time, but Sadie fought to keep it away for fear of what it would do if she opened up and let it all in.

Every face, every voice, and every smell asked to bring back memories, and now more than ever, Illinois was making it all come flooding back.

There was the longing, the familiarity, the regret, and the reality that trumped it all. She shook her head slightly, as if to clear the thoughts from it.

"I love this place," she said thoughtfully, peeking out of the car window as Sawyer pointed out places to her as they passed by them. As they passed the small town, she saw the rustic main street, with its aged signs and red brick sidewalks. She could see a cute pink and purple ice cream truck stopped by the park, with parents and children all lined up at it to get some ice cream. She smiled as she saw a little boy tugging on his mother's arm as she tried to tell him no to the creamy treat. Eventually, she gave in, probably equally as excited to grab a treat of her own. Just down from the little park was a library, with pillars out front and a swing by a fountain on the side of the building. She could see a couple sitting there, drinking coffee and enjoying time together, watching the water dance in the fountain. This town was like something from a movie, and she was in love with it already. It was everything she had dreamed it would be and more.

Her mind occasionally wandered off, the thought of Luke creeping in, and she wondered whether he would look for them. She hadn't reached out to tell him they were leaving for Stone Creek, nor when, and she was no stranger to the kind of reaction he'd usually have to things like this. He never allowed her to make decisions without first consulting him. Her parents had assured her that she could legally go wherever she wanted to since Luke had signed custody over to her, but she couldn't help but worry about what he may do if he found out.

Sawyer's response pulled her back from her wandering thoughts again.

"I knew you would. Even though we didn't end up doing this together, you were still my inspiration. I set my mind to it and followed through with what you and I had planned, all the while hoping and praying that you'd join me one day." Sawyer's hopeful tone made her smile.

"Miss Hazel," she turned her attention to the back seat for a moment, "there's my house!" she announced excitedly. Hazel popped her head up as high as she could to see out the window of the car. She giggled in anticipation of finally getting out to run and play.

Sawyer's house was nestled on the outskirts of town, surrounded by a lush garden bursting with vibrant blooms. The aroma of flowers permeated the air, adding to the welcoming atmosphere. A white picket fence framed the property, giving it a quaint and inviting feel. Leave it to Sawyer to have an *actual* white picket fence, Sadie thought with a smile. Reading her mind, Sawyer gave her a nudge. "Hey, it came with the house when we bought it!" she laughed, parking the car in front of the porch.

As they climbed out of the car, Hazel's eyes widened with wonder at the idyllic surroundings. The air was filled with the distant chirping of crickets and the gentle rustling of leaves, creating a soothing symphony of nature's sounds. Sadie could feel the summer breeze on her cheeks, and she was thankful for the promise of sun all day, and no rain. Hazel giggled her way through the flowers and shrubs, touching everything, pointing and asking more questions than could be answered at once. The most striking of them being whether they could live there forever, which had Sadie laughing. Things sure were simpler when you were four years old.

She looked at the beautiful house- it was a 2-story farmhouse-style home, but with modern siding, brick, and porches on the front and the back. The white of the house was a stark contrast to the beautiful green surrounding it. It was exactly as she had imagined it would be. Sawyer smiled as she led them up the porch steps, past a wooden swing that had a plaid-backed pillow that read 'Home' on the front. She opened the front door, holding it for them as they walked past her.

Inside, Sawyer's warm hospitality continued to shine. The interior was tastefully decorated with a mix of rustic and modern elements, creating a cozy and stylish ambiance. Soft, plush couches invited them to sink in and relax after their long journey. Sawyer's husband, Travis, emerged from one of the rooms wearing a very big smile. Seeing him now, for the first time, Sadie realized that she had missed the most important person in her best friend's life, and her heart ached to rewind the clock. He walked towards them, giving Sadie a hug and welcoming her to his home. Then, he turned his attention to Hazel.

"Well, if you aren't the cutest thing around then I don't know what is!" he said, smiling at her. "My name is Travis, and Sawyer is my beautiful wife!" he said, helping Hazel to relax a little.  He reached down with his arms, and Hazel looked at her mom with apprehension. After receiving a nod from Sadie, Hazel let him pick her up to carry her.

Hazel gazed at his face carefully, touching his sandy brown hair with her tiny fingers. She ran them through his hair, held up by a ponytail in the back. She seemed to be studying him closely, determining if he was safe or not.

Smiling affectionately, Sawyer said, "Babe, meet Sadie," and turning to Sadie, she said, "Sadie, this is Travis." Sadie could see how happy she was, and it made her wish she could feel that way too.

"Hi, Sadie, I've heard so much about you," Travis said, "I was beginning to wonder whether I should just travel to Seattle myself to meet you," he said with a bit of comedy in his voice. "The issue, you see, is that I melt in the rain, so Sawyer has seen to it I never have to do that." Sadie chuckled, the first genuine laugh since the journey began. Knowing her best friend, she instantly saw why Sawyer loved him. It wasn't simply because he was gorgeous, standing over 6 feet tall with deep blue eyes and cheek bones looking like they were chiseled. It wasn't even his low raspy voice. It was his laid-back personality and apparent playfulness. Sawyer always loved a good laugh, and apparently, Travis was quite the joker.

"And you're the gentleman who swooped in and won over Sawyer's heart." Sadie had a grateful smile, and it was, again, genuine.

Sawyer had spoken so highly of him during her visit in Seattle, and she was eager to finally meet the man who had captured her best friend's heart, and as soon as the door had swung open, and in walked Travis, exuding a vibrant energy, she knew he was perfect for her.

"And who is this cutie pie?" Travis turned his attention to the squirmy little girl in his arms.

Sawyer smiled and said playfully, "Travis, this is Sadie's daughter, Hazel. Oh, and of course, this is her furry companion, Cliff." Cliff barked as if he understood what was going on.

Travis shook Cliff's extended paw firmly, his business-like demeanor giving him away as a rather professional person, but his genuine kindness quickly softened the impression. "It's a pleasure to meet you all! Sawyer has told me so much about you. Hazel, I hear you're quite the adventurer, and Cliff, you're the true boss around here, right?" he joked, giving the dog a playful pat on the head while he wagged his tail in delight.

"He's just a dog, silly!" Hazel replied with a smile. Sadie knew by the way both Sawyer and Travis cared for Hazel, that she had made the right choice. Hazel's mind was at least taken away from bringing up her daddy, and she looked truly happy here so far.

"Okay! How about we bring these bags to your rooms? I bet you are both pretty exhausted from the ride," Sawyer chipped in, taking Hazel from Travis and leading the way as soon as she stole a quick kiss from him. They walked up the steps and stopped at the first door. "Here is Hazel & Cliff's room!" she said and then added, "Sadie, your room is right across the hall there. I figured you'd want to be close to each other."

Suddenly, as if remembering something she had forgotten, Sawyer turned to Travis and asked, "Oh, just in case I need your help with anything, where will you be while I get these three all settled in?"

"With me, ma'am," a friendly, deep voice called from the door.

"Oh, hey, Ryder, come on in." she responded with a laugh as she excused herself and headed back down the steps.

"Got visitors?"

"Yeah, my friend from Washington, the one I've mentioned to you before, came to visit." She turned to Sadie who was now in the room helping Hazel unpack her toys. "Sadie, can you come down here for a minute and say hi to a friend of ours?"

"My friend, you mean?" Travis joked, throwing a long arm over Ryder's shoulder.

As Sadie and Hazel made their way back to the living room, Ryder stepped forward and shut the door behind him. At first glance, Sadie was instantly impressed by what she saw. Ryder was built like a football player, she imagined, and had an easy confidence about him. Standing just a bit shorter than Travis, he had a rugged charm that she was sure most people probably found easily attractive. He had the most beautiful, tanned complexion and tousled auburn hair she had ever seen on a man. She was suddenly aware that she was staring, and she blushed as she turned her gaze to her daughter instead of the gorgeous man in the entry.

"You must be Sadie," Ryder said, extending a hand to Sadie for a handshake. As she shook his hand, he slowly lifted it to plant a kiss on it. She was acutely aware of her heart beating quickly in her chest. Her breath caught and she felt like her legs had gone to jelly underneath her. What was going on with her, she wondered. He had a sly and mischievous grin, revealing a dimple on the right cheek. He quickly turned toward Hazel.

Sadie couldn't help but notice Ryder's gaze as he looked at her. It was as if he was trying to see deep inside her soul, yet at the same time, there was a glint of amusement and something playful in his eyes. The combination of kindness and firmness in his demeanor made her feel at ease, but the five o'clock shadow tucked onto his shirt reminded her of Luke, and she found herself quickly withdrawn from his albeit easy-going nature, causing a confused bundle of feelings within her. The battle that her mind seemed to be having with her heart was making her tired, and she suddenly wanted a nap.

Ryder had a love for children, and it was evident from the moment he laid eyes on Hazel. He knelt to her level, his lazy stride turning tender as he interacted with the little girl. "Well, hello there. You must be Hazel! I've heard so much about you," he said, his playful tone immediately eliciting a giggle from Hazel. Much like her mother, however, she was torn between withdrawing from him and letting him chat with her. She looked up at her mother who reluctantly gave her an approving nod.

Sawyer glanced from mother to daughter, reading the room and seeing the worry in their eyes. She decided maybe they needed some time to get comfortable with their new surroundings and the people that filled them. "Come on now, let's get you washed up and ready for bed," she said, gently leading Hazel away.

Sadie couldn't help but smile at the sight of Ryder connecting with Hazel so effortlessly. His genuine interest in a child he didn't even know, and his ability to make her laugh, was endearing, and she could see why he and Travis were such close friends.

"It was very nice meeting you both," she said to Travis and Ryder. "I had better head up and help those two get ready their nap." Turning her attention to Sawyer, she added, "If it's okay with you, I may lay with them a bit, as we are all pretty tired after that long train ride."

"Of course!" Sawyer said, nodding her approval.

"I bet you're all pretty tuckered! Go get some sleep. We have lots of time to get to know each other." Travis said with a smile.

"It was nice meeting you, Sadie. I'm sure I'll see you around." Ryder added.

Sadie nodded and turned to head upstairs. She felt like she could sleep for days and couldn't wait to climb into the soft bed and finally let herself relax.

* * *

Night had fallen over the hillside, and the darkness was overwhelming. Sadie was exhausted, but Hazel was apparently even more tired than she was, because she had fallen asleep during dinner, causing her to get some of her 'basketti' in her hair. After excusing themselves, Sadie picked up the sleepy little girl and headed upstairs to give her a bath. The clawfoot tub in the bathroom near her room was stunning, with ornate golden claws at the feet of the cast-iron tub. She filled it up with bubbles and hot water, and hopped in with Hazel, helping her wash her hair and scrub her little toes. They played in the bubbles some, but Hazel was too tired to be her usual comical self.

Smiling at Hazel, Sadie washed her own hair and wiped her face, feeling the layers peel away and fall into the soapy water after two days of not showering during their journey. When they both felt clean and refreshed, they stepped out of the tub and dried off, putting their favorite pajamas on so they were ready for bed.

"Mommy feels so much better! How about you?" Sadie asked, giving Hazel a little poke on the nose playfully.

"I'm sleepy," she said, rubbing her eyes as a lazy yawn escaped her mouth. "Can we go snuggle now?"

"Absolutely! How about we rock for a little bit and read a book before I put you to bed?"

"Yes!" Hazel said in a partially excited, partially exhausted tone.

Sadie scooped the little girl up, giving her a kiss on the forehead as she lay her head on her mother's shoulder. They shut the bathroom light off and headed to Hazel's temporary bedroom. Sitting in the chair, they pulled a fuzzy blanket over themselves and read a short story. Then, she lay Hazel in her bed, tucking her into her covers and giving her a stuffed animal to snuggle. Cliff happily hopped up on the bed to lay next to her. Sadie moved back to the chair, looking out the window, catching glimpses of the serene landscape surrounding the house. The setting sun painted the sky with hues of pink and orange, casting a dreamy glow over Stone Creek. The grass shined with a fresh dew at its tips.

Stone Creek had a magical charm that seemed to cast a spell on Sadie, Hazel, and Cliff. The beauty of the countryside, the quaint small-town atmosphere, and the genuine friendship that had begun to blossom some more between Sawyer and Sadie made Sadie feel at home, finally. She knew she'd made the right choice in coming to Stone Creek.

"Mommy, are Ryder and Travis good guys or bad guys?" Hazel's unanticipated and abrupt question brought her from her trance.

"Sweetie, they are wonderfully kind men. If Sawyer trusts them, then we can trust them."  Sadie's heart sank at the thought of her daughter having to even ask that question. Satisfied for the moment with her mother's response, Hazel slowly shut her eyelids and surrendered to sleep.  As she watched her precious little girl sleep, Sadie felt the weight of the world aching at her shoulders. She knew the choices she had made had led them here, both good and bad. As she petted Cliff on the head and then tiptoed towards the door, she smiled at Hazel's sweet pudgy cheeks and the innocent look of her while she slept.

She slowly closed the door partway and then crossed the hall to her room.  She was here now, she told herself, and that was what mattered most. With time, Sawyer had told Sadie that she believed Sadie would heal from the trauma and impact of her abusive marriage. She hoped with everything in her heart that Sawyer was right.

She slipped her slippers off and climbed under the fluffy covers, savoring the feeling of the soft bed below her. She put one pillow under her head and the other one she cuddled in front of her. As she lay there, all cuddled up under the covers, her mind started to wander back to Luke, and to everything that had happened over the last couple of months.  As she settled her head on her pillow and closed her eyes, she decided she was going to give herself a break from thinking for one night. Tomorrow, she'd figure life out. Tonight, she'd sleep.

# Chapter Six

Over the next few weeks, Sadie and Sawyer spent countless hours sitting together and catching up.  Even though both had been on different paths, their lives seemed to merge back together seamlessly, as though time had stood still. Sadie loved sitting on the porch swing with Hazel, reading and singing and just spending time together.  She could easily get used to this life and the feeling of simplicity and joy that came with it. The rhythm of daily life on Travis' family's farmstead was wonderful, everything she had wanted back when they were teenagers in school, dreaming of the life they would create together here. As the days and weeks passed, Sadie found that she could feel the pain and sadness of her failed marriage being chipped away from her heart, making space for new possibilities. She started helping out at the winery, and she was in love instantly, and very thankful for the chance to work again. She had missed the conversations and being around people for the last few years. It was wonderful to feel as though she was providing for her family, something Luke hadn't allowed her to do.

Come to think of it, she hadn't thought about Luke much lately, but today was different. Her phone had rung while she was cleaning up after supper, but when she answered it the person on the other end didn't speak. After saying hello several times, she had hung up. She didn't recognize the number, but she could hear the person breathing on the other end. The whole thing had given her a very bad feeling, one that she couldn't shake as she gave Hazel her bath and read her a story. She laid Hazel down to bed and quickly headed to Sawyer's room. She shut the door behind her, knowing Travis was out bowling with Ryder, but wanting to be sure they weren't heard, just the same. Sawyer peeked out of the adjoining bathroom, her eyebrow raised in curiosity. "What's up?" she asked, toothbrush still lodged in her mouth.

"We need to talk," Sadie insisted, patting the mattress beside her where she sat.

Sawyer held up her finger in a gesture for Sadie to wait, then disappeared back into the bathroom to rinse out her mouth. When she returned, she chose to stand instead of sitting, a sign of restlessness and concern. Sadie had been doing great the past couple of weeks. She and Hazel had settled in perfectly, and even made a few new friends, so what could have gotten her friend so upset?

"You're making me nervous, Sade's! What's going on?" she asked, an obvious hint of worry in her voice.

"I think Luke called." she blurted out.

"What? Why? When?" Sawyer stuttered through, not sure which question she wanted the answer to most.

"A little while ago, when I was putting dishes away. At first, he was quiet and I thought nobody was there, but when I kept asking if anyone was there, I could hear some noise in the background. I think he got my number somehow!"

Sawyer could sense the fear in Sadie's voice. They'd spent the most of the time since she had gotten to Illinois catching up, and Sawyer had especially found joy in watching Sadie live a life away from the fear she had known in Seattle with Luke. Having that get ruined was not acceptable to her. Still, she was guessing that Sadie may just be feeling paranoid because she was so afraid that something would ruin the happiness she was learning to know and love.

"What if it was him, Sawyer? What if he changed his mind and wants Hazel back?  What if he becomes hostile and threatens to come down here? Oh my goodness, what if he is going to–"

"Relax, Sadie. Take a deep breath and back up for a minute. Let's think about this logically, okay? It might have just been a wrong dial by someone else. I mean, you didn't hear his voice, did you?"

Sadie's eyes widened, and she started pacing back and forth, the weight of the situation sinking in. She nervously put her left hand to her mouth, biting the nails as she tried to figure out the best course of action.

Sawyer interrupted the tense silence, her voice filled with concern and frustration as she watched her friend pace the floor. Obviously, this was really scaring her, and she hated seeing her like this. "Sadie, talk to me! What are you thinking?" Her emotions were evident as her lower lip quivered, and tears threatened to spill down her cheeks.

Sadie felt overwhelmed with fear and worry over what would happen if her worst nightmares were coming true. "I'm scared, Sawyer! I don't know what to do. What should I do?"

Sawyer walked over and grabbed her friend's shoulders, gently offering support and a plan. "I have an idea. First, we're going to sit down with Travis and let him know what happened so that we are all on the same page."

Sadie looked at her, seeming perplexed and confused. "OK, I guess that's fine, but what are we going to do to make sure we are safe? I will never be able to sleep at night if I don't know that Hazel is safe!"

Sawyer offered a comforting smile and a hug, trying to calm her friend down. "If you are truly thinking that it was Luke and you are scared for both of you, then I think it's time we talk to the police about how they can help protect you and Hazel. We are good friends with the sheriff, and he'll know more about how we can help keep you both safe."

"Oh, I don't think we need to tell the sheriff. I don't want to waste his time on my problems. I'm sure it will all be fine… I'm probably just overacting. Right?"

"How about this… we can hold off on telling the sheriff, but we definitely need to tell Travis, and you need to promise me that if you get any more of those calls, you'll go to the police and tell them everything!" Sawyer said, slight panic in her voice now to match Sadie's.

Sadie forced a small smile on her face. She knew she had her friend's support and guidance, and that gave her a glimmer of hope. With Sawyer by her side, they would face this challenge together, and Sadie felt reassured that she wasn't alone in navigating this mess. After all, she'd been there for her so far. The problem was, Sawyer didn't know Luke or what he was capable of, and neither did Travis, for that matter. Unfortunately, Sadie did.

Once again, the fear crept up and she couldn't stop herself

from voicing it. "Oh God. Sawyer, do you think he'd really come here? For some reason that possibility never entered my mind before today. How could I have been so naive? I thought we were safe here, but I also never really considered the fact that he may come after us at some point, or that he'd probably be able to figure out where to look since he knew I missed you and would want to come here to spend time with you."

"I highly doubt knows where you are or how to reach you. You changed your number before leaving Seattle, and you said you didn't tell him, right? And no one other than your parents know you're here… even if he figured out where you are, he'd still have no way to find your cell number, so that doesn't make sense." Sawyer hugged her comfortingly.

"Maybe he's been trying to find us, I mean, that's not impossible, is it?"

"You mean after he ghosted you and Hazel right after a divorce you didn't even get the chance to ask for yourself? I totally understand why you are worried, but I think it's a little too early to jump to too many conclusions. Plus, Trav said he got a call like that the other night, too. He said he thought it was a wrong dial, so maybe it's a telemarketer or something."

Sadie sighed. "Sawyer, not to change the subject„ but I have something else I want to talk to you about too, and I guess now's as good of a time as any. I've been meaning to talk to you about this for the last few days, but with business picking up at the winery I never got a chance to." Sawyer let her go and they both sat in her bed.

"Sure! What's up, Sadie? Did something else happen that I don't know about?"

"No, everything else is fine. Honestly, before *this*, everything has been perfect! Even so, I've been doing some thinking and I was wondering if you and Travis would be okay with Hazel, Cliff and I moving into the cottage down by the winery for a while? It's not that we don't like it here, because we all do! It's just that we are doing so good, and I think it's time for us to get out of your hair and start figuring out what comes next. Does that make any sense? I'm sorry if that upsets you, Sawyer, I just-"

"Come on, Sadie, you know you don't need to apologize for wanting your independence. To be honest, I wondered when you'd finally ask." Sawyer interrupted, smiling.

"You did?"

"Yes," they both chuckled. "But I didn't want to shove it down your throat. You are welcome to go wherever you'd like, but I'm glad you're going to start out at the cottage. Then we can still see each other all the time!"

"How do you always seem to know what I need before I do?" They exchanged a hug and Sawyer told her about the dreams she had had for so long about her friend living at that cottage and helping her run the winery.

"We used to talk about living right beside each other, and now we can!" Sadie said with more excitement in her voice.

"That empty cottage has been waiting for you for years. Sadie, and I'm glad you're finally here to enjoy it. You have no idea how happy this makes me, and how proud I am of you. I don't think I've expressed it well enough, but I frickin' missed you. I didn't even know how much until you got here."

"Sawyer. I'm so happy for you and all you have built here. You took a dream that two little girls had and made it a reality, and I couldn't be prouder of *you* for that."

"The winery was originally your idea, Sadie. It's been the

closest thing I've had to you, so I hung onto it in hopes that you'd join me one day. And thank God you got here in time for the busy season! You seriously have no idea how nice it will be to have your help this year! Now, when is it you want to move?" The two women laughed and hugged, and then laughed together some more. The genuine happiness Sadie felt was so refreshing, and it made her forget all about what had happened earlier, at least for now.

"How about this weekend?" Sadie eventually asked in a break of laughter.

"I think that is perfect! Oh Sadie, it will be so much fun getting the cottage ready for you and Hazel, and even more fun helping you move in! Just tell me what you need, and I'll have Trav and his friends get it for you." Sawyer was glad, at least for now, that Sadie's mind had been distracted from thinking Luke might be after her. Now, it was time to get to work.

* * *

"But if you were so scared, then why did you stay?"

"I loved him, and it's not like he was always waiting to hurt me. He just had a temper, and normally he used words, not his hand. There was only one other time he hit me, and that time wasn't really that hard."

"Sadie, you don't honestly believe that do you?" Sawyer wasn't being judgmental; she was just concerned. "I know you think he loved you, and I won't say he didn't on some level or at some point, but even *that* is not an excuse for what he did to you. Sadie, it was too–"

"Deep inside I know that Sawyer, it's just that it's hard for me to not feel that I had some part in the way he felt and acted. He told me all the time that it was my fault, that I was clumsy, or naive, or slow. Even though I know now that the way he treated me wasn't right, it will still take some time for me to truly believe it and live like it's true." It was so hard for Sadie to try to explain how she felt to someone who had never felt that way before. "And one more thing… I don't ever plan to let anyone do that to me again." Those were the words she needed to utter, but that was also only as good as it sounded.

Sawyer was helping her finish arranging and decorating Hazel's room. Hazel was thrilled to be moving to her own house, and she told them both that she didn't care what her room looked like as long as it was yellow and sparkly. She had stopped asking about her daddy, which made things easier, but Sadie knew she hadn't forgotten him either.

"Sadie, I'm sorry if it sounded like I was trying to rush you. I think it's great that you are starting to heal, and I know that it takes time. I do, however, want to be sure that you know that it's okay to move forward and stop looking back."

"I know, and I promise you that I'm doing my best. I'm a work in progress, I guess you could say!" Sadie said, nudging her best friend with her elbow playfully.

Smiling, Sawyer added, "I'm happy to hear that. One more thing, though… It's okay to try dating when you feel up to it, and I'd be happy to set you up with some pretty *eligible* bachelors around here, if you know what I mean!"

"Sawyer!" Sadie said with an exasperated laugh.

"Just saying… being spinsters was never part of our plan!" Sawyer laughed. "In all seriousness, though, *Luke* is not someone worth judging *every* man by, Sadie, and that's all I'll say about that for now."

Sadie finished positioning Hazel's little yellow table and chair set beside her window just in time for Hazel to come bouncing in the room, Cliff in tow. She cheerfully pulled out the chair and sat on it, smiling at her mamma in approval.

From Hazel's room, there was a picturesque view of the vast cranberry bogs in the distance. The serene beauty of the landscape added to the charm of their surroundings. Sadie knew that the view from that window would never get old. It was so different from the skyline in Seattle.

"Woohoo! Alright, ladies, we're all done! Before I go, remember we have that get-together thing tonight at the winery. Ryder's sister, Stacy, said she'd pick up Harriet from school, and then come get Hazel so she can play with Harriet while we're there, and then we can pick her up quick afterwards. I'll pick you up around 6 and you can ride with Travis and I, if that works for you."

Sadie didn't like the idea of being away from Hazel but saying no would only give Sawyer more reasons to think and worry about her. So, she agreed to it as cheerfully as she could. "Sounds great, I look forward to meeting all your friends from this area!"

"Yahoo... I can't wait to play with Harriet!" Hazel's excitement was palpable as she explored her new home. She absolutely adored her own room, which had been carefully decorated in beautiful shades of yellow that made the sun's rays bounce all around it. The cheerful hue brightened up the space, creating a warm and inviting atmosphere for the giggling little girl.

* * *

The cottage had a short wooden fence surrounding the property, providing peace of mind for Sadie as she watched Hazel play outside. The fence added an extra layer of security, allowing them to enjoy the beautiful outdoor space without any worries. Since she had no car of her own, she had to resort to walking the short distance to the winery or Sawyer's house. She didn't mind, though, as she loved to walk, and so did Hazel. She grabbed her cell phone out of her pocket before sitting on the porch swing to watch Hazel play on the swing set that Travis and Ryder had put together for her. She hit the button to call the only person she knew would understand how she was feeling that afternoon, someone she missed very much.

"Hello, mom!" Sadie said as her mother answered.

*Oh my goodness... Sadie! I miss you! How are you girls doing? Are you all moved in?*

Sadie could tell that her mother was excited to hear from her. She felt guilty for not calling the last few days, but she had been horribly busy trying to get everything done so they could move into the cute little cottage.

"Yes, we just finished a couple of hours ago actually. It's perfect, and Hazel loves it too. Honestly, this is a pretty big step for me," Sadie told her mother, "But I am finally getting some fresh air and it's definitely helping me to see things more clearly."

*Oh, that's great honey. What about Hazel? How's she taking it there?*

"Hazel is... well, Hazel– she's a child, innocent, trusting and full of giggles." They both laughed.

*Has she made any friends?*

"There's a little girl here about her age close by, and I think they've already hit it off. Her name is Harriet, and she's Ryder's niece."

*Oh, well that's wonderful. Ryder's one of Travis's friends, as I remember…the firefighter who loves kids, correct?*

"Yes he- Wait…who told you that he loves kids?" Sadie glanced at Hazel, pulling her dolls around in the little red wagon Stacy had given her to play with. As Hazel smiled and waved her chubby little hand at her, she suddenly realized who had told her.

"Hazel told you. Of course, that explains a few awkward moments we've had so far. When did you two talk about Ryder?"

*A little while back. She called me while you were in the shower… she sure has figured out how to use your phone!*

"That little stinker… Yes, sometimes I think she knows more about it than I do!"

*She told me all about the people she has met, and how much she loves it there. Sweetheart, I should also tell you that she also asked about her daddy.*

"I'm going to need to find another lie sooner or later, mom, and I'm not sure what to say."

*Sweetheart, she's a child. She may have witnessed what happened between you two, but she probably doesn't understand much about it. Just tell her whatever you think is right. I'm sure she will be okay, just like you will be.*

"I know. But she hasn't asked me for a while now. I suppose she's already used to the answer I keep giving her. Anyway, how's dad?"

*He's good. He ran to town to have coffee with some friends and then was picking up some groceries on his way home later. I'll tell him you called.*

"Thanks mom. I love you."

*Love you, too. Give my kisses to Hazel and tell her I'll send her some of her favorite pancakes and syrup soon!*

"Mom, you do know I can just make it for her, right?"

*No hard feelings, sweetie, but nobody makes it like grandma does.*

"Alright, mom, you, have a nice evening. Tell dad I said hi.

*I will, sweetheart.*

"Bye, mom."

Sadie placed the phone on her bedside table and looked around, then hesitantly walked towards her closet. She looked through, touching and pushing aside every single outfit. It was a "party-ish", as Sawyer was calling it, which apparently meant hanging out, drinking fruity drinks with cute little straws in them, and playing a game or two. Sadie finally made her choice, but not without the help of Hazel who had come bouncing into the room and insisted that she wear a short black dress with little yellow flowers on it. She also picked out a pair of cute, yet comfy, sandals to match. A serious lack of motivation for leaving the cottage deterred her from considering any other options. Instead, she brushed her teeth, put on some lip gloss and a little dab of eye shadow, and headed into Hazel's room to get her ready to be picked up by Stacy and Harriet.

After packing her things into a little bag, Hazel and Sadie sat on a bench by the front window to watch for Stacy. The evening was fast descending over the cottage, but for some reason, the darkness soothed Sadie. She loved to watch the sun set over the hills as the moon rose over the valley. It brought a sort of peaceful feeling to her, and she loved that.

When the car pulled up, Hazel leapt off her lap and practically sprinted out the door. She laughed, helping her into the car, buckling her in and giving her a kiss. She had thought she might need to persuade Hazel she wouldn't miss her, and that she would have so much fun with Harriet, but there was no need for that. The two little girls seemed to already have a special bond, one that only children can form in such a short time.

"Thank you very much for taking her tonight, Stacy. I really appreciate it." she said, leaning her head in the door so she could exchange smiles with her.

"No problem at all! These two can play so I can maybe get something done for once!" Stacy replied, laughing as she watched the two girls giggling away already.

Sadie shut the car door and waved at Hazel as they drove down the driveway. After going back inside and shutting the door, Sadie stood for a moment and enjoyed the silence. She could hear a couple of squirrels outside the window rustling in the tree. She loved how close nature was to her in the quaint cottage. She walked to her room and sat on her bed, left alone with her own thoughts. She imagined that as the days passed, she and Hazel would settle into their new life in the valley. That they would spend time exploring the winery, enjoy leisurely walks through the cranberry bogs, and take in the breath-taking scenery around them. The peaceful ambiance of their surroundings already made their new home feel like a haven of tranquility.

Each evening, they would sit on the porch, savoring the view of the bogs as the sun dipped below the horizon, painting the sky with vibrant hues of orange and pink. The distant sound of crickets chirping, and the gentle rustling of leaves would add to the soothing symphony of nature around them. She loved the fact that you could hear the most incredible sounds around you if closed your eyes and just listened. In Seattle, you just heard cars honking, people talking, and the distant sounds of ships arriving at port to deliver shipping containers or their daily catch of fish or crab.

The valley's beauty, combined with the comfort of their cozy cottage, made Sadie and Hazel feel like they had found a slice of paradise in Illinois. Sadie knew that the sense of belonging and safety within the confines of this fenced cottage would allow them to relax and embrace this new chapter of their lives with hope and contentment. She wanted nothing more than peace and the quiet, and she knew this was the place to find just that. Even so, she was also glad that it was September, which meant it was the busy season at the winery and the farm, because she could easily get lost helping out where she was needed.

"Ahem! Hey," Sadie jumped, her heart feeling as though it had just leapt across the room. She had been so lost in her own thoughts that she hadn't realized that Ryder had opened the door and was standing in the entryway. "Umm, you okay?" he asked, keeping his distance so as not to scare her any more than he already had. "I'm sorry about that. I can be light-footed sometimes. It's just that you weren't answering, and your door was unlocked so I let myself in to be sure everything was okay. Being a firefighter, it's kind of a hazard of the job-always worrying that something might be wrong."

Ryder's explanation was understandable, but Sadie didn't think it was necessary. "No, I'm sorry, I was just... thinking, I guess."

"Yeah, I figured as much." He smiled at her, instantly making her legs wobble.

"Are you giving me a ride? Sawyer said she was going to be here at 6…" she said, obviously confused at his presence.

"Yes I am. Sawyer had to… um…" he stuttered, seeming uncomfortable in his own boots. "Well, I'm honestly not sure *what* she had to do, but she asked me to pick you up, so here I am. I hope that's okay."

"Yeah, that's fine. I really am sorry for not hearing you knock. After all the noise of the city for so long, I get *so* lost in the quiet sounds of nature all around me here, and I seem to lose my ability to think, and apparently to hear, too."

"Well, as I said before, no need to be sorry. I hope it's okay if I tell you that you look beautiful tonight." His dimple peeked out as he put that mischievous grin she found so appealing on his face. She suddenly found herself wondering what it would be like to kiss that mouth. The thought had her internally shaming herself and getting quite flushed in her face. She hoped he didn't notice.

"Oh. Hazel picked it," Sadie said, blushing more deeply. The awkwardness she felt tightened around her belly. "And the sandals too."

"Well, I better try to remember to thank her then, because she has great taste!"

"She does. Of course, there's some yellow on it." she said as she pointed to the little flowers on her dress.

"Yeah, I was actually thinking she'd have you in a sparkly yellow dress, or something of the sort!" Sadie laughed, and for the very first time in what seemed like an eternity to her, she felt a sense of freedom escape her throat. "Where is she, anyway?"

"Oh, they already left."

"Right, Stacy. Totally skipped my mind. Well then, after you," he said, pointing toward the front door. Sadie took a deep breath as soon as he turned around, thankful that she had a moment before he was looking at her again so she could regain her composure. There was something about Ryder that aroused feelings within her, feelings she didn't' feel that she had any right to feel this soon after her divorce. Besides, there was no way he felt them too. She felt like her life was a mess, and there was no man that would want to take that on, especially with a little girl involved. It was a conflict within her, and there was a lot of fear and skepticism in it. From the very first day she'd met Ryder, it had been that way, and she was so confused and scared by it. He seemed to be able to turn her into a nervous little schoolgirl with a crush, just by giving her a look or a flash of that smile of his. How could he do that so easily? She was far from a schoolgirl, and not innocent in the relationship department, so what was it about this man that made her so on edge, yet also so excited, all at one time?

# Chapter Seven

In the heart of Stone Creek, a cozy and rustic bar named Quinn's, after Travis's great great grandfather, had become the gathering place for Travis and his friends.  The bar exuded warmth with its dim lighting, exposed brick walls, and wooden furnishings.  Framed vintage posters and old photographs adorned the walls, reflecting the town's rich history. There was a photo of Travis's great great grandfather, great grandfather, grandfather, his father and himself on the wall in ascending order, oldest to youngest.

As Sadie and Ryder stepped inside, they were greeted with the inviting aroma of wood and the faint scent of fresh flowers on the tables. The soft glow of hanging Edison bulbs created a warm ambiance, casting a golden hue on the faces of their friends. As Sadie and Ryder walked in the door, it felt as if all eyes fell on them. They both instantly felt self-conscious and awkward. They hadn't said much on the 10-minute drive from her house, mostly making small talk between them. She couldn't figure out why it seemed so hard to relax around him.

Sadie scanned the room, quickly finding Sawyer, and excused herself to head toward her.

The bar had been reserved exclusively for them, a gesture from Travis and Ryder, to give them a private space to unwind and enjoy each other's company. Sawyer and Travis's friends, including Ryder who had joined them, had already gathered over by the pool table, laughing and chatting animatedly. There were already a few empty bottles of beer and half full glasses of wine sitting on tables. After a few minutes of talking to Sawyer, she glanced over and saw Ryder walking towards her.

"Drink?" Ryder asked, offering Sadie a glass. "Fruity, just like you like it," he explained, and a smile formed on the corner of Sadie's mouth.

"Thanks. And I'm sorry for taking off. I just needed to talk to Sawyer quick," she said, accepting the glass. "Wait... how did you know I like fruity drinks?

"No need to apologize, and Sawyer mentioned it to me once when she was walking about a new wine she was creating after your taste. Anyway, you girls have fun sipping your frilly drinks while I go use the men's room and then find Trav doing whatever he's up to." Sadie blushed as he smiled at her before leaving them. The smell of his cologne lingered in the air, and she found herself wishing he had stayed.

Small wooden tables were scattered around the room, adorned with flickering candles and flowers, creating an intimate setting. Sadie looked around for a perfect spot, one that would allow her to talk with Sawyer for a few minutes without others hearing.

A chalkboard behind the bar showcased the evening's special drinks, each uniquely crafted to suit the tastes of everyone present.   Soft, melodic tunes played in the background, providing the perfect backdrop for their "party-ish."  The soft melodies allowed them to talk without shouting over the music.

In one corner, a group of Sawyer's friends that Sadie had either only met once or a few times, had a lively game of darts going, their feminine laughter filling the air. She recognized Lily Stanton, Daisy Miller and Karen Cooper, and the others were women she hadn't met yet.  In another area, Travis's friends, Landon Magee and Charley Hagen, among a couple of others she didn't know, gathered around a vintage board game, lost in playful banter and friendly competition.

The bar itself was a work of art, handcrafted with care, showcasing a collection of spirits from local distilleries. The bar counter appeared to be made from a slab of wood that she guessed had come from a beautiful cedar tree. She could smell a hint of cedar in the air, and it mixed well with the men's cologne she was smelling in the air. The bartenders, masters of mixology, expertly crafted the guests' favorite drinks with a flourish, adding a personal touch to each concoction.

Sadie's heart fluttered uncontrollably as she stole glances at Ryder, who now stood behind the bar, flashing his charming smile and tending to their friends with ease.  He looked comfortable and sexy as hell behind there, with his sleeves rolled up to show the masculine strength of his forearms beneath. She found that she wanted to run her fingers along the lines made by the veins in his arm, to explore where they led.  She wanted to look away, afraid she'd be caught staring, but something had her eyes stuck to him like glue. Finally pulling away, she saw Sawyer smiling at her, obviously knowing who she was gawking at.

It was obvious to Sawyer that Sadie had feelings for Ryder. She had been looking at him like she wanted to eat him for dessert ever since they had arrived together. She smiled, hoping her plan would work. She had planned this little get-together in hopes that Sadie being in this relaxed and playful setting would help her to meet new people and intensify those feelings she obviously had for him. Ryder had so much charm, and he was built like an athlete. She had grown to love him, and she knew that he would be such a perfect match for Sadie. Best of all, he was the most patient man she knew, and that would be needed if he was going to have any sort of luck with Sadie, especially after all she'd been through.

"Has anyone told you he wrestled in high school?" Sawyer eyed her, making a face that suggested she knew what was going through her mind.

Sadie paused briefly, blushing as she contemplated whether to give Sawyer a predictive response or just to say nothing at all. "Oh my gosh, Sawyer, seriously." Sawyer laughed, then excused herself to go find Travis.

As she stood there taking in the room, Sadie fell back into her thoughts, observing everything and everyone in the bar. This was the best part of her night so far... being left alone. She never was a party lover. She enjoyed time with her close friends and her family but wasn't a fan of groups of people she didn't know. It made her nervous and uncomfortable. The atmosphere was filled with love and camaraderie, as each group raised their glasses to toast to friendship, love, and whatever else they had to toast to.

"What happened to your partner?" Ryder's unmistakable, friendly voice asked, taking the stool next to her.

*Where in the world had he come from?* she thought.

"Did she bail on you?"

Sadie smiled involuntarily, "More like got tired of me," she said, drinking from her glass.

"I highly doubt that," he said, smiling. "Can I fill that up for you?" Sadie hadn't realized her glass was empty, but before she could say anything, Ryder took the glass from her and went to fill it up, giving her a minute to think clearly. Something about him always seemed to put a pause to her brain, and as good as that felt, it also happened to remind her of what it felt like to lose control of herself, which terrified her. The odd thing was that, at the same time, it felt exciting. More than anything, though, it was confusing, and she wasn't sure that she liked that feeling at all.

As the night went by, Sadie felt a sense of belonging she hadn't experienced in a long time. The weight of her not-so-past life seemed to lift, being replaced by the joy of being surrounded by new friends who seemed to accept her as part of their group. She was amazed that so many people who she had just met could already appear to care so deeply for her and Hazel. She had always felt everyone's eyes staring at her in judgment in the past, so this new feeling of acceptance was so refreshing. Luke's constant belittling had made her feel as though she was inferior to others, as though they were all looking at her and laughing or talking behind her back. She finally started to realize that maybe he had wanted her to feel that way, that maybe they weren't really doing that at all.

"Sadie," Once again she nearly jumped out of her skin as she awoke from her thoughts to the rumbling, yet whiskey-smooth sound of Ryder's voice. As she looked over to him, she saw he had someone with him. "Have you met Carson Holton yet? He's the sheriff of this town we all love so much, and he also happens to be my best friend and my partner-in-crime since we were teenagers." He playfully nudged Carson with his elbow.

"Oh, no I haven't actually. Hi, Carson, I'm Sadie. I've heard Sawyer and Travis talk about you a little, but it's nice to meet you finally."

"A little? That's all?" Carson joked, "Just kidding. It's a small town, so I've heard about you, too. And Miss Hazel too, of course." Sadie lit up at the knowledge that the town's sheriff knew of them.

"I'm really sorry I haven't been able to officially welcome you and Hazel to Stone Creek, but I promise I will treat you both to some basketti and chocolate milk soon." Sadie laughed, and for the second time in one night, it was from her heart.

"Hazel and I would definitely love that." She cast a quick glance at Ryder, and he reciprocated her smile. She was grateful to him, but she couldn't bring herself to say it– yet. It was sweet to know how much Ryder knew about she and Hazel, and how much he apparently talked about them as well.

Carson's phone alerted him to a text, and he glanced at it quickly. "I'm sorry to do this, but I have to leave." He pointed the phone towards them and sighed. "Duty calls. I apologize, Sadie, but I need to steal Ryder here for a moment. If you don't mind."

"Yeah, sure. I'll go find Sawyer. She couldn't have gone too far away, I wouldn't think." Carson went for a hug, which Sadie awkwardly accepted. Everyone here was so friendly, and she wasn't used to all the attention or the flamboyant gestures of friendship.

As the evening continued to unfold, Sadie engaged in very few activities while everyone else wholesomely played games, laughed, and shared stories. Being new to the group, she preferred to watch and learn.  She truly enjoyed the comradery and found herself laughing easily at the jokes and antics of these people who shared such a special bond.  Her new favorite drink, a refreshing cranberry cocktail, perfectly complemented the party for her.

The bar had quite successfully transformed into a haven of joy and happiness, where Sadie watched Sawyer, Travis, Ryder and their friends relax, be themselves, and create hilarious moments that would one day become precious memories. It was in this cozy and welcoming atmosphere that Sadie's growing crush on Ryder seemed to deepen way more than she was ready for. She struggled with it, but the sight of him also made her feel a glimmer of hope for her own future. Somehow, she had started to believe, without even knowing, that peace and happiness were well within *her* reach, too.

She finally found Sawyer over by a table picking up glasses and putting them in a wash basin. She walked over to her and helped her clean the table off.

"So, how was the ride?" Sawyer had a naughty smirk on her face.

"The ride? Oh, you mean the one you purposely bailed on in order to set me up with the fireman? It was… safe. At least if there had been a fire, he would have been able to save us both!"

"Ah! You've still got it in you, girl." Sawyer drank from her bottle of beer at the bar.

"Got what?"  Sadie said, playing with her glass of fruity deliciousness.

"That adorable sense of humor you always had. You know… shy, with a little bit of fun thrown in?"

Sadie rolled her eyes playfully. "This seems a bit 'calm' for you… when does the actual party begin?" she diverted.

"Ha! Nice try on the subject change! I've been watching you since you got here. You haven't taken your eyes off him, and I can't say as though I blame you."

"I barely even know him, Sawyer." Sadie looked away, slowly sipping from her glass.

"Okay, fine, I'll let it go for now, but you can't deny it forever, Sadester!" she surrendered.

"So, what do you have planned next?" Sadie tried again to change the subject.

"Trav's over there with a bunch of the guys, let's go sit with them. The next game is for everyone, truth or dare! I hope you're ready for that!" Sadie grimaced, looking at Sawyer reluctantly.

"It been a while, but it's not my first time, you know."

"Great, since you're not into spilling the beans about your feelings for Ryder, let's head on over!"

"Wait," Sadie grabbed her hand. She took a deep breath, looked around the bar full of only friends of Sawyer and Travis's, then back at Sawyer.

"This is probably whatever's in this drink talking, but fine, I'll spill. What do you want to know?" Sawyer was shocked, she had been joking around with her and wasn't expecting Sadie to open up here, of all places.

"I want to know everything, Sadie. I want to hear what's in your heart, especially why you are so afraid to feel whatever you are feeling for Ryder. I mean, I'd love to know what those feelings are too, with all the juicy details, but that's probably best left for a later time!" Sadie laughed, thankful to have such a caring, yet nosy, best friend.

"OK, I *do* like Ryder," she confessed, "But I'm really scared, Sawyer. I don't want to repeat my mistakes, and I can't stop thinking about all the things that are wrong with me. I seem to have this crazy crush on him, but I highly doubt he feels the same way about me. I come with a lot of baggage, and I can't imagine that Ryder, who just so happens to be the handsomest man I've ever seen in my entire life, would possibly want me!"

"Sadie, he-"

"Please, Sawyer, I have to finish this while I still have the guts to spill…"

"Okay, okay," she surrendered, hands in the air as a sign. "Spill away."

"To be honest, I'm not sure I would want him to if he did. I just, I don't know. I guess I'm overwhelmed by the thought of getting into a relationship so soon after everything that happened with Luke," she said, seeming to choose her words carefully.

"Sawyer, I want to let every good thing possible into my life, because I know that that's what someone who's been through what I have needs to do, but I can't ignore all the conflict going on in my mind. It's like a tug-of-war of sorts that never stops no matter how hard I try to make it go away."

Sawyer held her friend's hands, a lovingly empathetic smile warming her face. "Sadie, I know none of this is easy, trust me. The thing is, I want to see you happy again, and I honestly believe that you are getting there. At the very least, you're taking the right steps to get there at your own pace. I also want you to feel safe, so trust me when I say that Ryder is an amazing guy. I've known him since I moved here with Trav, and he is, *by far*, the nicest guy you could ever meet. Even so, I understand that you need time, and I'll do my best to respect that."

Sadie sighed, relieved, but only for the moment, and perhaps, that was enough to get her through the night.

"Okay, I'll try to remember that. Now, do we really have to play truth or dare?" Sadie pleaded.

"Nice try! Come on, let's go have some fun."

* * *

"Okay before we continue, you guys, go easy on her," Sawyer said, pointing at Sadie. "My best friend's first return to truth or dare better not be too heated or *every one* of y'all will have to answer to *me!*" Ryder stole a glance at Sadie as Sawyer addressed the group, doing her best to sound intimidating.

"I have a feeling you aren't too excited about this," he whispered near her ear.

"Getting personal with people I just met is kind of nerve-racking," she whispered back shyly. The intimacy of him whispering near her ear made her want to lay her head against his face, allowing him to nuzzle her ear closer. She shook her head lightly, trying to erase the naughty thoughts from her brain, unsuccessful as usual.

"I see. In that case, if you feel like quitting at some point, just let me know."

"Really? How?"

"Just give me a sign, any sign, and we'll be outta here."

"We can do that?" Sadie asked, surprised.

"Anything for you," Ryder replied, making her blush wildly. She really hoped nobody else had noticed.

"Who's going first?" Daisy, one of Sawyer's friends asked.

"We'll start with Tucker, then circle back from the left until we get to Sadie," Travis said, and everyone agreed.

"Okay!  Tucker, truth or dare?"  Sawyer asked excitedly. Tucker, a fellow firefighter of Ryder's, thought briefly before answering back, "Truth!"

"Hmm… When was the last time you cried and why?" Sawyer asked him with a sly grin.

"Um, that'd be two Fridays ago. Couldn't save a cute little puppy from a fire on the other side of town.  We got the other two but couldn't find the third." Collectively, the group expressed, "Ahh, that's so sad!"

After a pat on the back from Ryder to Tucker, the game moved on. The atmosphere buzzed with a newfound sense of excitement as they dove into the game.  Daisy, the town veterinarian who was vivacious and outgoing like Sawyer, took the lead next. "Alright, everyone, let's lighten the mood again, okay? Who's up next?"

Lilly, with a mischievous glint in her eye, jumped in, "I'll go! Dare!"

A devilish grin entered her face as Daisy contemplated her options. "I dare you to dance on the bar counter for a whole minute!"  Sadie looked around, her eyes and mind seemed more interested in observing the players than engaging. She was happy to be enjoying everyone's company and laughter, but it also had her thinking about how much she had missed the past couple of years, and how differently things could have been for her. The occasional cheering and shouts were enough to jolt her back to the game, or sometimes it was Ryder's gentle touch as his arm brushed hers that brought her back.

"Are you having fun?"  Sawyer mouthed from across the

table. Sadie nodded yes.

With laughter and cheers from the group, Lilly confidently climbed on top of the bar and busted out some impressive dance moves, earning applause and whistles from her friends.

Next up was Sawyer, who chose "Truth." Tucker asked her, "Alright, Sawyer, spill the beans! What's the craziest dream you've ever had?"

Blushing slightly, Sawyer giggled and shared a hilarious tale of flying llamas and cotton candy clouds, leaving everyone in stitches. Although nobody had any idea what the dream could mean, the group thought it was indeed crazy. Only Sadie and Travis knew what the dream was about, and she smiled a knowing smile at Sawyer to acknowledge her understanding.

Travis, ever a playful one, picked 'dare' and was challenged to sing a love song to his wife. Sawyer and Ryder both protested vehemently, having suffered the terror that was Travis's voice too many times to count, but everyone else insisted, including Sadie. With a voice so very far from melodious, he serenaded her, melting her heart and causing a collective "aww" from the group. Well, amidst mocking laughter of course.

"Alright, Ryder's next," Charley, a farmer who helped with the fall harvest at the winery, said. "What's it going to be, fireman?"

"You know I love me a good challenge, so I'll take a dare!" Charley looked around for anyone who would take the call, and quickly jumped right in.

"I dare you to either tell everyone here who you currently have a crush on *or* do a pole dance with an imaginary pole."

"Ooh that's a good one!" gasped the whole group. "Yes!"

Ryder got up and cleared his throat. "Well, I'm not one to kiss and tell, so pole dancing it is!" he declared, laughing along with the cheering of his friends.

With a quick look around the bar for imaginary support, Ryder found his invisible pole. He approached it with the confidence of a seasoned dancer, even though it existed only in the realm of his imagination. To the amusement and delight of the group, he began to sway and move his hips with flair, playfully mimicking the motions of a pole dance routine. His friends hooted and clapped, thoroughly entertained by his enthusiastic performance. As the imaginary music played in their minds, Ryder executed a series of graceful spins and daring dips, all while maintaining a charismatic charm that had everyone laughing and applauding. Sawyer through a few dollar bills his way, causing another round of hoots, hollers, and even a few catcalls.

"You've got some serious moves, fireman!" Charley called out amidst the laughter, acknowledging Ryder's quite surprising prowess in pole dancing, even if it was entirely make-believe.

His eyes fell on Sadie, looking at him with a heart-warming shy laughter he had ever seen, and he got motivated to do a few more moves, just for her. He found himself wanting to keep going just so he could see her smile like that at him. It was almost as if he craved it. Blushing with a contagious smile, Ryder took a playful bow, basking in the joy of the moment. "Thank you, thank you!" he replied with a mock seriousness. "I'll be here all week!"

The bar erupted in laughter and cheers, and she was almost certain that Ryder's spontaneous pole dance would later become a legendary tale among their group of friends, a much-told addition to the cherished memories of their times together.

"I had no idea you could do *that,*" Sadie said in a low voice, the happy laughter still silently plastered on her face.

"Is that your 'I'm so pleased with your performance' face?"

"I guess you could say that." Sadie tucked some hair behind her left ear, quickly looking away in a bit of shyness. Ryder touched her hand affectionately, a move that made her entire body tingle, making her very thankful that nobody else could see the exchange.

"You know, I used to try different things as a kid. I hated being told I couldn't do something, especially if it was coming from my sister." Sadie giggled, unsurprised. "Unbelievable, I know, but though there was a downside to that, and the downside was that she dared me to do all sorts of stuff, including some pretty emasculating things."

"Wow, that must have been hell for your ego," she amused.

"She sure did enjoy it, and so did you, now, apparently."

As the game continued, the dares became more outrageous, and the truths became more revealing. Karen, owner of the local hair salon, who was apparently known around town for her sense of adventure, did an impromptu karaoke performance, and her husband, Joe, confessed his most embarrassing moment.

Landon, another firefighter and the apparent joker of the group, hilariously re-enacted a famous movie scene, and poor Charley was forced to confess his secret crush on a local barista.

Finally, it was Sadie's turn. Sawyer's friends, sensing Sadie's apprehension, opted for a light-hearted question. "Truth or Dare, Sadie?" Daisy asked.

Feeling grateful for their consideration, Sadie chose "Dare." Lilly asked her, "Okay, then, Sadie, I dare you to take a shot of

Trav's best whiskey!"

"Wait… that's too easy!" Sawyer cut in.

"Do you think you have something better?" Sadie challenged her friend.

"Absolutely!"

"Fine, let's hear it then," Sadie responded with a little more confidence.

"I dare you to kiss Ryder!" Sawyer said, sitting up and tapping her fingers together in anticipation. Everyone was silent for a moment, followed by cheering, encouraging Sadie to go for it.

"Wait a minute, Sadie, you-"

"It's okay, Ryder," Sadie interrupted with a deep breath.

To Ryder's astonishment, and Sawyer's too, Sadie turned to him, grabbed the collar of his shirt gently, and pulled him towards her. In a gentle, but somewhat rebellious manner, she kissed him. Not a peck as everyone had assumed she would, not a quick brush on the lip even, but a whole five second kiss. Everyone was counting, and that moment instantly became the highlight of the day's games.

As she moved away from him, Sadie touched her lips softly. Had she *really* just done that? She shyly glanced at him, fearful that he would be upset, and was shocked at the look in his eyes. She wasn't quite sure what the look meant, but she almost thought it looked like desire. Was that possible? She hadn't seen that in so many years that she wasn't sure she was even capable of making a man feel that way. She quickly looked away as if his gaze would burn a hole right through her.

The game wrapped up and goodbyes were shared. On the drive home, Sadie reminisced about the evening she'd just had. There was a different feeling in the air, and she couldn't quite define it. A soft smile, along with a new flush feeling, entered her face as she remembered the kiss she'd planted on Ryder's mouth. It had been electrifying. She glanced towards him and realized he had a smile on his face too as he caught her glance. Although he had told Sawyer he would drive her home, Sawyer had insisted on tagging along, and, in true Sawyer fashion, she had no intentions of being quiet during the ride.

"You know, Sadie, you should really be thanking me," Sawyer said, catching the silent exchange between Sadie and Ryder in the front seat of his truck. Sawyer hadn't seen her smile like that in *so* long, and she felt elated that her little 'plan' had worked.

"And what should I be thanking you for, exactly?" Sadie asked her wonderfully nosy friend with a grin.

"Well, look how much fun you had tonight! If I hadn't convinced you to come with, you would be sitting at home feeling sad and bored. Instead, you are happy and smiling," Sawyer said proudly.

"Oh that! OK, Sawyer, thank you very much for dragging me along," she dramatically added, causing Ryder to laugh out loud and Sawyer to roll her eyes playfully. "And thank you, Ryder, for the ride tonight and for offering to bail with me!"

"Wait, what?" Sawyer asked, confused.

Ryder and Sadie shared a glance and then laughed together, causing Sawyer to join in. She didn't care that she had missed something, she was just overjoyed to see her best friend *finally* allowing herself to be happy.

# Chapter Eight

Amidst the vibrant colors of autumn, the Quinn family's winery, Cranberry Creek Farms, bustled with life and energy. The air was filled with the sweet scent of ripening grapes, and the vineyard's leaves showcased a stunning palette of red, orange, and gold. Rows of grapevines stretched into the distance, their luscious clusters waiting to be transformed into exquisite wines.

Sadie, fully immersed in the winery's busy season, moved gracefully between the barrels, helping to oversee the fermenting process, and checking on the quality of the wines. She was learning so much about the wine-making process, and she loved every minute of it. Sawyer, with her bright smile and welcoming demeanor, welcomed guests to the winery, guiding them to the tasting area.

Customers, both local residents and tourists, mingled under a canopy of grapevines adorned with twinkling fairy lights. The atmosphere was alive with laughter and the clinking of glasses, as the guests sampled the winery's finest creations.

Sadie hadn't realized how much she missed being able to do things for herself until the season came with September. That amount of engagement and busyness was much needed for her. She decided it was a good time to take a break from her wine making duties, so she joined Sawyer in the wine tasting area, sharing her knowledge and passion with the visitors. Her friendly personality and insightful explanations won the hearts of the guests, who appreciated the personal touch she brought to each tasting. She didn't talk a lot, but enough to explain why every single variation was unique and worth the try.

One couple, wine making by the *Cranberry Spice* wine Sadie recommended, struck up a conversation with her. "This is amazing! Do you have any recommendations for a white wine?" the woman asked eagerly.

"Absolutely! Our *Cranberry Cork* wine pairs beautifully with the local cheese platter," Sadie replied warmly, leading the couple to a nearby table where they could indulge in the winery's delectable offerings. Meanwhile, little Hazel, with her curly brown hair and freckled cheeks, dashed around the winery's spacious courtyard, attempting to mimic her mother. Her infectious laughter and playful energy brought a smile to everyone's face.

"That sounds wonderful!" the man exclaimed, his eyes lighting up with excitement. "We'll have two glasses, please."

"Coming right up." Sadie said with a smile, turning to Sawyer, who was staring at her having the time of her life. She smiled at her friend, headed over to the counter, and returned with two glasses of chilled *Cranberry Cork*, the golden liquid glistening in the sunlight. As she placed the glasses on the table, the couple thanked her and took their first sips, savoring the crisp and fruity flavors.

"Oh, this is fantastic!" the woman exclaimed, taking another sip. "It's refreshing and really *does* enhance the flavor of the cheeses."

"I'm so glad you like it," Sadie replied, genuinely pleased to see the delight on their faces. "Our *Cranberry Cork* wine is made with a combination of handpicked grapes from the vineyard and cranberries from the bog, with just a hint of coconut and lemon, and we take *great* care to create a balanced and flavorful wine.

Sawyer was so happy as she watched Sadie interact with the customers. All her friend needed was the chance to live the life she had always wanted, the one they had planned for and dreamed about as young teenagers, girls who had no limitations, no experience, and nobody telling them they couldn't fulfill their wildest imaginations. She was already looking so much more confident, and happier, than she had in the time since she had arrived.

Sadie left the couple while they enjoyed their wine and cheese, but not before they struck up a conversation with her about the winery, the harvest season, and the beauty of the surrounding countryside. Sadie happily shared stories about the wine making process and the passion that went into crafting each bottle.

Across the courtyard, Ryder and Hazel were engaged in their own little world of fun. Since the 'wine season' had officially begun, he'd taken on several different roles for Sadie and Hazel. In addition to Fire Chief of Stone Creek and Uncle to Harriet, he'd shown up when Hazel needed someone to stay with, provided he didn't have a shift at work. Otherwise, he made a safe environment for her so she could spend time playing while her mom went about her business at the winery. He loved spending time with Hazel, and it didn't hurt that he got to steal moments with her mom whenever possible too. She was slowly warming up to him, and he had come to realize that she was worth the patience it was taking to take things at her pace and not rush.

Today, Ryder was on full 'Uncle' duty, and he had fashioned an impromptu scavenger hunt for Hazel and Harriet, leaving clues that led them to hidden treasures among the grapevines near the winery. Hazel's eyes sparkled with excitement as they discovered each surprise, and Ryder couldn't help but be enchanted by their infectious joy. He made sure the hunt was simple enough for their young minds, but not without a few challenges along the way. At the end of it was a 'treasure' that he had made for them. He couldn't wait until they solved the final clue so he could see their faces light up as they discovered the little wooden doll beds he had made for each of them, complete with a tiny blanket and pillow that he'd had his mother sew, each in the favorite color of the little girl they were intended for.

As he waited for them to find their last clue, he glanced towards the winery, hoping to steal a glance at Sadie. It was almost noon, and the sun was casting a warm glow over the winery, and the atmosphere was filled with laughter and happiness. He loved days like this, the way the sun felt on his face. He knew that soon enough there would be clouds and snow on the ground, and he much preferred the sun and the warmth it provided. In the distance, the soft sound of a local musician performing to the guests gently filled the air, adding to the magical ambiance of the afternoon.

All of a sudden, he heard loud shrieks of joy coming from

the little girls behind him. He turned to see their faces lit up with happiness as they discovered their doll beds. He couldn't believe the incredible warmth he felt in his heart as he watched the two dance around and sing. This was what his mother had told him about so many times before. This was the feeling that every man dreamed of feeling one day. He had grown to love Hazel, and he realized it suddenly. He smiled and re-joined the two in their excitement.

After their treasure hunt, the girls were tired, so Ryder scooped them both up in his arms and carried them to Sawyer's house so they could lay down and take a nap. He left the beds behind, telling the girls that he'd come back for them while they napped. Satisfied, they both laid a head on his shoulder, one on each side, and he felt his heart grow even fuller. It was incredible to him the amount of joy that a child's love could put in a man's heart. He was definitely going to walk slowly so he could enjoy every minute of their snuggles.

Back at the winery, the dinner hour was quickly approaching, and it was busier than it had been all day. Cranberry Creek Farms was big enough to accommodate over 100 people, but it got pretty crazy inside when it started to fill up. Guests were eager to experience the charm of the winery and sample its exquisite wines. The winery staff worked seamlessly, attending to the guests' needs and ensuring that each visitor had a memorable and enjoyable time while they were there. Sawyer personally interviewed and selected all of her staff members, and great thought was put into how their personality would mesh with the other staff. She believed that if you treated your staff well, they'd be happy to be there, and they would then treat the customers well. If you treated the customers well, they would be more likely to come back, so it all came around full circle.

Sawyer walked around checking in with guests as they enjoyed their wine and other goodies at the table. One young couple near the side door thanked Sawyer for her hospitality, their glasses now empty but their smiles full of contentment. "We've had a wonderful time here," the man said, "Your winery is truly a hidden gem, and we can't wait to come back soon. We have a few friends that would love this place too, so we'll have to make a day of it!"

Sawyer beamed with pride, grateful for the kind words. "Thank you so much! It's been a pleasure having you here, and we'd definitely love to have your friends visit us as well," she replied. Sadie had walked up to thank the couple as well, so Sawyer gave her a side-hug. "This place was born of a dream in the heads of two teenage girls, and now we are standing here together, watching the dream come true."

"That's incredible! It must be so special being able to be here together and watch the fruit of your labor come to fruition!" the young woman said.

"Yes, we couldn't be happier." Sawyer smiled at Sadie who was grinning back.

As the couple bid their farewells and moved on to explore more of the winery and shoppe, Sadie took a moment to soak in the beauty of the scene around her. The winery was alive with laughter, love, and the simple joys of life.

"I'm starting to wonder if it's the wine or if people are genuinely this happy," Sadie said, and in that moment, she felt a deep sense of gratitude for the community that had formed around them here, for the friendships she had now inherited, and for the love and happiness that were slowly but surely finding their way back into her life.

In that moment, also, with a renewed sense of hope and contentment, Sadie walked over to the window and looked over to where Hazel and Harriet were sharing a laughter-filled moment. Her heart swelled with warmth, knowing that her daughter had found a dear friend in Harriet, something she'd never had in Seattle. She was also immensely thankful for Ryder's kindness, and she was amazed that the man seemed to have the patience of a saint. She appreciated his friendship, and she was excited, yet nervous, for whatever would become of the feelings that were trying to sneak into her heart more and more each day.

"People are, and can be, genuinely happy," Sawyer finally said, breaking the silence as she walked up to her by the window and looked out herself.

"You know, Sadie, as the evening goes on, the winery will only continue to bustle with more and more activity and laughter," she added. Sadie looked at her questioningly.

"Trav's got it from here, how about you and I take a little walk down to our favorite spot for a while." Since Sadie had come to Stone Creek, she had Sawyer had found a beautiful and quiet corner by the vineyard that had quickly become their favorite place to go for some time together. "We can just sit and talk while the sun makes its way down the horizon."

"I'd love that," Sadie agreed as they quietly slipped out the door. "Let's go!"

"It's been a wonderful day," Sawyer said, her eyes shimmering with happiness as she gazed at the valley's beauty.

Sadie nodded in agreement, a sense of peace settling within her. "Yes, it really has. I'm grateful for everything, Sawyer. For this winery, for Hazel, and for the incredible community of Stone Creekers you and Trav have here. I'm happy to be a part of it, a part of all these. I don't even deserve half the understanding and kindness I've received here."

Sawyer smiled warmly, knowing the depth of Sadie's journey and the courage it took to even get to this point in her life. "You deserve all the happiness in the world, Sadie. People make mistakes, in different shapes and forms, and you, of all people, deserve all the good things of life over and again. If it's one thing I've learned since marrying Trav, it's that marriages take daily work by both people. Every relationship story has two sides, and mistakes are made by both. You may have made mistakes, but it wasn't all you. In the end, *none* of it gave him an excuse to hurt you... *ever.*"

"I'm realizing that more and more each day. Thank you for saying that."

"I know I haven't said this before, Sadie, but I'm so glad you trust me enough to allow me to be a part of your journey."

Sadie and Sawyer raised their glasses in a silent toast while the sun made its way down the horizon, casting a golden glow over the winery.

"I haven't told Trav this, but this winery has been a source of healing for me, too," Sawyer sighed deeply. "I don't know how I would have been able to survive without this place, coming to work here every day, having something to care for and to nurture. I needed it, and even though you weren't here in person, I've carried you with me the entire time," she said with a mixture of sadness and nostalgia as she spoke.

"I never knew how much you wanted a child, Sawyer," Sadie said. "It wasn't until the Truth or Dare game the other night that I realized it. I remembered that silly dream of yours from when we were younger, except, it doesn't seem as silly now, now that I realize it was a real desire of yours." She smiled and offered a supportive hug. "Hazel has been my anchor, Sawyer. Without her, I don't know what would have become of me, so I know how much this must mean to you. Is there anything I can do to help?"

"I don't know," Sawyer lied, but Sadie knew her too well, so she assured her, "Whatever you need, Saw, I'd be more than delighted to help."

"I see how happy Hazel is playing with Ryder and everyone else, the way she makes people light up, and it makes me yearn for a child of my own," Sawyer admitted, her eyes glistening with unshed tears. "I love Travis with all my heart, but this longing never seems to fade."

Sadie placed a comforting hand on Sawyer's, offering her support. "You're not alone, Sawyer," she said softly. "I'm here for you, and we'll figure this out together. You deserve all the happiness in the world, and if having a family is what you desire, then you better believe we will find a way!"

* * *

Sadie found herself thinking more and more about Ryder as the days went by, her ability to suppress the feelings becoming harder and harder with each passing moment. Most of the time, Hazel was their excuse for seeing each other, but there was no deceiving anyone else, they were into each other. They'd steal quiet moments together, sitting under the shade of the vine-covered pergola, stealing stolen glances and enjoying light conversation as they watched the girls playing nearby.

Sadie was washing the last of the tables on the patio as the sun began to set in the sky. Tonight, the horizon was painted with hues of pink and gold, a beautiful palette that only nature could create. With the winery slowly winding down for the day, Sadie and Ryder suddenly realized they were alone. At some point, Sawyer, had discreetly stepped away, giving them a moment of privacy. She had a way of doing that, Sadie thought with a silent laugh.

With a motion from Ryder, she joined him to sit on a wooden bench overlooking the vineyard. As they sat, Ryder gently reached over and placed Sadie's hand in his, the warmth of his touch sending a mixture of comfort and electricity through her body. "What a beautiful night. I could sit right here all night and watch the stars. Well, only if you were right next to me, of course," he threw a flirty wink her way. "How about you?"

"You are too sweet, Ryder, but I *do* certainly agree that it is a beautiful night," she shyly responded. "And, I very much enjoy siting with you, too," she added as she looked at their hands, amazed at how strong, yet gentle, his was in hers. There was something about those hands… strong, with small scars and veins that looked like a maze. They made her feel something deep inside her gut, something she'd never felt before, and she wasn't sure what it was. She only knew that she wanted him to hold onto her forever with those hands, and she had to shake away the thought she had about where she'd like those hands to travel next. After a moment, she hesitantly asked "Ryder, can I ask you something? It's personal, so if you don't want to answer you certainly don't have to!"

"Absolutely, I'd love to know what's on that beautiful mind of yours," he replied softly, his eyes reflecting the colors of the sunset.

A hint of a blush filled Sadie's cheeks, her heart fluttering with a mix of feelings. She'd never been able to have talks like this with Luke, always afraid that she would upset him and that he would hurt her in his anger, his choice of weapon usually being his mouth and the words that slipped from it, directed towards her and making her feel inferior and small. The problem was, with all that fear in her past, it made it hard to trust that she could ask Ryder something personal without him getting mad at, or annoyed by, her too. She took a deep breath, as if trying to decide whether to ask or not.

"Sadie," he interrupted her thoughts, "Whatever it is, there's no need to get so worried about it. I'm an open book when it comes to you, just ask." He squeezed her hand gently, as if to will his own courage into her.

"Ryder, you've been so wonderful to Hazel and me, and I'm so grateful for everything. Knowing that Hazel is safe with you, and with Stacy and Harriett, means the world to me."

"You don't have to thank me, Sadie," Ryder said, his gaze unwavering. "I care about you, and I want to be here for you and Hazel. You both are very important to me."

She smiled at him, then hesitantly went on. "The thing is… it makes me wonder how a wonderful guy like you isn't married already. I guess I'm asking this; Did something happen, or do you just not want to get married?" she finally spit out, her voice filled with apprehension. It pulled at his heartstrings that she seemed so nervous to ask him, like she thought he was going to attack her for asking or something.

"I'm not sure if I really know how to answer that question, but I can sure try. I think it's kind of like how you're this sweet, thoughtful, loving person, and even though I don't know a lot about you yet, I do know that you're not here in Stone Creek, a single, beautiful mom, by the way, because you want to be alone. These things just happen sometimes. I've been in relationships, several shorter ones and a long one as well. I learned a lot from each one of those, but each ended for its own reasons. The longer one ended because she simply developed feelings for another man too, and when I told her she needed to commit to one or the other, she chose the other."

Sadie sighed, looking at her feet. "I'm sorry that happened to you, and I'm sorry if I made it seem like I was trying to–"

"Please don't apologize, Sadie. You didn't do anything wrong, and I'm not upset about that anymore. I know that she simply wasn't the right woman for me, and I wouldn't be sitting here. enjoying this time with you, if she had chosen me." he said, playfully nudging her shoulder with his own.

"I suppose that's true. I guess I should probably thank her then," she said, laughing softly and earning a laugh from Ryder.

"Now, since you asked me a question, can I ask you something in return? I've wanted to ask for a while now actually."

"Um… yeah, that's fine," Sadie said, feeling shy.

"It's not a big deal, but I noticed you apologize a lot. I know that, for some people, it's because of how they grew up and that it's a habit basically, so maybe that's it, but can you maybe explain why *you* feel the need to apologize or take the blame for misunderstandings, no matter whose fault they really are?"

"Oh, um, I just, I don't know… I guess that with Luke, my ex-husband, I was always made to think I was at fault for *everything*. Now, no matter what happens, I tend to think it's my fault in *some* way. It's just how I have learned to think, I guess." Sadie rambled a little bit. "Does it bother you when I do that? I'm *really sorry* if I-"

"It's fine, Sadie, I'm not judging or anything. I just wanted to understand how your mind works a little bit better is all. It's okay, really." Ryder ended the conversation the moment he noticed that his question was making her nervous. He wasn't sure what had happened to her back in Seattle, but it must have been pretty rough. Sawyer and Travis had said that Sadie would have to share those things with him, because it was her story to tell, and he had respected their decision on that. He suddenly wanted… no, *needed* to find whoever had hurt her and make sure they felt the same pain she had. He wasn't sure where such a fierce sense of protection over her had come from, and it unsettled him a bit. Maybe he was falling harder than he had realized, he thought.

He took her other hand in his and turned her towards him. He gently touched her chin as he lifted her eyes to look at his. "Would you like to take a walk with me?" he suggested, and she nodded her agreeance to him. As they started down the porch steps, Sadie's mind wandered off slightly. She hadn't thought about Luke for a long time, and the conversation they were having had reminded her of him, sending chills down her spine. It brought back memories that she had been trying to bury, and instantly changed her mood.

"Actually… would it be okay with you if I take a rain check on the walk? I'd like to just head back to the cottage," she said apologetically.

"Yes, of course. I hope I didn't say anything that upset you, Sadie."

"Oh, no, Ryder. It's not that. I'm just feeling kind of tired, that's all," she fibbed.

"OK, but would it be okay if I at least walked you there?"

Sadie nodded. As they walked, she asked "Do you believe

that people can heal from wounds in their past and allow themselves to be open to love and happiness again?"

"I sure do. I know that some wounds are deeper than others, but I also know that humans are strong and resilient. I think that if you are open to it and willing to work hard, you can overcome anything and, in turn, open your life up to happiness and love," he told her, both of them looking around themselves at the beauty of the darkening landscape that was surrounding them.

Sadie thought for a moment, "I find myself in this incredible place, a place I have only dreamt about for so many years and feel like I've begun to hope that my heart will find solace and joy again. Sometimes I think I have, or that I'm on my way there, but it doesn't last. Something always happens that makes me question it again."

"Sadie, what *does* last?" Ryder asked her. When she looked at him curiously, he attempted to clarify, "Like, when the hope for happiness is questioned, are there any feelings that last through the doubt? What is it you hope for that you are so scared to pursue?"

For some reason, his question had her feeling nervous and as though her stomach was doing flips. Was he trying to figure out how she felt about him? Should she tell him? What if he didn't reciprocate her feelings? She was almost positive there was no way he could possibly feel the same way as she did… maybe he liked her and cared about her, but she doubted it went any farther than that. She wasn't sure her heart could handle that kind of rejection. Even worse, what if he felt bad and things got awkward between them. That would be awful.

"I'm not sure if I know the answer to that," she lied, hoping he'd drop it.

"I guess I'm asking you how you feel about me, Sadie," he prodded, gently.

"Oh," she said, obviously uncomfortable with this line of conversation. "Ryder, I need a little time with all of this. I'm not-"

"Never mind, I'm sorry for trying to push you. I would never want to make you feel nervous or uncomfortable around me," he apologized.

"It's not that, Ryder. I'm just scared to tell you how I feel because I don't want to ruin our friendship. It's not just me I worry about. You are so kind and thoughtful, and you have brought endless joy to Hazel, who, by the way, adores spending time with you more than with me now, I think." They both laughed.

"That little girl loves nothing, and no *one*, more than her mamma… trust me!" he said.

"I guess, to answer your question, the feeling I get when I watch you two together lasts.  You've become Hazel's favorite playmate, her confidante, and the source of countless smiles and giggles. The way you join her in her imaginative adventures and make her laugh with your silly jokes is so sweet. She's grown to trust and love you as if you are a part of our little family, and I could never repay you for that kindness."

"First off, you don't need to repay me for anything. I spend time with her because I love being around her, and her mother too, for that matter. Second, I can see that, in a way, me being close to her scares you. Why is that, Sadie?"

"We just… I can't let her be-"

"Too attached? Because you think something might happen? Or is it that you don't think you'll be able to stay in Stone Creek?"

Sadie's quietness told Ryder he was on the right trail. Those things must obviously be big fears of hers, and he was guessing Sawyer didn't even know all of this. "I know it sounds crazy and ridiculous, and I'm sorry if you expected me to say something else. I just absolutely *have* to protect Hazel at all costs, even if it means pushing my happiness and my needs to the side. She means the world to me, and she *has* to come first."

Ryder took her hand and gently rubbed the back of her palm. The intimate simplicity of it made her suddenly shudder as if the chill of the fall evening had finally caught up with her. "Sadie, I may not be a father, but I *do* understand your concern. I hope you know that I'd never do anything to hurt you or Hazel, at least not on purpose. I'm a man, so you can expect me to screw up, but I'll never allow anything to happen to either of you if I can help it. I feel the same way about my sister and Harriet; I will always do whatever I can to protect them, even if it means standing against my brother-in-law."

"I want to believe that, and I think I do, but it's so hard for me. I wish I could find the words to help you understand."

"It's okay, I'm not going to try to pressure you into anything. Trust is earned, and I will show you any way I can that you can trust me. I don't know the details of your life before you came here, Sadie, but I need you to hear from me that I mean you and Hazel no harm."

Sadie stopped in front of her cottage and stood by the door. She took a deep breath of the fresh night air, trying to clear her mind, if she could, of the thoughts running all over it. She looked up at the stars filling the sky before closing her eyes to take in the sounds and smells around her. In that moment, Ryder didn't think he had ever seen something or someone so beautiful in his whole life. Something in his gut caught, and he felt the breath leave his chest. She was stunning in her own natural way, and he knew right then and there that he needed to have her in his life, no matter how slowly he had to take the path to get there.

"Thank you for today, Ryder." Sadie interrupted his thoughts. "I really appreciate everything you've done for me and Hazel these past two months. It means a lot to both of us."

He gave her an assuring nod, "I'd do anything for you, beautiful. And, I happen to adore that little bundle of sunshine sleeping inside the cottage as well," he winked.

His term of endearment sent a chill down her spine. How did he do that? He didn't even need to touch her to make her feel like that- all it took was a sweet word and that mischievous grin he was so good at. "Um, I should go in and see if Hazel's still awake," she said, heading for the porch steps quickly. She needed to get inside before she made the mistake of allowing him to kiss her. She wasn't sure she could stop if so. "I'm guessing your sister would like to head home soon."

"Sounds like a plan," he said, smiling. "Give her a peck for me, will you?"

"Yes, of course," she said, wishing she could get a peck of her own.

Ryder turned to leave, but Sadie turned back towards him, suddenly adding, "Wait, Ryder. We're okay, right? Um, I'm sorry if I said anything that didn't come across the right way. I'm just really concerned for my daughter. Well, and me, maybe. I mean, I think you're an amazing person, and I'm sorry if I made you think I felt any other way."

Ryder sighed, "Please, Sadie, you don't have to apologize for looking out for Hazel or yourself. Ever." He blew out a breath, releasing his frustration. He really wished she'd stop doing that all the time. He looked up the step at her and was amazed at the way the moonlight was reflecting off her hair, casting a soft glow on her face. He felt like someone had socked him in the stomach. He knew he needed to go slowly, but damn it, he was still a man and he only had so much restraint. The urge to hug her and take all her fears away was so strong that he couldn't stop himself.

Before she could figure out what was happening, he closed the gap between them, causing her to flinch as he got within reach. Her heart skipped a beat. Ryder stopped dead in his tracks, looking at her with bewilderment. He felt like his heart had suddenly shattered a bit. He hadn't meant to scare her. What kind of ass hat was he anyway, moving towards her so quickly and terrifying her? More importantly, what in the hell had happened to this poor woman before she got here?

"I didn't mean to scare you, Sadie. I was just going to hug you goodnight," Ryder explained before slowly pecking her on the cheek and stepping back. "I better get going. I'll see you tomorrow."

As she watched Ryder walk off, back towards the winery and his truck, Sadie held her chest in one hand, and walked into the cottage. She was worried that if she let go of it, her heart might jump right out. After shutting the door gently behind her, she let herself lean back against it and take a few deep breaths. She needed to slow her heart rate down a bit. When she was satisfied that she could walk on her wobbly legs again, she headed for Hazel's room so she could check on her. She kissed her twice, one from her and the other from Ryder. She sat at the foot of Hazel's bed and thought about what had just happened. She had seen the look on Ryder's face when she had flinched. The thing was, she hadn't done that because she thought he'd hit her, she had done it because she thought he was going to kiss her! As she recalled the humility of the moment, tears filled her eyes. She couldn't explain it, but she had simply gotten scared at the moment, worried more than anything that she would disappoint him or something. She hadn't kissed a man in a long time, and, although she really wanted to kiss Ryder, she still worried that he'd reject her. Boy, she was way more of a mess than she had realized! There was no way he would ever want to kiss her now, that was for sure. He may never hurt her the way Luke had, but she was beginning to think that this kind of hurt may be worse.

# Chapter Nine

They say dreams are made up of things we experienced during the day, but sometimes nightmares come in the most unexpected ways, forms and times. Sadie's peaceful slumber was suddenly disrupted by a haunting dream, one that dredged up painful memories from her past, mixed with the worst version of her fears for the future. Whether it was real or not, she had no way to know. It wasn't every day a woman's verbally and physically abusive ex-husband materialized at the doorstep of the place she now called home, but in her dream, that's the story that was unfolding. Panic coursed through her veins as he demanded to see their precious daughter, Hazel. Their confrontation escalated quickly, and Sadie found herself trapped in a nightmare of the worst nature.

Although her body was trying to awaken, her brain continued telling a vividly terrifying story, *"Hazel's asleep, Luke. I'm not going to wake her up in the middle of the night. Besides, you can't just show up here uninvited and make demands! You know that's not okay!"* Luke's anger flared, and he lashed out violently, his hand connecting with her cheek in a stinging slap. The force of the blow sent her stumbling back, crashing against the wall, her head striking it with a sickening thud.

Sadie screamed in pain, finding herself in a similar situation as before, this time Luke was madder, and this time, he wasn't stopping there. As she struggled to clear her dizzy head, she saw him step forward and reach for her. He put his hands around her neck and began to tighten them.

Gasping for air, Sadie struggled to free herself from Luke's clutches, her heart racing as terror gripped her. She felt herself sinking deeper into the darkness of this reality, fearing this was the end because his grip was too strong for her to escape. Just as she felt herself starting to lose consciousness, she saw Hazel appear in the doorway. She wanted to scream for her to run, but Luke's hands were too tight. Her eyes fixated on the hatred in his, and she found a sudden surge of strength within her, shoving him off her.

Sadie gasped for air as she woke up with a start, drenched in a cold sweat. She was grabbing her neck and feeling for Luke's hands, not finding him anywhere as she looked around her in desperation and fear. Her chest heaved as she realized that her torment had been merely real in the realm of her own dreams, yet still trying to breathe through lungs that felt like they had forgotten how.

Shaken by the vividness of the dream, Sadie reached for her phone on the nightstand. Her trembling fingers dialed Ryder's number, the urgency in her voice betraying the turmoil she had just experienced.

"Ryder," she squeaked out a whisper, her voice shaky. "Can you... can you please come over? It's *important*."

It was 2 in the morning, but Ryder had picked up after the

first ring. His concern was evident even through the phone. "Of course, Sadie. I'll be right there. Are you okay?"

Tears welled up in Sadie's eyes as she clutched the phone. "I'm really sorry for waking you, I just... I just need someone here." Ryder assured her he'd be right over, and he kept to his word. Within what felt like both an eternity *and* an instant, Ryder arrived at the cottage, his presence a reassuring anchor in the storm of Sadie's ever-changing emotions. She opened the door, her gaze locking onto his concerned eyes, and without saying a word, she fell into his welcoming arms, wrapping herself around him tightly, seeking solace in his embrace.

Ryder caught her in his arms and could feel her body shaking in his. "It's alright, I'm here," he said calmly, gently closing the door behind him with his free hand. He could see terror in her eyes, and he wanted to know what put her in such a state in the middle of the night, but asking was less important than simply making sure she was alright.

"I'm so sorry for waking you up, Ryder," she said through her sobs.

"No need to be sorry, Sadie." He rubbed her back with his hands, hoping to help her stop shaking. "I told you to call if you ever needed anything, and I meant it." Ryder held her gently, his strong arms offering a sense of security, which she clearly had needed desperately. "Shh, it's alright. I'm here." Sadie held on, her hands shaking less and less with each passing second that she had Ryder's arms wrapped around her.

"Hazel's asleep," she said without being asked. "I checked on her after calling you and she was fine," she added. He could see that she was exhausted, but also that she was worried about her daughter, so, after a few moments, Ryder guided her back to her bed and tucked her in, promising he'd go check on Hazel for her. His tenderness was evident in every gesture, and she had never felt so protected and cared for by a man, other than her father. She knew when she had more time that she'd need to revisit those thoughts, but not now. "Try to get some rest. I'll be right here on the couch if you need anything," Ryder added softly as he walked to the door.

Sadie nodded. "Ryder, after you check on Hazel, is there any way you'd come back and stay with me a little bit? I know it probably sounds silly, but I don't want to be alone right now, and I think I can sleep better if I know you are here."

"I sure can. I'll be right back." He stepped across the hallway and peeked in on a precious sleeping Hazel. He had always been awed by the peacefulness of a sleeping child. He had a fierce urge to scoop her up and hold her while she slept, but he knew her mamma needed him more right now. He softly closed the door and crossed back to Sadie's room.

"She's sound asleep, probably dreaming of yellow glitter and unicorns," he softly chuckled. Sadie smiled sleepily.

"Thank you, Ryder," she yawned.

Ryder took his shoes off and sat in the chair Sadie had near the window in her room. "You just get some sleep. I'm not going anywhere."

Slowly, Sadie closed her eyes, a combination of gratitude and relief washing over her. She let herself be enveloped by the warmth and security of Ryder's presence, a stark contrast to the icy grip of the nightmare she had just woken up from.

* * *

The warm morning light shone through the windows, casting a glow over Sadie's room, and waking her. She slowly opened her eyes, the memories of what happened last night distant from her consciousness. She smiled at the sound of a morning dove just outside her window, announcing that a new autumn day was beginning. She got up, stretched her legs and arms, and walked across the hall to Hazel's room. As she looked in, she saw that Hazel was still sound asleep, so she gently closed the door partway and headed to the kitchen to make some tea.

Her heart stopped in her chest as soon as her gaze fell upon the figure sprawled on the couch. For a brief, heart-stopping moment, her mind played back on the horrors of her nightmare, and she thought it was Luke lying there, as if her dream had somehow seeped into reality. She let out a screech, looking all around her, fully ready to grab anything she could find to defend herself.

Hearing her, Ryder opened his eyes and jumped so high he almost fell off the couch. Looking towards the sound, he found Sadie's terrified eyes staring at him.

"Hey, it's just me," he said as Sadie wiped her eyes involuntarily. As her foggy mind cleared, the truth settled in, and everything started to come back to her. It was Ryder, his features softened by sleep, his chest rising and falling in a steady rhythm. Sadie's breath caught in her throat as she remembered that she had called him in the night to chase away the specters of her past, and he had willingly stepped into the role of her protector, banishing her demons with his mere presence. Enough for her to fall asleep again, anyway.

Ryder noticed her initial confusion and terror, and he reluctantly sat up, giving her enough time to take in the reality staring her in the face. He had no idea what was going on in the pretty head of hers, but it was too damn early to sort it all out now. He just wanted to figure out how to take whatever it was away from her so she could smile again.

A small, tearful smile tugged at the corners of Sadie's lips as she watched Ryder rise from the couch. He walked to her slowly, touching her arm gently. "Hey," he said, "Are you okay?"

"Yes, I'm fine. I'm sorry I screamed… I just forgot you were here for a second there, and I thought it was someone else."

"No problem. I look a bit like a bear in the morning, so it was probably my fault." He chuckled. "Hope you slept well?" Sadie nodded, acutely aware of his body close to hers and his hand touching her arm. She blushed as she realized the intimacy of their position.

"You were pretty troubled last night. You were shaking like crazy! Did you have a bad dream or hear something outside or something?"

Sadie stepped back. "Yeah, um, I had a nightmare that seemed too real. I'm sorry for waking you up but thank you for coming over and for staying while we slept."

"It was no problem. I'm glad you called me." Ryder tried to take steps closer to her, but she just kept taking some back. "Is everything alright?" he asked, confused by her retreat.

"Yeah, why?"

"Well, you keep backing away from me…"

"Oh, I'm sorry, there's a lot going on in my head right now, and I just kind of want to be alone to figure it all out," Sadie said, confusing him the more.

"Okay, but first, can you tell me what's going on?"

"Nothing's going on. I just had a rough night, and I'd really love to have some time to think. I'm sorry, I hope you can understand?" Ryder was befuddled, but if what Sadie wanted was time alone, then that was exactly what he was going to give her. However, he was not going to leave without making one thing clear.

"Sadie, listen very closely to me. I am here for you, whenever you need me. I think it's about time you know the truth about how I feel about you. You are such an amazing woman, beautiful on the inside and out and a wonderful mom to Hazel. You make my stomach hit the floor every time you walk in the room, and I find myself constantly wanting to take you in my arms and kiss you until your knees go weak. I am doing the best I can to be patient and give you the time you need, but I can only do this for so long. At some point, you need to tell me if you feel the same way or not." He paused, taking a deep breath and softening his tone. "Also, at some point I'd really love for you to trust me enough to tell me what happened to you in Seattle. I won't force you to, but I think it's important that you do. Until then, I'm a phone call away if you need me." With that, he turned, threw on his sweatshirt and shoes, and walked out the front door.

Sadie stood there, her feet glued to the floor, and watched him leave. It was as if she had been paralyzed with emotion. She wanted to run after him and tell him she felt the same way, but she couldn't get her feet to move. The tears were slowly falling down her face. Hearing his truck drive off, she closed her eyes, wishing she had handled that differently. After everything he had done for her, he hadn't deserved to be treated like that. *What is wrong with me?* she thought. *Am I ever going to be free from this prison Luke stuck my heart in?*

She finally found the strength to walk to the kitchen and make herself some tea. She sat at the little white dining table by the window and pulled her phone from the pocket of her robe. She dialed the familiar number she had known since childhood. With slightly trembling hands, she held her phone to her ear. "Dad?" she said immediately as he picked up.

"Sweetheart, good morning!" her father answered excitedly, oblivious of his daughter's plight. He went on cheerfully until she cut him off.

"Dad- Have you seen Luke lately?" Sadie asked, interrupting her father. The question took her father by surprise, and he paused for a moment.

"No, honey. Why? Is anything wrong? Is Hazel insisting to see him or something?"

"No, she's doing great. I think we have enough distractions here to keep her mind on other things for now."

"Well, what brought that question on then?" he asked, curious about her current line of questioning.

"I'm afraid our stay here might be cut short." Sadie held her hand between her knees and locked it to manage the shakiness.

"Okay, Sadie, take a breath sweetie, and tell me what the heck is going on. Slow, deep breaths, okay?"

Sadie listened to her father and did as he said, taking long, deep breaths until she steadied enough to speak again.

"Okay, now that you are a little calmer, go ahead and tell me what the problem is. Your mom went to breakfast with some friends, but I can do my best to help with whatever is going on, and when she gets home, I'm sure she will call you."

Hearing her father talk about her mom settled her some more, and she felt the anxiety leaving her body. "I dreamt about him, dad," she started to say, "And he wasn't any different. Not even in my dream, and after all this time. He was furious at me. And he... um, he tried to... dad, it really scared me!" Sadie broke down and began to sob quietly.

"Sadie," her father finally said after a few seconds of thought about how to proceed. He had learned a long time ago that she usually needed to get it out for a bit before she could calm down and talk to him, so he was allowing her that time.

"This isn't good for her, daddy. For Hazel, I mean. Everything was so perfect and now it all feels like it's about to end. Like we're about to have to go back to Seattle before we are ready to go. Honestly, I was beginning to think we may stay here forever, daddy, but now we may have to give that up to stay safe."

"OK… I think you need to calm down for a minute and not make any decisions until you can think a little more clearly. Emotional decisions are rarely good decisions, darling."

Sadie took a few more deep breaths to try to control her panic. She needed to calm down and think clearly, her father was right. After she felt more stable, she asked him "Dad, I need to ask you something, and I need you to be honest with me, can you do that?"

"Well, I can't promise but I can sure promise to try," he replied, already knowing what she was about to ask.

"Dad, I need you to tell me what happened between you and Luke that day. He just suddenly disappeared, only returning one message I sent him after he filed for divorce. He never even messages to check on Hazel. When you told me he'd never bother me again, what did you mean?"

Henry sighed, he had hoped that he could keep her from all of this, but clearly, Sadie wasn't going to let it go. He supposed he had himself to thank for that one since he had always taught her to be strong, yet cautious, to always be aware of others and their intentions to help keep yourself safe. Obviously, she hadn't felt safe with Luke, and he had made sure that she wouldn't have to deal with him ever again after what he had done to her.

"Honey, it was a dream, you're safe. I'm going to call Sawyer and have her check on you, okay?"

"Dad, you're not answering the question. What happened to Luke?"

"I got him to let you be, honey. Your old man is a retired Captain from the US Army, and I did what any father who loves and cares for his kid will do." Sadie stayed silent for a while, her stomach sinking as she processed what he had just said.

"Dad, is he—"

"No! God, no, Sadie! Even *I* would never do *that*. I simply told him to leave you and your little girl alone. Well, I guess I *thoroughly warned* him, if you prefer more accurate words." He could hear her breath of relief, and he was sorry that she had gone through such fear and such heartache. "You're safe, honey. Luke knows better than to bother you or your sweet little girl, and he knows he'd answer to me if he ever did."

Sadie sighed, "Okay, dad. I believe you. This whole thing is just so scary, and I wish I could go back in time and choose to tell you sooner so we could have kept things from getting so bad."

"I know, sweetheart. No use going back to a bunch of 'what ifs' and such. Just do everything you can to be happy and safe now."

"Thanks, Dad. I think I better head in and wake Hazel. She's usually up by now, and we need to get going soon."

"Sounds good, honey. Give her a kiss for me! I think I'm going to head out to the garage and take a gander at my car. It's been making a funny noise the past two days and I haven't had time to check on it myself. I promised your mom she won't be hearing it sing the next time she rides in it," he laughed.

Sadie chuckled at his antics. "Okay, I love you."

"I love you too, sweetheart."

Sadie ended the call, got up and walked to Hazel's room. It troubled her that she was not yet awake, so she went over and kissed her forehead. Stretching herself, Hazel woke up and hugged her instinctively, melting away all the worry. Sadie hugged her back– very tightly. As she was helping her hop up and out of bed, they heard a knock on the front door.

"Who's that, mommy?" Hazel asked curiously.

"I'm not sure… should we race to the door and see together?" she asked her, letting the little girl get a head start as they raced for the front door. For a brief second, Sadie felt a pang of fear as she got to the door, but she quickly pushed that out of her mind so as not to worry Hazel. She hesitantly opened the door and saw Ryder standing on the other side, holding a white nylon bag in his right hand. A rush of relief flooded over her, and she smiled.

There was an awkwardness between them, and very visible to Hazel, even, who against her desire to run to Ryder and hug him, stood by her mom, staring up at her questioningly, obviously not sure what to do.

"Hi," Ryder spoke up first. "Um… I picked this up for you. Last night, I got hungry and wanted to make a sandwich and realized there were some things on your grocery list hanging on the fridge that weren't crossed off yet, and there was no bread either," he chuckled, lifting the nylon. "You were also short on cheese. And, there were no hot dogs, which I know Hazel really likes." Ryder seemed to be rambling a little and she couldn't help but find it cute. Suddenly, Hazel started to tug at Sadie's hand to get her attention.

"Mommy, can I have a hotdog and chocolate milk for breakfast? Please?" she asked in a voice that Sadie had a hard time saying no to. "Yes, Hazel, just a second." Sadie reached out and took the bag from Ryder. Her first instinct was to ask him to come in, but she couldn't, not after what happened earlier. She wasn't sure what to say to him yet, she needed some time to think about what he had said.

"Thank you," she said, Hazel tugging at her arm still. Ryder looked down at Hazel, a smile making its way across his face. "Enjoy your hot dogs!" he said to her. She waved a tiny hand at him, partially hidden behind her mom, still confused by the odd feeling in the air.

"I should go," Ryder said, even though what he really wanted to say was, "Can I come in?" Sadie nodded, looking away from him. The tension wasn't gone, not completely, and she just wanted things to go back to the way they were.

She closed the door gently behind her and headed to the kitchen with Hazel and the groceries. As she put them away, her thoughts were interrupted by Hazel's tiny voice asking if Ryder was coming back soon.

"No, baby," Sadie said apologetically. Hazel pouted sadly. Her hands worriedly played with her nightgown.

"But mommy, he promised to get me chocolate milk," she said, with an adorable little pout. She turned towards the bag of groceries and grabbed some out. Ryder had been so thoughtful to go grab her some groceries. That was one of her favorite things about him- that he was always thinking about how he could help people, especially her.

"Chocolate milk! He remembered!" Hazel said excitedly, grabbing it from her mom's hand, who was still staring at it curiously.

"Baby, when did he promise you chocolate milk?" she asked, and Hazel hesitated for a while before giving it up.

"Last night, when you were asleep."

Sadie's heart skipped a beat. "What happened last night, baby? Where did you see Ryder?" Sadie was panicking deep down, her assumptions seemed to heighten by this revelation. If something had happened, then it would destroy her to know that she hadn't protected her.

"I heard a sound in the kitchen, and I thought it was you, but it was Ryder. I was thirsty and I wanted chocolate milk, but it was all gone. He made me a little sandwich because we only had a little bread left, and he got me some water. He said he'd get me some chocolate milk in the morning.

Sadie hugged her, relieved, and so thankful that Ryder had taken such good care of her little girl while she was getting some much-needed sleep. She instantly felt guilty that she had even considered a thought that Ryder may have hurt her in any way. What was wrong with her anyway?

"Well, that was very sweet of him, wasn't it?" she smiled softly.

"Mommy, do we like Ryder?" Hazel asked very matter-of-factly.

"*Yes,* sweet pea," she patted Hazel's hair. Ryder had bought bread, cheese, more chocolate milk for Hazel and some vegetables for Sadie. Sadie sighed. She wasn't sure what was going on in her head, or her heart for that matter, but she did know that she needed someone to talk to about it. She needed to know she wasn't going crazy, and talking to Hazel was not going to help that, unfortunately.

* * *

As the brisk autumn day went by, Sadie busied herself with work in the cottage. She and Hazel washed the breakfast dishes up, dried them and put them away. Then, they went to Hazel's bedroom and made her bed, placing every stuffed animal she could find by her pillow. She tidied her own room, and then ran a load of laundry through the washer and dryer. Just before lunchtime, Hazel had gone to town with Stacy and Harriet, affording Sadie some quiet time to herself. She was sitting in the living room folding the clean clothes, her thoughts still swarming her brain, forcing her to try to sort through them and make sense of their meaning. The events of the past several hours had left her grappling with an unsettling paranoia, a lingering fear that had woven itself into the fabric of her newfound peace.

After folding the last little outfit of Hazel's, she walked over to the window, gazing at the falling golden leaves, her fingers tracing the rim of her iced tea absentmindedly. Ryder's patient and understanding demeanor, combined with the confession he had made that morning about how he felt about her, should have been enough to quell her apprehensions, yet doubt gnawed at her heart like an insidious whisper. Had she let her past trauma blind her to the genuine kindness that other around her exuded? Was she so far broken that she couldn't even feel anything *real* anymore? Did she even deserve someone like Ryder anyway?

Her mind replayed the moments she had treated Ryder with unwarranted caution, her reservations a result of the scars that Luke had etched into her mind and body. Sadie's heart ached as she acknowledged the unfairness of her actions, a sudden surge of regret threatening to engulf her. She closed her eyes, trying to clear her head. She felt as though a million little people were running rampant in her brain, each one trying to tell her something that contradicted what another one had already said. She couldn't figure out how to muddle through it all, how to sort out the reality from the fear-driven falsities.

Had she just made the worst mistake of her life? In her quest to protect herself and Hazel from any potential harm, had she unknowingly pushed away a man who could have brought joy and healing to her shattered world? Her chest tightened at the thought of losing Ryder, more than anything, his incredible friendship. A man who had shown her nothing but patience and unwavering support. A man who she wanted to explore every possibility with, both emotionally and physically.

She clenched her hands into fists, frustration welling up within her. The battle between her desire to move forward and the weight of her past had left her torn, each step forward marred by the lingering shadow of doubt. The hardest part for her to get past was the fact that Luke had once been kind, too. She knew, now, that he was only kind to trick her, but that didn't really matter in her head… in her head there was still a chance that Ryder could be doing that same thing, and the thought made her sick to her stomach. She desperately wanted to quiet the trauma of the past so that she could move forward, leaving all of it behind her.

As a tear slipped down her cheek, Sadie's gaze fell upon a photograph on the mantel – a snapshot of she and Hazel, and she was reminded, yet again, that it was her love for her daughter that had endured the darkest of storms, a love that had survived the onslaught of Luke's torment. Perhaps, she thought, this time she could let that love aid her in overcoming and confronting her fears. Would it really be so bad to take a leap and trust that Ryder wouldn't hurt them, and that his intentions were true and transparent? Maybe, if she could just figure out how to compartmentalize it… to be ready, just in case, but to keep those parts locked up, only to be used if she needed them. If so, could she *actually* have a chance to be happy?

# Chapter Ten

As Sadie walked towards the winery, the morning sun cast a warm, soft glow over the valley. The lingering chill of the autumn breeze nipped at her cheeks, causing her to pull the collar of her jacket a little tighter. Mid-October draped Stone Creek in a tapestry of golden hues, as the air turned crisper and the days grew shorter. The small town, nestled amidst rolling hills and lush landscapes, was alive with the vibrant colors of fall foliage. Falling leaves fluttered like confetti, carpeting the ground in a mosaic of reds, oranges, and yellows. The charm of the season was unmistakable, casting a spell over the tranquil countryside.

She loved this time of year- the air always felt so clean and crisp, smelling new, like pine and dirt mixed with the smells of hay and harvest. She let her eyes wander over the picturesque setting, the winery standing in the center, shining like a beacon of hope and prosperity. The sun-dappled vineyards from across the shoppe, now grape-less after the harvest, exuded an earthy fragrance that mingled with the sweet aroma of fermenting fruit. Rows of vines stretched towards the horizon, their leaves a mosaic of green and gold. The winery's rustic buildings, adorned with clusters of ivy, blended seamlessly into the landscape, their red-tiled roofs contrasting against the azure sky. Beyond the buildings lie the rows and rows of cranberry bogs, now empty and solemn, awaiting their winter coat of snow.

The winery's courtyard would soon be transformed into a lively hub of activity. Tables adorned with crisp white tablecloths would be scattered under the open sky, each one laden with bottles of the winery's finest offerings. Visitors and buyers, both locals and tourists, would mingle with an air of anticipation, savoring the chance to sample the fruits of the land. Laughter would waft into the breeze, intermingled with the low, soft strains of live music that would float from a corner stage. It was a familiar scene; one she was growing to love.

As she neared the winery's shoppe, she saw a light on in the window. She climbed the steps of the porch and entered the already-unlocked door. To her surprise, being inside the store felt like a relief, for some reason. She felt it as soon as she stepped through the vine-covered archway, the earthy scent of the vineyards greeting her like an old friend. Her steps were measured, her movements slower than usual, as if carrying the weight of the restless night that had come before. She listened for Sawyer, finding her around a corner near the register, ensuring that everything was ready for the new day.

Sawyer's eyes lit up when she spotted Sadie, and she hurried over, her voice infused with genuine warmth. "Sadie! You're here bright and early. I saw you a few times last night, but never got a chance to talk to you, it was so busy."

Sadie managed a weak smile, her eyes still tinged with the shadows of sleepless nights, battles in her heart and mind, and fears showing up in every corner of her dreams. "I've been searching everywhere for you too. I didn't want to bother you last night because I know how busy it was in here," She hugged her, thankful for this time with her friend. "Do you have a little bit to talk?"

"Yes, of course!" Sawyer said, worry in her tone. "Just give me a second to make sure Trav covers the door for me when people start to roam around. He's around here somewhere," she excused herself to go find her husband.

When she returned, Sawyer led Sadie to the office area and closed the door. Her brows were furrowed with concern as she sat down by Sadie, her jovial demeanor giving way to a more serious expression. "OK, I'm all yours, is everything alright?"

Sadie hesitated for a moment; the words caught in her throat. She cleared her throat, her voice soft but laden with emotion. "I… I had a rough night."

"A rough night how?" Sawyer asked.

"I had a terrible nightmare about Luke… It was so vivid that it was hard to separate it from reality."

Sawyer's eyes softened, empathy radiating from her gaze. Without a word, she enveloped Sadie in a warm embrace, the kind of hug that conveyed understanding and support without the need for words. Sadie clung to her friend, the vulnerability of the moment spilling over in the form of tears that she had held back for too long.

"There's more. I think I saw him the other day in town. I was grabbing a few groceries with Stacy, and I could have sworn I saw him in another aisle. It really scared me, and I got out of there as quickly as I could. I didn't see him again, but I don't know… Sawyer, am I going crazy? I mean, I know I had that nightmare, but seeing him around here seems even more insane! My dad said he won't bother us again, but if he figured out where we are and came here, we may be in a lot of danger!" She was bordering on hysteria now, and she was really worrying Sawyer.

"I'm so sorry, Sadie," Sawyer whispered. She was honestly not sure what to think about all of this. She had spoken with Henry, too, and he had assured her that Luke didn't have the balls to make a move after he had threatened him, but now she wasn't so sure he was right about that. What if he *was* around here? "Do you think you could you tell me more about these nightmares you are having? Maybe it will help to tell me about them."

Sadie's voice wavered as she recounted her nightmare, the memories of Luke's abuse still vivid and haunting. "I thought I was done with this, Sawyer. I thought I had moved on."

Sawyer's hand found Sadie's, her touch gentle and reassuring. "Sadie, I'm so sorry you have to go through this, and I'm *always* here for you. But honey, healing takes time. You've come so far, and I can't even begin to tell you how proud I am of you. You truly inspire me. You've been brave through all of this, especially for Hazel who, by the way, really looks up to you. She's always watching you, following your cues about who to trust and what is safe. You have a very smart little girl! The thing is, even with all that work and all the leaps and bounds you've jumped, you're going to have some setbacks. What matters is that you're strong and resilient, and you have an army of friends who love and support you right here."

Sadie nodded, tears glistening in her eyes as she found solace in Sawyer's words. "I just… I don't want my past to ruin my chance at happiness moving forward, but I can't help but feel scared."

Sawyer's eyes held a fierce determination as she spoke. "How can I help you, Sadie?" Sawyer asked, knowing her friend and how her mind worked. "What do you need me to do?"

"I need you to tell me if I should be scared. Should I ignore the nightmares and forget about what I thought I saw? Do I just do my best to go about my day without worrying?"

"First thing's first… Never ignore your gut. Still, I think you have to talk to someone about what happened to you so that you can find a way to move forward without the weight of the past anchoring you there," she advised, "In terms of moving on, I think you need to listen to your heart in that area. Trav and I see how you and Ryder look at each other. He is head-over-heels for you, Sadie. Do you realize that?"

"Yes, he actually told me the other day. I didn't react very well, Sawyer. I think I blew it. I got scared and backed away from him, making him get a really defeated look on his face. I feel horrible about it. I don't know what to do."

"Wow… I had no idea he told you! That's great, Sadie!" Sawyer replied excitedly.

"Don't get so excited, Sawyer. Like I said, I'm pretty sure I sent that ship out to sail."

"Nah… I know Ryder. He knows you are worth fighting for. Most importantly, you need to remember that Ryder is not Luke. He's proven that time and again to you, and you need to decide if you can believe he is safe or not. You deserve happiness, and you deserve to let go of that fear. I'm not saying you don't have a billion reasons to feel afraid, I'm just saying that you can't let those fears obstruct your life and the happiness you deserve."

Sadie absorbed Sawyer's words, deep breaths following, a spark of hope ignited within her. She looked into her friend's eyes, gratitude and determination intermingling in her gaze. "Thank you, Sawyer. I wish you could have been there these past few years… You were always there for me, and I forgot just how much that means to me."

"And you were there for me even more, Sadie, let's not forget who the actual queen of being there was– and still is. I never stopped being there for you and I never will, and that's all that matters. One last thing… I think you really need to think about sitting down with Ryder and telling him everything you just told me. He is a big boy, and he can handle hearing it. Plus, I think allowing him in like that will draw you closer to one another. Think about it, will ya?".

"I love you, Sawyer. Thank you for being here. For me and for Hazel. And yes, I'll think about it."

Sawyer smiled, her heart radiating warmth. "Always, Sadie. We're in this together."

* * *

"Not only do we have a large variety of wines, but we also use the freshest fruits in our wines, all of which are grown here in the valley," Sadie told Jake, a customer who was asking her about using their wines for his wedding. Over on the other side of the room, talking to Travis, was Ryder. She was trying to keep an eye on him, feeling like a schoolgirl with a crush or something. She needed to snap out of it!

"Um, we offer a wonderful package deal for weddings if you're interested," Sadie said mindlessly. She hadn't seen Ryder since he brought her groceries the other day, and she couldn't believe how much she had missed seeing him and talking to him.

"That sounds nice. Honestly, this wedding is costing a fortune, so any discounts definitely help sweeten the deal for me!" Jake responded, trying to figure out what she was looking at over to the right. "Is everything okay?" he asked.

"What? Oh, I'm so sorry, I was just distracted for a second," she replied, feeling terrible for not giving him the attention she normally gave to customers. "Jake, we would be honored to have you choose your wine from Cranberry Creek. Trust me, you won't be disappointed, and neither will your guests. Our reputation precedes us, and I'm sure you already knew that, or you wouldn't be here now."

"I really appreciate you taking the time to talk to me, Sadie. You definitely know your stuff!" Jake genuinely told her.

"Thank you, I appreciate you saying that. Um, would you mind if I excused myself for a minute? I need to make a quick phone call."

"Absolutely! I want to check out a few more options before I head out anyway. Thank you again for all your help!" Jake said, all lit up and smiling. This made his day, and Sadie was about to be a major inspiration for his honeymoon. Somewhere during their conversation, he had made the decision that it would be in Stone Creek. Not only had he found the small town quite endearing, but he'd had the best experience, however briefly, with Sadie's natural gift with words. He was glad his fiance had left the decision for their honeymoon solely in his hands. He knew she was going to *love* this place too.

"Thank you for understanding," Sadie said, extending her hand to shake his.

"Oh, no! Thank you, Sadie! You have no idea what you just did for me," he said, pulling her in for a friendly hug. She nodded and walked towards the front door, quickly glancing in the direction she had last seen Ryder. He was nowhere to be seen, so she snuck out the front door and walked to a swing near the courtyard. Even here, in the fresh autumn air, the scent of aged oak and rich blends lingered in her senses. The sun hung low in the sky, casting a warm and golden hue over her. Seeing Ryder had thrown her emotions into a tailspin, and she needed to take a few minutes to gather her thoughts.

When she was ready, Sadie pulled out her phone and dialed her parents' number, As she listened, waiting for her mom to pick up, Sadie's mind raced, her thoughts a whirlwind of doubts and hopes. When her mother's warm voice finally filled her ear, she took a deep breath, her voice trembling slightly. "Hey, Mom."

*"Sadie, sweetheart! How's everything going?"* Her mother's enthusiasm was unmistakable, a clear reflection of the love she had for her daughter.

"I'm doing okay," Sadie replied, her voice tinged with uncertainty. "Do you have a few minutes to talk? I have to get back to work in a bit, but I wanted to talk to you about something quick, if you have time."

A concerned note entered her mother's voice. *"Of course, honey. I've always got time for you. Dad told me you called the other day, is this about the nightmare you had, sweetie?"* her soothing voice slowly calming Sadie's current mood.

Sadie thought for a second about that nightmare, realizing

she wasn't quite so worked up about it anymore, for some reason. "Not really, not anymore anyway. I'm so happy to hear your voice mom," she said, a smile slowly filling her cheeks.

*"Oh, I'm so happy to hear yours too, sweetheart. If that's not it, what has you sounding like you're all worked up?"* her mother asked, obviously knowing something was up.

"I… I think I really like Ryder, mom. Like, *really* like him. The problem is that these feelings I'm having are scaring the heck out of me," she explained, her words a mix of vulnerability and honesty.

*"Why do they scare you?"*

"Well, mostly because I keep worrying that he will turn out to be like Luke? I mean, I really want to believe that I can trust him, but I thought the same thing about Luke, remember? Sawyer assures me Ryder would never be anything like Luke, but how could anyone be sure?"

*"Because Ryder isn't Luke. As a matter of fact, sweetie, most men are not like Luke! Take your dad, or even Travis, for instance,"* her mom chipped in quickly. There was a chopping sound in the background, telling Sadie she must be cooking something for dinner. *"Neither of them would ever hurt the ones they love!"*

There was a brief silence on the other end of the line before her mother spoke again, her voice soft and soothing. *"Sadie, sweetheart, we understand your fears. But you can't let the past dictate your future. Ryder has proven to you time and time again that he cares and that he won't hurt you."*

"I know that Mom, but for some reason my brain and my heart are fighting over this and I can't make them stop. Remember, Luke was kind to me at first too. As a matter of fact, he didn't change until we had been together for quite a while really. How do I know that Ryder won't eventually get sick of me and do the same thing?" Sadie had tears welling in her eyes, threatening to fall if she didn't calm down.

*"Sweetie, I need you to listen to me for a second, okay? There is a huge difference between Ryder and Luke, one that you haven't probably considered yet. Luke's family, co-workers, and others around him saw the signs and knew he had a violent temper, they were just too afraid to say anything for fear of his response. For some reason, your father and I missed it, but I think that's because he made sure we didn't see it, just like he did with you,"* her mom continued softly. *"Has any person in that town led you to believe that Ryder has the same issues?"*

"No, not at all, but-"

*"Okay then, if you combine that with all the wonderful things Sawyer has told you about him, how can you still question his motives?"* she asked her daughter matter-of-factly.

Sadie thought for a moment. She had never even considered that possibility. How had she missed that?

"I've never really thought of that, mom. I guess my fear of putting Hazel and I through that same horror again is really clouding my judgment, isn't it?"

*"Oh honey, that's totally normal after everything you've been through."*

Sadie closed her eyes, taking comfort in her mother's wisdom.

*"I'd love to hear more about these feelings you're having about Ryder, if you are ready to share them with me..."* her mother urged gently.

With a deep breath, she began to share the details of her experiences with Ryder. Her words flowed freely, a mix of cherished moments woven together with love and care, with a bit of humor sprinkled on top.

Sadie's voice stopped quivering as she finally relaxed and spoke freely to her mother, her admiration for Ryder evident in every word. "Mom, he's been so amazing to us. It's not just about the big things; it's the little things he does that show how kind and caring he is."

Her mother listened attentively, a smile forming as she recognized the genuine affection in Sadie's voice. *"What kind of things does he do for you?"*

Sadie's eyes sparkled as she recounted the moments that would help her mother see her belief in Ryder's goodness. "Well, for one, he's incredibly attentive. Whenever we're together somewhere, he makes me feel like I'm the only person in the room. It's like he genuinely listens to every word I say, and he remembers even the smallest details."

Although she couldn't see it, her mother nodded in approval, understanding the significance of such gestures. *"That's definitely a sign of someone who values you and your company. A good man listens, Sadie, and he doesn't talk at you, he talks with you."*

Sadie's voice grew animated as she continued. "He's not just attentive to *me*, Mom. He's been so caring towards Hazel too. He takes care of her sometimes when I'm working, and he takes her and Harriet on these adorable little picnics by the courtyard. He sets up this cute little spread with all of Hazel and Harriet's favorite snacks, and the 'conversations' they have make me laugh."

A fond smile curved her mother's lips. *"He sounds like a pretty great guy to me, Sadie. Especially if Hazel sees it, you know how great of a character judge she is!"* she laughed.

Sadie's heart swelled with pride as she shared another example. "He also takes time to answer Hazel's million and one questions, and he doesn't act annoyed by her like I'd expect a man with no children to feel. If she struggles with something, he patiently sits with her for a long time, explaining and showing her until she finally gets it. The smile on her face at the end of the day, Mom… It's always so priceless. It seems like he can do something that even I cannot do for her. I really appreciate that."

*"Sounds to me like he is a better man than Luke ever was,"* her mom encouraged, *"And I can tell you from experience that a man who invests time and effort in the people he cares about is a man worth holding onto."*

*"She ought to know, sweetheart, she definitely landed a good one!"* Sadie heard her dad chime in from somewhere across the room, causing her to laugh out loud. She wasn't sure where he had come from, but apparently, he'd felt the need to chime in on the subject.

*"Henry John Archer… keep moving along! Sadie and I are having some girl-talk time."* She could hear the laughter as her parents shared a familiar moment of comradery. She loved when they went back and forth like that, it reminded her of her childhood, and that made her smile as she reminisced. After a few seconds, she heard her father give her mother a quick kiss and then head out the door.

Suddenly, her mind wandered back to the night she had the terrible nightmare, and Sadie's voice became more hushed. "I know Dad told you about the nightmare, but there's a part I left out. When I woke up, I was terrified, and I called Ryder," she confessed.

*"You did? What happened?"*

"Without a second thought, he showed up at our cottage. He sat with me, comforting me until I fell back asleep. The next morning, I was still so shaken and scared that I forgot he was there, and he scared the living crap right out of me! I got *so* confused by everything that I asked him to leave. To be honest, I wanted to run to him and hold on tight, because he made me feel safe for the first time in a very long time, but instead I asked him to leave. He looked confused and hurt, and I felt *terrible* for that. Then, a little later that morning, he showed back up with some groceries he had seen I needed."

A warm smile played on her mother's lips. *"Boy, he sounds like a pretty amazing guy, Sadie. He obviously is a man who will be there for you, no matter what. Does that sound like a man who would treat you like Luke did, honey?"*

"No, it doesn't," Sadie admitted.

*"I agree. He also seems like a man who would face a problem the right way instead of throwing punches,"* Rose said.

"Well, Luke only hit me twice, Mom, and I am pretty sure Ryder would never do that."

*"Sadie, verbal abuse is just as bad, sometimes worse. Luke played mental games with you, making you feel like you were lesser than him, like you were worthless. All of that abuse over the time you were married left bigger scars than him hitting you did, and you need to realize that. I think that may be one of the keys you need to be able to face the past and move into the future."*

Sadie's voice held a note of resolve as she concluded, "You're probably right, Mom. Honestly, he's been a rock to me and Hazel. Through the good and the bad, he's shown me what it means to have someone who cares deeply and is willing to stand by me, but that terrified me for some reason."

*"This is just my two cents, so take it as that, but I think you got scared because you are realizing that you have something to lose now. With Luke leaving, it meant you were safe, and you didn't lose*

*anything but fear. With Ryder, if he left it would mean something entirely different to your heart. That should tell you a lot about how you really feel, Sadie."*

Sadie thought about those words, how true they were. Her mom knew her heart and she was so thankful she had called her. Her mother's soft voice interrupted her thoughts, *"Sweetie, it's pretty clear to me that Ryder has shown you his true colors – colors that paint a beautiful picture of care, patience, and unwavering support. Don't let your fears overshadow the wonderful person he is."*

Sadie's heart swelled with gratitude as her mother's words sank in. "Thank you, Mom. I really needed to hear that. I miss you and Dad very much!"

*"We miss you and Hazel too!"*

"I love you, Mom."

*"I love you too. Okay, now that we got that part out of the way, tell me more about this fireman of yours. Does he look good in a uniform?"* her mom asked her, making Sadie laugh out loud for the first time in several days. Leave it to her mom to ask a question like that!

After goodbyes were said, Sadie ended the call, a renewed sense of clarity washing over her. She stepped back into the wine shoppe, her gaze sweeping across the familiar surroundings. Jake was standing with Travis and Sawyer, engaged in a rather hearty conversation, standing amidst the bottles and the laughter of patrons. All three glanced at the door when she entered, and Jake paused to wave at her. Sawyer gave her two thumbs up, behind his turned back, with an excited expression.

Sadie smiled at the group, but she was preoccupied with her her search for Ryder. After a few moments, her heart sank.

He seemed to have disappeared. It must have taken her too long on the phone, and now she would have to wait to see him or talk to him until later.

Disappointed, she sighed and turned to head back to the tasting room to help wherever she was needed. Sadie spun around and ran smack dab into what felt like a brick wall.

"I'm so sorry, I wasn't look-"

She stopped, the words getting lodged in her throat suddenly as she realized who she'd run into. There he stood, right in front of her, a tender smile curving his lips. "I thought maybe you were running from me, and now you ran right into me!" he said playfully.

Sadie's eyes sparkled with awareness and embarrassment. A soft gasp escaped her lips as she found herself face to face with Ryder. She was acutely aware of the masculine smell as she pulled away from his chest. His cologne, mixed with a hint of mint soap, created a potion that seemed to take away her ability to think or speak. Jumping back like he had stung her or something, she looked up into his eyes. She blushed furiously, feeling weak with need. *Oh boy, I've got it really bad,* she thought. With a deep breath, she decided it was time to take a leap.

# Chapter Eleven

Like a wave, it dawned on Sadie that the man before her was a portrait of rugged handsomeness and effortless charm, every detail about him a vivid and enchanting picture. She had done her best to avoid allowing herself to study him like this, but now, things were different.

He stood a little shorter than Travis, yet he could easily outshine his taller friends. Ryder's athletic build exuded an aura of strength and confidence. The sunlight kissed his tanned complexion, casting a warm glow that highlighted the contours of his face. His auburn hair, adorned with loose curls tousled atop his head, seemed to dance in the gentle breeze, framing his features with a touch of playful nonchalance.

As his dimpled smile extended up his right cheek, it was impossible not to feel a flutter of warmth in her heart. His grin, sly and mischievous, held the promise of shared secrets and private jokes, as if he held a treasure trove of laughter and naughtiness, just waiting to be unlocked. Sadie wondered how she had possibly let fear and doubt keep her from noticing his stunningly handsome features before now.

Ryder's movements were a captivating blend of casual elegance. She had noticed before that he walked with a lazy stride; A confident swagger that spoke of a man comfortable in his own skin. Yet, when his eyes met Sadie's now, his posture transformed, his lazy gait giving way to a determined stride, a subtle hint of excitement in his steps. His handshake was firm, a tactile reassurance of his steadfast presence.

Clad in well-worn jeans and a comfy sweatshirt donned with the fire station's name and logo, Ryder effortlessly merged his rugged charm with casual style. It dawned on Sadie that although she was not usually a fan of cowboy boots, they suited him perfectly. Somehow, without her knowing, each step Ryder made left an imprint on her heart, adding a touch of rustic authenticity to his ensemble. She also loved when he had a baseball cap perched atop his tousled hair. She loved that it seemed to complement his effortless charisma.

But, in this moment, it was the way he gazed at Sadie that truly captured her attention. His eyes held an enigmatic depth, as if he was peering into the very core of her being, attempting to unravel the mysteries that lay beyond her eyes. Yet, there was a hint of mirth, a glint of amusement that danced in his eyes.

Suddenly, she realized she was staring at him, and she blushed furiously.

"You look like you've just seen a ghost or something, are you okay?" Ryder asked, smiling at her in a way that weakened her legs. He seemed to be able to hypnotize her with a look, and it was a bit unsettling. Still, she seemed to be enchanted by them, no matter how hard she tried to pull herself out of it. "Hazel was looking for you, but I was able to distract her when I saw you step out for a call."

"Oh, where-" Sadie blinked rapidly, looking around.

"Don't worry," he interrupted, seeing her instant concern for her daughter, "she's coloring in the other room with Harriet."

Sadie couldn't help but feel a rush of warmth. Ryder's love for his family was evident in every gesture. His protective nature, born from a genuine and heartfelt place, resonated with her on a profound level. She often saw his interactions with Hazel, the way he took an immediate liking to her, his eyes lighting up when he made the little girl giggle. It reflected how kind and compassionate he was, and even more, it was a reflection of his innate ability to nurture and protect. She was finally starting to see that, and she was realizing how much she wanted him to do those things for her too.

Oblivious of the activities around them, Sadie and Ryder stood face to face, everything else around them seeming to blur, leaving only the two of them in a kind of personal bubble. "Ryder, I need to-"

"Sadie, before you say anything, I have some things I need to tell you," Ryder cut in. "Can we go for a little walk so we can talk?"

"Yes, I think that would be good. I have some things I want to talk to you about too. I need to grab Hazel's bag from the cottage anyway, so we can head there. I'll just go let Sawyer know we will be right back." As she walked off to find Sawyer, he couldn't help but watch her with a grin. He wasn't sure what she had been thinking about before when she'd bumped into him, but he had enjoyed watching her look him over. He just hoped she had liked what she saw. He felt something shift, like something in her had changed suddenly, but he wasn't sure what that was. When she came back, she grabbed her light jacket, and he held the door for her as they exited the shoppe.

"Sawyer said that she is taking the girls to get some ice cream, so we don't have to rush back. Travis has everything covered for now."

"Perfect," he responded, smiling at her.

They walked together, side-by-side, for a little bit, until they were a little way from the winery. He reached over and held his hand out for Sadie to take, and she accepted. It was such a simple gesture, but she was sure he had no idea what it meant to her. She was letting him in, and she found herself thankful that it wasn't scary like she thought it would be. His hand felt warm in hers, and it seemed to be sending electrical shocks through her, making her very aware of his body so close to hers.

As they rounded the corner towards her cottage, he looked into her eyes and said, "Sadie, you are such an amazing woman. I'm not sure what happened before, but I know how I feel, and I know what I see. I want us to have a chance, but I think you need to tell me about what brought you here so that I can know why you are so afraid of letting me in. I don't want to push you, but I really hope you'll trust me and tell me, whatever it was. No judgment here."

Sadie fought back the tears that attempted to flow through her eyes. As he stopped walking and stepped closer, the distance between them gave way, and Sadie felt a surge of emotion that made her heart race. Ryder's presence became what it had been after her nightmare, a beacon of light, a constant reminder that there was beauty in vulnerability, and strength in opening one's heart to love. As his fingers brushed against hers, the electric spark of their connection sent a shiver down her spine, and she couldn't help but smile. His gray eyes locked onto hers in a silent declaration of feelings more powerful than words could describe.

"Ryder," she replied, her own voice filled with regret and apology. "I am so sorry about the other morning. I was really shaken after my nightmare, and I reacted very poorly. I never meant to hurt you."

Ryder's eyes held a tender gaze as he reached out his hand and touched her cheek, his touch intended to be a reassurance. "I'll always be here for you, Sadie. No matter what," he said, and in response, Sadie sighed and seemed to melt into his hand as she closed her eyes and lay her cheek into it. He wanted to kiss her, right then and there, but he knew she wasn't ready yet. He had to be patient and hear her out, as hard as that was. After a moment, she grabbed his hand again and they finished the short distance to the cottage. They climbed the steps and sat together on the porch.

"Thank you. I want to try to help you understand, but I'm not sure I can find the right words. You see, everyone I love keeps telling me the same thing, but I have this hurt deep down trying to dissuade me from their words. Before today, I kept listening to that hurt, but I'm done doing that."

Ryder stared at her attentively. "Well, that's good, right? Do you care to share?"

"The phone call I made was to my mom. She helped me to see that you are a good man, and that I need to stop comparing you to what I knew in the past. And, she was right," she said, smiling that smile he loved so much.

"I'm so glad to hear you say that. You can trust me, and I'll spend every day trying to show you-" Sadie closed the gap between them and kissed him, her palms holding his head in place. Her hands felt like ice on his face, a stark contrast to the soft, warm lips that graced his. The kiss was short, but it left him needing more. "You're not alone, Sadie. I just wanted to say that. You are never alone, and I love you."

Sadie's heart started to beat fast, and she began to breathe in the way of her heartbeat. "Then kiss me again, Ryder," she said. He put one hand at the back of her neck, and another around her waist, then kissed her, his dream finally a reality.

* * *

The night sky was extraordinary with her shades of red, pink and orange. The moon shone brightly, illuminating Ryder's small forest green house. It had beautiful brick around the lower half that made the green of the siding look rich and deep. There was a mum on the porch steps, something she assumed his mother had put in place since Ryder had a 'black thumb," as he put it the other day. She took a deep breath and walked up the steps. She couldn't believe she was actually going to have dinner with Ryder tonight. Sawyer and Travis had taken Hazel for the night and were excited for an evening of Go Fish and chocolate milk. She smiled at the thought of Travis on the floor playing cards with Hazel. The last time she spent an evening there, Travis ended up with a hilarious face full of gaudy make-up and lipstick. Of course, she was pretty sure he'd deny that to his death if anyone asked.

As she got to the door, she took a deep breath. "Here goes nothing," she said to herself with an attempt at calming her leaping nerves. She knocked gently on the door and could instantly hear Ryder's footsteps approaching. As he opened the door, her heart leapt. He was stunning in his jeans and tee, and she found herself wanting to kiss him, forget dinner, and do the things she had been dreaming all week about doing with him. Instead, she moved past him, noticing the smell of his woodsy cologne and wishing she could move closer.

Ryder's house was cabin-like, and she instantly loved it. He had old fireman's hats on the wall, displayed with pride and nostalgia. There were some photos on the fireplace mantle of Harriet, more proof that he obviously loved her very much. He had a small table that was near the kitchen, a simple space with very few decorations. The kitchen opened into a small living room which he had a couch and a comfy recliner placed in. It was practical and clean, and exactly as she had expected it to be. She placed her coat over a chair at the table and turned toward Ryder, not realizing he had already closed the gap between them and was standing right behind her.

His hands were instantly on her face, gently caressing and bringing her lips closer to his for a kiss. The kiss was soft and sweet, but with an urgency that she met whole-heartedly. She was lost in the taste of him, this man that she was falling hard and fast for. As she parted her lips, he slowly filled the space with his tongue, exploring and tasting. She met his and their mouths became a haven for their tongues to dance within. After what felt like an eternity, they parted, each taking a moment to get their breath and figure out what to do next.

Ryder stepped back a bit, his mind reeling from their encounter. He had fully planned to make Sadie dinner, talk about things and get to know each other better, and then maybe watch a movie together, but apparently his body had a different idea. If he didn't slow this down a bit, they were going to end up in his bed, eventually hungry from missing dinner. "Wow, I'm sorry I just pounced like that. I have been thinking about doing that all day, and I told myself I'd try to be a gentleman, not a tiger," he said apologetically.

She laughed, obviously still not on solid ground either, "I actually rather like your tiger side," she said, with a flirty sound she didn't even know she had in her.

Somehow, her feet started to move, and she pushed her body up to his again, looking at him in a way that made him forget all reason and all previous plans.

"You'd better be careful, Sadie. I'm trying hard to be good here, but I am a man, not a saint."

"Well," she said in that throaty voice again, "Maybe you shouldn't try so hard."

That was all the encouragement he needed. He scooped her up and took her to his bedroom, kissing her the whole way. She giggled with delight as he kicked at the door, stubbing his toe and swearing under his breath, completely unashamed of the excitement she felt. Her mind threatened to go to a place of insecurity and fear, but she pushed it aside. *Not tonight,* she thought. *Tonight, I am going to live in the moment and savor every second I get with this wonderful man that I care so much about.* She had been thinking all week about how it had felt to be in Ryder's arms, and she was about to find out how it felt to be in his bed as well. He sat her onto her feet on the floor in his room.

He gently kissed her again, this time with a sense of calm and sensuality. A kiss that showed her that he was so much in love with her. For Sadie, the feelings he was invoking in her felt new and exciting- as it if was her first time all over again, only this time was so much better than it had been before.

Ryder was different, and in that moment, she realized that she loved him too. She wasn't ready to tell him yet, but she knew it was true.

"Sadie," he looked deep into her eyes, "I need to hear you say that you want this, too. I don't want to-"

"Yes, Ryder, I want you to make love to me," she whispered in his ear with more sensuality than she ever realized she had. She smiled when she felt him shudder against her, feeling more powerful than she had ever felt before.

Ryder slowly moved his hands over her hips, sliding her dress up and over her head. He kissed her shoulders before moving up her neck, making her nerve endings roar with excitement. As he kissed her, he slowly turned her so she was facing away from him, giving him access to the back of her neck. He slowly slid his tongue up the nape of her neck, causing her to shiver as he tasted his way over her. She thought her legs would give away underneath her, and he sensed it. He put one hand on her belly and held her against his body as his other hand gently undid her bra. Using his teeth, he moved each strap slowly off the shoulder it was held by, kissing its path as it fell. She had never known she had so many places to kiss before, and she found herself gasping at each new sensation.

As her bra fell to the floor in front of her, she felt Ryder's hands move up her belly to gently cup each of her supple breasts. She thought she may literally die as his fingers moved to flick and play at her nipples. She couldn't believe she was here right now, with this man that she loved, and feeling so safe and happy. As he turned her towards him, her mouth found his and she kissed him, slowly moving from his lips to his ear. "My turn, fireman," she whispered in his ear between nibbles.

As she explored his neck with her mouth, she unbuttoned his shirt and moved it off his shoulders to the floor. His chest was tanned and strong, with contours and lines that she couldn't wait to explore. She slowly moved down his neck, enjoying the groan she heard from him as she stopped at his nipple and ran her tongue over it. As she started to unbutton his jeans, he took her hand from his fly and kissed it.

"If you do that, this will be done before it starts," he said, his face filled with need.

Instead, he lay her gently on the bed, treating her as though she was a fragile piece of glass that may break under his fingers. With a smooth flick of his wrist, he unbuttoned his jeans and pulled them down, removing each leg from the denim. She watched with awe as he removed his boxers next. His erection was firm and large, and she felt an excitement in her groin that had her aching to touch and explore more of him. "Do you see what you are doing to me?" he asked, loving the intense gaze she had when she looked at his body.

Sadie felt a sense of power that she had never known before. Had *she* really turned this beautiful man on, just by being herself? She didn't even think that was possible! Just as she was about to say something, he reached down and pulled her panties off. She felt exposed, and suddenly embarrassed. What if he didn't like what he saw? He was so handsome, and she felt far from his level.

Sensing her hesitance, he reached down and slowly slid his hands between her knees, spreading her legs gently. He reached down and kissed her right knee, looking into her eyes. "You are so beautiful, Sadie. I want to explore every part of you. I've been wanting to do this for so long…" he said in a voice sounding like leather. He slowly traced his fingers down the inside of her thighs, making her shake with delight. "I'd like to start with these…" he said, following his fingers with kisses.

Sadie's embarrassment instantly faded away, replaced by a need to feel the warmth of Ryder's body on hers, suddenly feeling like she couldn't live without it. He lowered himself to her, their body's close but not touching. He kissed her, his tongue teasing her mouth, before moving his lips slowly down her neck, stopping at her breasts. He took a nipple in his mouth and suckled it. She arched her back towards him in delight. He was igniting feelings in her that had long been buried, and she couldn't wait to see what else he could dig up.

"Please, Ryder, let me touch you," she begged.

"Sweetheart, next time I'll let you explore whatever you'd like. Right now, just lay back and let me pleasure you."

She was happy to oblige. As he placed kisses up and down her body, she felt a passionate release building inside of her. As if he could sense her getting close, he used his tongue to flick the nerve endings between her legs, sending her over the edge with a shout of ecstasy. Her body jerked with strong currents of sensation, leaving her both numb with satisfaction and wanting more, all at the same time. He moved his kisses back up her torso, stopping once again to flick and tease her nipples. When she felt like she couldn't take it anymore, she begged him, "Ryder, please, I-"

"Yes, beautiful, what would you like me to do?" he teased, an unfamiliar and exciting look in his eyes.

"I-" she tried, but the words were caught in her throat. Spreading her legs, Ryder adjusted his firm, muscular body so it was above hers. He looked deep into her eyes, enjoying the intimacy they were sharing together, and wanting to see her face when they made love for the first time. "Please, Ryder…" she said, squirming beneath his body, putting her hands on his back and gently pulling him towards her.

"I love you, Sadie," he whispered, kissing her softly as he slipped inside her.

Sadie threw her head back, feeling every inch of him as he slowly entered her body. She had never known such an ecstatic feeling before. He was deep inside of her, but she wanted more. She didn't want this feeling to end, ever. She adjusted her hips so she could raise her legs to wrap around his hard, sweaty body. The motion brought him even deeper inside her. She gasped in joy as he began to move, slowly, in and out of her. She began to move her hips to match his rhythm, as if they were dancing together.

Ryder could feel the blood pooling in his groin, knowing he would climax soon, wishing he could continue forever inside of Sadie. He looked into her eyes, wanting to see her face as he came inside of her. He kissed her, slowly and gently, needing her to know how much he loved her. Breaking the kiss, he looked at her as she brought her hands to his face, caressing him, the sensation ever so sweet.

"I love you too, Ryder," she said, sending him over the edge with a gasp, pouring his love deep inside of her.

* * *

Sadie sat in front of a beautiful mirror, exactly her height, while combing her shoulder-length wavy hair. The gentle morning light filtered through the windows of Ryder's house, casting a soft and warm glow across the room. As Sadie sat before the mirror, her reflection framed by the mirror's elegant edges, she felt a sense of peace and happiness that she hadn't felt in so long that it seemed foreign to her.

With delicate precision, Sadie combed her hair, the strands intertwining like a composition of mahogany and auburn. Her movements were deliberate, almost therapeutic, as she untangled any knots with patient strokes. Each pass of the comb seemed to be a gentle affirmation, a way to reclaim control over something as simple and personal as her own appearance. It was a habit she had grown into in the past five years of her life. But on this day, a smile formed on her face as she reminisced the evening before. How could it be that she had absolutely loved doing something that was so uncharacteristic of her? Even now, she couldn't believe how things had unfolded in the last 24 hours.

The quiet serenity of the moment was interrupted as Ryder emerged, his presence a welcome interruption that elicited a soft smile from Sadie. "Morning, beautiful," he greeted, his voice was warm, deep as it often was in the early hours of the morning.

Sadie turned her gaze towards him, her eyes meeting his in fondness and affection. "Morning, Ryder."

His lips quirked into a playful grin as he stepped closer, his eyes lingering on her reflection in the mirror. "You know," he began, his voice laced with a teasing undertone, "I was always taught to comb my hair in the bathroom. Hair maintenance central, my dad called it."

Sadie's cheeks tinged with a light blush, she was unable to hide the embarrassment in her eyes. "Oh, really? Sorry about that. I didn't know."

Ryder's response was delivered with an ease that spoke volumes about his character. "Oh, come on, no need to apologize. I was just teasing you. I don't even understand it myself, but my dad raised us kids to always deal with our hair in the bathroom. Refusal to do so would result in him telling my mom, who would then nag at us, and oh, you don't want to be nagged by my mom."

As he spoke, the absence of grievances, anger, or any hint of meanness was striking. Ryder's calm demeanor seemed to radiate a kind understanding, the sort that made Sadie's heart swell with appreciation. She nodded, a small smile gracing her lips, and turned her attention back to her hair.

As she began to brush, Ryder stepped behind her, his voice holding a hint of curiosity as he spoke. "Hey, Sadie, can I ask you something?"

She paused, looking up at him in the mirror. "Sure, fireman. What is it?"

His eyes locked onto hers in an intent gaze that made her pulse quicken. "I've asked you this before, and I know you gave me an answer, but I notice that you have a unique need to often apologize. Like just now, for not knowing where to comb your hair, which isn't a big deal at all. Did you think I'd get mad or something?"

Sadie's gaze lowered from his, her fingers absently twirling a strand of hair. Her voice was soft, almost a whisper, as she spoke. "I guess I… I tend to do that. It's just a habit, I suppose."

Ryder's expression softened as well, his eyes as gentle as his hands. "Sadie, you don't have to apologize for every little thing."

A tender smile tugged at Sadie's lips, gratitude shimmering in her eyes. "Thank you, Ryder. For being so kind and gentle with me."

He came around the chair and held his hands out to her, lifting her from the chair and walking with her to the couch. Sitting, he centered his gaze on hers once again, his voice remaining a gentle reassurance. "Can I ask why you do it? Apologize, I mean. I really do want to know, Sadie. Last night you said you wanted to help me understand, but then we ended up getting a little side-tracked, if you know what I mean," he said with that mischievous grin she loved so much.

Sadie hesitated for a few seconds, her look momentarily fixed on the floor before she met his eyes with a quiet vulnerability. "It's... It's something that's stuck with me from before I moved here. My ex-husband, Luke... he used to tell me everything was my fault. It was like I was always doing something wrong and could never do anything right. Even if he did something wrong, he somehow had this way of flipping it so it was me who was in the wrong in the end."

Empathy filled Ryder's eyes. "I'm so sorry you had to go through that, Sadie."

Her voice quivered slightly as she continued, the weight of her past slowly becoming evident in her words. "He was abusive, Ryder. Emotionally and verbally, and in the end, physically... I felt like I was constantly walking on eggshells, always afraid of doing something that would set him off. He would curse easily, call me names, blame me for everything, threaten me with words or by using my fear of Hazel being hurt to control me." Her voice cut, and he wanted to scoop her up in his lap and hold her, but knew she needed to get this out. "I could never figure it out, could never understand why he seemed to hate me so much instead of loving me like he said he did in the beginning. I thought it would get better, but

I found out in the end that I had thought wrong."

Ryder's expression darkened with both anger and concern. "Oh, Sadie. I'm so sorry for the pain he put you both through. I wish I knew how to go back and take it all away for you."

"I appreciate that, Ryder. Unfortunately, there's more. In the end, he hit me so hard that he sent me to the hospital. The worst part of it all was that Hazel saw. I felt like such a failure- what kind of mother can't protect her own daughter from someone who would do that? What if he had hurt her?" Sadie was crying now, willing the tears back but losing the battle.

"Oh Sadie, please don't cry. I'm sorry I made you talk about this stuff. I can't imagine how hard it is to think about it all over again." He reached over and hugged her, willing the bad thoughts to leave her body and enter his. How could any man ever think of hitting a woman? If he ever saw him things were not going to end well. *I wonder how tough he'd feel with a full-grown man to fight*, Ryder thought.

"You never have to feel that way with me... ever! I'm not him. I've never been, and I'd never be. Please trust me on that. You have no reason to be afraid with me, I promise."

Tears continued to fall from her swollen eyes, her voice laced with emotions. "I know, Ryder. It's just... it's hard to shake off those old habits, you know?"

Ryder's hand reached out, his fingers gently wiping away the tear from her cheek. "You're safe now, Sadie. I'm here with you, and I promise you'll never have to apologize for being yourself. For being human. For making mistakes. Or for anything at all."

Sadie stared at him, her eyes glistening with a newfound hope. It felt like Ryder's words held the power to heal her wounds, and she had never wanted anything in her life to be truer than she wanted that feeling to be.

"I'm not going anywhere," he added, his fingers brushing against her cheek, a sense of protection washing over her. "I'm going to do my best to make sure you always feel safe, and we'll fight the ghosts of your past together, but I can't do that if you don't talk to me, okay?" Sadie nodded. Her parents were right, and so was Sawyer… Ryder *was* trustworthy, and he meant her no harm.

As if reading her thoughts, Ryder pulled her onto his lap, his arms encircling her with so much intimacy and reassurance. Nestled against him, her head on his shoulder, Sadie felt a comfort and safety she hadn't experienced in years coursing through her.

When the tears stopped, she looked out the window near them, amazed at the morning sunlight that continued to bathe the room in its soft embrace. Sadie snuggled into Ryder's arms, basking in the realization that the journey she embarked on a couple months ago was tied around this amazing 34-year-old fireman. With him by her side, every step forward felt a little less daunting, and the prospect of a future in which there was less fear and more love and safety finally stared her in the face.

# Chapter Twelve

The bright autumn sun wasn't the only thing that revealed the true beauty of Stone Creek. Even at night, though a small town, Stone Creek was beautiful in its unique way. Ryder made his way down the familiar path that led to his mother's house. He hadn't been there in a couple of weeks because she had been sick with the stomach flu, insisting he stay away so he didn't catch it. He had called her yesterday and told her he was stopping by to check on her, no matter what she said. Ryder didn't often go more than a few days without seeing his widowed mother, but between nights with Sadie and her sickness, he felt like it had been forever.

The Mack residence stood nestled amidst a grove of trees, its white-painted facade exuding an air of timeless tranquility. The two large apple trees to the side of the main entrance were empty, yet still drooping down after their recent harvest. His mother loved to bake, and he imagined that she had a full freezer stocked with apple pies, cobblers, and sauce, all things he absolutely loved to receive from her whenever she felt like giving some up.

As Ryder stepped onto the welcoming porch, the soft creak of the wooden floorboards under his feet hinted to the passage of time. The porch itself was adorned with vibrant hanging baskets overflowing with colorful blossoms, evidence of his mother's love for all things natural and beautiful. The scent of freshly baked cinnamon rolls lingered in the air, one of his mother's favorite recipes, and one that had his stomach grumbling for a taste.

After a gentle knock, Ryder announced his presence, his heart swelling with anticipation. The door swung open, revealing a figure that radiated kindness and love. Annie Mack, a bit plump, and definitely vertically challenged, as she liked to say, oozed a sense of maternal warmth. She looked up from the counter she was wiping to see her son walk in the room.

"Ryder, my boy," Annie exclaimed, her beautiful smile lighting up her face. She embraced her son, her soft and wrinkling hands offering a comforting touch that held years of love and care.

"Hey, Mom," Ryder greeted, "How are you feeling tonight?"

Annie stepped back, her soft complexion illuminated by the light. Her dark brown hair, worn short and wavy, framed her face in a way that seemed to accentuate her timeless beauty. Her choice of attire, a long skirt paired with a button-up blouse and moccasins, had more to say of her practical elegance and her personality. Her heart necklace, a precious memento from her late husband, and her simple wedding band on her finger held stories of a love that had stood the test of time. Even now, over 5 years later, she refused to remove it.

"Come in, come in," Annie urged, her voice filled with so much warmth. "I was just making some spice cakes. I'm feeling much better, thank you for asking!"

Ryder stepped into the cozy interior, removing his shoes before entering the kitchen. The familiar sights and sounds of home always wrapped around him with a sense of nostalgia. The living room, to the left of the kitchen, was adorned with quilts and crafts, thanks to Annie's creative spirit. A framed photograph on the wall captured a moment from his childhood. Standing on each side of him were Wyatt, his younger brother, and Stacy, his younger sister.

His mother motioned for him to sit at the kitchen table. Cinnamon rolls, golden fried chicken, and a steaming bowl of mashed potatoes adorned the table, flanked by ears of corn on the cob. A pitcher of lemonade completed the picture, not lost on Ryder that they were all Annie's favorites.

As they sat together indulging in the delicious meal set before them, they easily conversed, and laughter filled the space between them. Ryder savored every bite. It was usually all of them sitting at the table, Wyatt, Stacy and her husband, Rick, and Harriet. Tonight, though, it was just the two of them. As they caught up, Annie could tell he was bothered about something, even amidst the laughter and jokes he told just to make her laugh. Even so, she had learned long ago that she had to let Ryder come to her when something was wrong. Stacy and Wyatt had to be prodded, but not Ryder. She knew he'd share when he was ready to.

After they finished their meal, Annie pulled the spice cake out to cool, and they decided to go sit on the porch swing to enjoy the beautiful fall evening. They sat together swinging for a bit before Ryder finally broke the silence. "Mom," he began, his voice tinged with hesitance, "I've been spending a lot more time with Sadie over the last few weeks. "

"I see…" She interjected briefly.

He hesitated, then went on. "The thing is, there's something that I need some motherly advice about, but it's very personal for Sadie, so it has to stay between us, okay?"

"Ryder, you can always trust me to keep your secrets… from me to the grave, dear." She smiled and squeezed his hand for reassurance.

"It's Sadie, Mom. We've been getting to know each other more and more, but… she apologizes all the time, for the smallest, and often oddest, things."

Annie's expression loosened, her gaze filled with curiosity. "Apologizes? How so?"

Ryder sighed, his frustration evident. "Like for practically everything, Mom. She apologizes for not knowing something she thinks she should have known, for not being sure, for just being wrong about something, for making a mistake. Sometimes she apologizes for apologizing! I want to understand, and I want to be patient, but it's driving me insane that I can't help her stop."

Annie's smile was knowing, she had a clue as to why Sadie was doing that, but she needed to hear it from her son. "Ryder, I am sure there's a reason behind that. But I believe you already know what it is. You probably just don't understand it completely. Do you think Sadie would be okay with you sharing the whole story with me? Maybe I'd be able to help you understand better if I knew more about what she went through before coming here."

"Um, I think I can give you some basics, but it's really *her* story to share with you one day, if she wants to. I *can* tell you, though, that she was married to an abusive husband. He did a lot of horrible things to her, things that no man should *ever* do to a woman, especially one he claims to be in love with."

She could see the anger welling up in her son's eyes, and the sadness that closely followed. She was so happy that he was finally in love- he didn't have to tell her, she just knew by the way he was talking about Sadie that he had fallen in love with her. And, more than that, she was so proud of the man she was seeing in front of her, proud that he had learned to be respectful and kind to women, something both she and his late father had worked hard to teach their sons.

"Ryder, when someone goes through the kind of abuse that Sadie has endured, they learn to doubt themselves. They're made to believe that they're always wrong, that they need to apologize for their actions, their thoughts, everything. It's a survival mechanism, and you will only make it worse if you keep getting angry at her for trying to make things right."

"So you're saying I have to just let her keep apologizing?" he asked, perplexed.

Annie nodded, her voice gentle as she continued. "Yes, honey. I know you mean well, but when someone goes through what she has, they're constantly seeking forgiveness, especially from those they care about. It's a way to avoid conflict, to placate the other person and prevent further harm. My guess would be that she was made to apologize, no matter who was to blame, and that it became the only way for her to control her ex-husband's temper. Like I said, it's a survival skill, and it is ingrained in her now."

"But, she doesn't have to do that with me. I would *never* hurt her, Mom."

"*I* know that, and *you* know that, and on some level even *she* knows that. Still, you have to allow her to express herself, and learn to respond to that expression with understanding and empathy more than correction. With time and patience, she will learn to apologize less. She will learn to ask you first before expressing that part of her. She will learn what needs to be apologized for and what doesn't, eventually," she said, hugging him, knowing this was a lot for him to be taking on, but also knowing he had a heart of gold, one that would be capable of a great love with this woman if he could only remain patient. "After all," she added, "I'm sure she wasn't *always* like that."

A sense of comprehension washed over Ryder, and his heart suddenly ached for Sadie's pain on a level he hadn't felt before. "I… I had no idea, Mom. I knew she was hurting, but I wanted her to stop because I felt like she was saying I was just like him or something, and it really frustrated me. Thank you for helping me see it in a different way," he said with a nudge, "What would I do without you, anyway?"

Annie patted his back. "You'd be just fine… hungry, but fine," she said with a laugh.

After they sat in silence for a moment, she added, "Honey, one more thing. Try to do your best to understand that her heart has been through a lot. It's learned to be cautious, to expect to be hurt. Even so, she's allowing herself to be with you, to trust you as much as she can right now. That's a big leap for her."

"I want to earn her trust, Mom. I want to show her that I'm not like her past, that I won't hurt her. I know it sounds silly, but I want to love her so much that she forgets all about that horrible life she lived with him and only knows the joy of a future together, with me."

Annie's smile held an indication of pride as she met her son's eyes. With a hand on his cheek, she winked, "You're a good man, Ryder. I know you will try your best not to hurt her, and I think deep down, she knows it too. Just keep being patient, keep showing her that you're different. She'll come to see you for who you truly are."

* * *

Outside the cottage was a long walkway leading to the winery on the left, and away from the cranberry bog and toward the town's exit on the right. Sadie loved taking walks with Cliff while Hazel was either away or asleep. She often took the path that led towards town as a change of scenery from her walk to the winery for work each day. She took the opportunity to think, to reinvent a future for Hazel and herself, one where they were happy and safe. Today, of all days, was perfect for such a walk. She'd left Ryder's house two days prior, as he had a night shift at the firehouse and then was going to visit his mom. She had returned to the cottage to spend a day to herself before Sawyer returned Hazel to her.

She'd taken walks like this with Cliff when she was in Seattle, and it had been very helpful to her, giving her time to gather her thoughts. It was quieter in the small town of Stone Creek, which was why she loved taking walks like this. Before she knew it, an hour had gone by, and Sadie had walked over 2 miles. She looked around for Cliff who had wandered down the path a ways, chasing a squirrel in fun. She called him, but he didn't come. She called again, but still no Cliff. She started to walk back towards the house, calling for him every few seconds, trying to remember when she had last seen him run off the path. After a few minutes, she began to worry. She listened but heard nothing. She turned back the way she had come, thinking maybe he had run down the pathway towards town and gotten lost. As she neared the edge of town, she stopped dead in her tracks. There, in the back of a cab, was a familiar face, one that made her shake to her core with fear. She jumped behind a bush, praying he hadn't seen her.

Was she seeing things? It couldn't be Luke, could it? She had to get to her house, find her cell and call Ryder right away! Turning and making one last attempt to look for Cliff in the bushes nearby, she made the decision to get out of there. She'd have to enlist the help of her new friends to find him as soon as she got back to the cottage.

As much as she tried, it became impossible to walk, even at a fast pace, so she picked it up to a steady jog, covering 2 miles in less than a half hour.

As the cottage came into sight, she felt relieved to see a familiar figure sitting in a wooden chair on her deck. Seeing her move closer, Ryder got up and walked to meet her. He had so much to say, and it was written all over his face. His beautiful gray eyes begged for intimacy, to express something strong and passionate, and Sadie wanted it. But she had to tell him what she had seen right away! He was about to say something when he saw the look of terror on her face.

"Ryder, I think I saw Luke!" she choked out, clearly shaken. Ryder held her in a reassuring hug, making her feel safe and helping her to calm down a bit.

"Tell me what happened, Sadie," Ryder said when she had calmed down enough to talk to him.

"I was walking, and I lost Cliff. He ran off to chase a squirrel or something and never came back. I walked all the way to town looking for him, and when I got to the edge of the path, I saw a cab going down second street with a man in the back. It looked so much like Luke… I keep trying to convince myself I saw wrong, but I have this feeling deep inside that it was him, Ryder!" she recalled the moments leading up to her run back home.

"It's okay, I've got you," he said, smoothing her hair with his hands. "We'll get to the bottom of this, and we'll find Cliff, I promise!"

Tears filled Sadie's eyes as she realized that Ryder believed her. She was so lucky to love a man that would drop everything to make sure she was okay. They had to find Cliff… Hazel would be heartbroken if he didn't come home. What was she going to tell her if she got home before they found him? She didn't even want to think of that right now. She had to concentrate on keeping her daughter safe, especially if what she thought she saw was true.

"I'm going to give Carson a call. As the town's sheriff, I'm sure he'd be able to do some digging and see if your suspicions are correct." Ryder assured her.

"Ryder, you were going to say something," she remembered suddenly, "I'm sorry for interrupting you." This time, regardless of her apology, Ryder smiled. He turned back to her and held her hands in his.

"I wanted to tell you that if you're angry about something," he started to say, "tell me. If I do something wrong, tell me. If you're unhappy about something, tell me. You can tell me anything and everything, Sadie. Express yourself however you want, but never be sorry for being human. Also, if you think I'm angry or offended, ask me. If you think something is wrong, ask me. Never be afraid to call me out, and never take the blame for something you didn't do just because you don't want things to escalate. Just be you and be honest and we'll be just fine. I *will not* hurt you or let you be hurt if I can help it in any way."

Sadie was speechless, she heard his words, but didn't know what to say in response, so she just listened as he continued, "I know you remember what it was like before Luke, the way it was at home when you were a young girl. It's the same here… We can talk about things, including conflicts, and you will still be safe with me. I will never do to you what he did to you, and I'm willing to prove that to you every single day we have together."

Sadie still seemed lost for words, so she put her hands on the sides of his face, running her fingers through his tousled curls, and kissed him, needing to show him how much she appreciated what he was telling her. There was no way he could possibly know how much his words meant to her, how much each one melted and chipped away at the pain and hurt that Luke had created inside her.

After kissing him, she laid her forehead against his, absorbing his love and enjoying his masculine scent. Smiling, she pulled away and asked, "Do you want to come in and make spaghetti with me? Hazel will be home later, and I wanted to have it all ready for her when she gets here. I think I may have a beer or two left, too."

"Uh… by beer do you mean that fruity stuff you like, or actual beer?" Ryder teased her, grabbing her waist from behind playfully as she walked towards the front door. Ryder could see that she was still shaken by the man she saw in the cab, so he did his best to distract her.

"I have a game we can play while you make spaghetti and I enjoy my drink," Ryder said.

"Oh. What game is that?" Sadie asked, curious.

"Well, basically, it's a question-and-answer game."

"That sounds interesting. I do have a few questions I wouldn't mind asking you. Are there any rules to this little game of yours?"

"Just one- I get to ask the questions, and you provide me with the answers."

Sadie laughed. "That's cheating, Ryder. How's that a game?"

"Hey, my game, my rules," he said, joking around. "You in?"

"Okay, fine. I'll play, but I get to pick the game next time!" She laughed as she passed through the front door, Ryder in tow.

Ryder started off easy, asking Sadie personal questions meant to get to know her better. He wanted to know the things Sadie loved to do before she got married.

"Did you participate in any sports or clubs in high school?"

"Yeah, Sawyer and I played softball together, actually. It was my favorite sport, and I played every chance I got. She was *way* more competitive than I was, but we loved challenging each other, and playing in tournaments all summer each year gave us a lot of time together outside of school."

"That's awesome! I knew you two went to school together, but not that you played softball. Trav and I used to play football together. We were definitely competitive with each other, but Carson and I were even more bull-headed. We loved every chance we got at puffing our chests out and letting the testosterone flow," he said with laughter. She could picture them all running around as teenagers and suddenly felt sorry for their mothers.

Next he asked about her hobbies, her interests, whether she loved surprises, how she preferred to celebrate her birthdays. He wanted to know the things she wanted to do in life and what her biggest dream was. She told him that all she had ever wanted was to be happy while loving someone that was also her best friend.

"I hope that's me you're talking about," he teased with a wink.

"Maybe... I guess you'll have to stick around and see," she joked back.

"What about your most embarrassing moment?" he asked.

"Hey now, I thought you were going to be nice?" she tried to avoid the question.

"I am! You can tell me... go on now..." Ryder encouraged her with amusement in his eyes.

"Fine. When I was in 6$^{th}$ grade, I was in Sunday School, and I peed my pants in front of the whole class! It was mortifying! I was too stubborn to ask to go to the bathroom and boy did I learn my lesson!" she said, her face red with embarrassment.

Ryder started to laugh, covering his mouth, but losing his composure. He could picture her dancing around in front of the class with pee dripping down her tights. He felt bad for her and thought it was hilarious, all at once.

"Hey... that's not nice!" she said, trying to fight her own laughter.

"Ah, I'm sorry, beautiful," he said as he came around the kitchen counter to pull her into his arms. "Is there anything I can do to make it up to you?" he asked playfully.

"Well, maybe... Why don't you try something, and we'll see if it works." she said as she looked at him with a spark of challenge in her eyes.

She squealed with delight as he lifted her off her feet and swung her around. He set her butt on the counter, turning the oven off with his free hand so the spaghetti wouldn't burn. He kissed her, this time with purpose and heat. She could feel his manhood throbbing between her legs, causing need to course through her veins. He pushed his groin into hers, making her heartbeat throb in her center. His hands roamed over her back, settling on her bottom. Giving it a squeeze, he plucked her up off the counter and into his arms. He carried her through the living room and into her bedroom, reaching behind him to close her bedroom door. Just as the door started to close, they heard a knock at the front door. Hazel was back.

"Shit!" he muttered, putting Sadie down so they could both get their clothes back around themselves correctly. Silently, he told himself to remember to thank Sawyer later for her wonderful timing.

Ryder walked into the kitchen to give his body time to settle back down after their impromptu make-out session. His groin had some pretty different plans for the afternoon, and he needed a minute to convince it to put the feelings on hold. Sadie went to the door and met Hazel's joy as she jumped into her arms and hugged her. She wasn't used to being away from her mamma, so she was obviously very happy to be home. Thinking about what he had been about to do to that very beautiful mamma made him blush a bit. Oh well, at least he had succeeded in keeping Sadie's mind off Luke for a while.

Now that Sadie was busy with Hazel, he politely excused himself so he could walk Sawyer to her car. He needed to tell her about Sadie's walk earlier, and they needed to get a group together to try to find Cliff.

# Chapter Thirteen

Ryder sat on his porch looking out over the valley. Normally, the view relaxed him, but today it did nothing to calm his nerves. After talking to Sawyer about getting a group together to find Cliff, he had said his good-byes to Sadie and Hazel, got in his truck, and headed home to call Carson. He took the 10 minutes it took to get home to think about everything Sadie had told him about her walk, trying to decide just how worried he should be about her seeing someone she assumed to be Luke. Although he had never met Luke, he trusted Sadie's description of him and knew from her stories that he was dangerous. Now, he sat in his chair, staring blindly into the field, his phone to his ear.

Why wasn't Carson picking up, dammit? He needed to talk to him about all of this. Carson was always a good judge of both people *and* situations. It was a necessity in his line of work, and Ryder needed his take on all of this. Plus, he needed to let him know that Cliff was missing so he could have his deputies look for him on their shifts. As he heard Carson's voice on the automatic message, he cussed and hit the button to end the call. Inpatient and frustrated, he dialed again, again getting voicemail. Just as he was about to hit the call button for a third time, his phone started to ring.

"What the hell took you so long to answer?" Ryder spit out, a little more curtly than he needed to, in Carson's opinion.

"Good grief, Ryder, can't a guy take a leak without his phone going off twenty times?" Carson replied, annoyed by the intrusion and the rudeness in Ryder's voice.

"Sorry, I just need to talk to you about something important. Do you have a few minutes so we can chat?" Ryder asked, his voice calmer now.

"Well, I don't reckon I have much of a choice at this point," Carson replied with a chuckle.

"Earlier this afternoon, Sadie took Cliff on a walk between the cottage and town. Cliff ran off, chasing God knows what, and she went all over trying to find him."

"Did she ever find him?" Carson asked, clearly assuming that was the issue that Ryder needed help with.

"What? Oh... no. That's one of the things I need help with-can you let your guys know to be on the watch for him? It was over by the old Jantry place, on the South edge of town," he told Carson, knowing he'd let people know to be on the lookout.

"OK, I'll send a message to the crew that's on now and the crew taking over at 7," he assured Ryder. "Did something else happen? You said that was only one issue..."

"Yes, and this is the part I need your expertise on. When she got to the edge of town, a cab drove down the street, and Sadie is almost positive that her ex-husband, Luke Benson, was in it." Ryder recalled the story she had told him earlier.

"OK... I'm not too sure where this is going, Ryder. Are you worried that she'll go back to him or something?" Carson asked, a bit confused by his friend's worry.

"No! It's not that. We should have told you this a long time ago, Carson, but Sadie's ex-husband was abusive. He put her in the hospital once. He is a dangerous man, and this has Sadie really spooked," he explained.

Carson's tone went from playful and confused to serious in a heartbeat. He knew that abusive spouses were never something to mess around with, and you couldn't take their intentions for granted. "So, do you believe that it was him, Ryder?"

"I don't know, man. I trust her... I just also know that she is really scared of him, and she's had some pretty scary nightmares about him coming for her and Hazel. I honestly don't know what to think about all this," he said, sighing as if to release the confusion from his body.

"Well, if you want me to do some digging around, I sure can. If he's around here, it shouldn't be too hard to find him. It's not that big of a town, and everyone around here *loves* to talk, as you know." Carson added, "I'll see what I can find out and let you know. Does that work?"

Ryder felt relieved to know that Carson was going to look into this for him. He knew he'd be able to find something, if there was something to find. "I really appreciate that, man. I've got a shift tonight, and I want to be sure someone is keeping an eye on this for me. Plus, Hazel is going to be a mess if nobody finds that dog, you know?"

"Yeah, I'm sure we'll find him. He probably just took off after an animal and couldn't find his way back to the trail. Tell

Sadie to try to relax and let us look for him, okay?" Carson did his best to assure his friend that he would take care of it for him.

"Thanks, Carson. I'll keep my phone near me in case you find anything. Talk later."

"Wait… I'm getting another call and it's from the vet clinic. Let me take this quick and then I'll call you back, okay?"

"Sounds good," Ryder said, ending the call. He hoped like everything that it was a good call, one saying that Cliff had been found, safe and sound. He knew it was a long shot, but he still hoped it was true. He headed inside his house to find something to snack on while he waited. He was starving, and he needed to keep up his energy if he was going to pull a full shift after this.

Within minutes, his phone was ringing again, Carson on the other end. "Ryder? They found Cliff!"

"Thank God! Where is he? Is he okay?" Ryder asked, releasing a breath that he hadn't even realized he'd been holding.

"He's at the vet's office waiting for you or Sadie to pick him up. He's fine, just hungry and tired. It sounds like he wandered up to a house about 5 miles out of town earlier today, and the elderly woman who lives there fed him and called into town to see if she could find his home. She dropped him off at the office there and left him to be checked over."

"I'm so glad to hear that. Do me a favor and don't tell Sadie, okay? I want to go get Cliff and surprise her and Hazel!" he said, excitement replacing the worry he had felt only minutes before.

"Sounds good, man. Head on over… they'll be there for a little bit and I'll let them know you're on your way soon, okay?"

"Thanks, Carson." Ryder hit the button and ended the call. He felt much better knowing that Cliff had been found *and* that Carson was going to dig into this whole mess for him. Now, he had to head over to the vet's office to get Cliff so he could bring him home to the two people who loved him most in the world. He couldn't wait to see their happy faces. On the drive, he thought about everything that had been happening. He had to find a way to get this nervous feeling out of his gut. He had too much to get done with Sadie's birthday only a few weeks away. He and Sawyer had big plans, and he didn't want this whole thing with Luke to ruin her first birthday in Stone Creek. Luke had taken enough joy from her; he wasn't going to let him take this too.

* * *

Sadie was exhausted. She had been worrying all day about Cliff, and telling her sweet little girl that her best friend was missing had definitely not been easy. Before finally falling asleep in her mamma's arms, Hazel had cried for almost an hour, rocking in the chair, clutching her doll to her chest. Her little 4-year-old heart was broken, and Sadie felt terrible for being the one that had broken it. If only she had been able to keep a better eye on Cliff on their walk... then this probably wouldn't have happened. She hated being the one that hurt the people she loved. Yet, she seemed very good at it.

She was drifting off to join Hazel in sleep when she heard a loud horn honk from the front yard. Startled, she jumped a bit, making Hazel readjust in her arms. She listened, trying to make sense of the sound, and then she heard it again. She carefully moved Hazel onto the couch next to her, got up, and walked to the window to peek out. She saw the bright lights of a truck, making her heart instantly jump. Then, realizing it was Ryder, not Luke, she smiled. What was he up to, anyway? She saw him get out, so she stepped over to the front door and opened it. Just as she got the door open, a familiar sound had tears filling her eyes.

"Cliff!" she shouted, dropping to the porch floor to hug him as he pounced at her. She fell back onto her butt, laughing the whole time.

"Shit, Sadie, are you okay?" Ryder asked, concern on his face as he helped her back up.

Laughing, she said, "Yeah, I'm fine. Where in the world did you find him, Ryder?" she asked, looking at him as though he had saved the world.

"I wish I could take credit, beautiful, but it wasn't me. An older lady about 5 miles away found him. He was hungry and lost and she brought him to the vet so he could get checked out and find his home," he told her, accepting her hug and returning it gently. He wasn't sure he'd ever felt so happy in his entire life as he did when he saw Hazel jump up from the couch, now awake from the noise, and see her pup for the first time. She screeched with excitement as she grabbed Cliff and held on tightly. Cliff's tail was wagging with pure delight as he got doted on. Ryder was glad he had been the one to return the mutt. This made his day for sure.

"Uh, I'm sorry to have to do this, but I have to head out, Sadie. I have a shift tonight and I really need to get to the station. I just wanted to be sure Cliff made it home safely before I headed in," he told her, a big smile on his face.

Sadie turned to Hazel who was running around the living room, Cliff close behind her, both having the time of their lives. "Sweetheart, I have to talk to Ryder quick, I'll be right back, okay?"

"Yeppers!" the little girl shouted, obviously void of any care in the world at the moment.

Sadie and Ryder stepped onto the porch a little farther, and Sadie closed the door a little so they could have some privacy. When she was sure they were safe, she reached up and put her hands on Ryder's face, looking into his eyes. She leaned in and kissed him tenderly. "Thank you, Ryder. You don't know what this means to both of us."

Ryder leaned down and kissed her again, this time with more urgency and need. Sadie opened her mouth and let his tongue explore hers. She loved the taste of his mouth on hers, loved the feeling it gave her in the pit of her stomach. She wrapped her arms around him and deepened the kiss, this time thrusting her tongue into his mouth, running it over his tongue and tasting his unique flavor. She suddenly needed him like she needed air, and she gasped slightly as he pulled away, putting some space between them.

"I love you, but if I don't go now, we are going to end up in a very awkward position on your grass, and I don't think they'd like it much if I totally blew off work. They both laughed, out of breath and turned on. She glanced at his midsection, seeing his erection bulging in his jeans. Her body instantly reacted to the sight, and he laughed as he guessed what she was thinking. "See… that's exactly what I mean. Keep looking at me like that and I'll have no choice but to take you, right here, right now," he said, kissing her one more time before forcing himself to turn and get in his truck.

Sadie watched him drive off, so much in love with the man who had just made her and her daughter so unbelievably happy.  How could she possibly have gotten so lucky? Just months ago, she thought her world had ended, that she would never have a chance at happiness again, and now she was standing in her yard, watching her insanely handsome love drive off, anxiously awaiting the next private moment she could spend with him. She turned and walked back into the cottage, shutting and locking the door behind her.

"Time for bed, sunshine!"  she told Hazel, who was still playing with Cliff.

"But Mommy, I want to play with Cliff!" Hazel whined.

"You'll have all day tomorrow to do that.  Now, let's race and see who can get to your bed first. Ready, set… go!" she yelled, letting Hazel get off to a hefty head start. Cliff followed the little girl, barking and wagging his tail in pure puppy joy. Hazel squealed with delight as she beat her mom to her room, earning her some tickles and a twirl in the air before being set down on the bet to get ready for sleep.

After getting Hazel and Cliff settled for the night, Sadie laid her head on her pillow and closed her eyes.  She needed to sleep, and she knew it, but her mind kept wandering back to the kiss she and Ryder had shared on the porch earlier. Her body was still tingling, and her mind was wandering to the scenario that the two lovers hadn't had time to let play out. Hazel was going to sleep soundly tonight, but her mother *definitely* wasn't.

* * *

Sawyer and Ryder had spent the last 2 hours planning the party of the century for Sadie. They both wanted her to be happy, and they couldn't think of a better way to celebrate her new start here than by surrounding her with fun. Besides, they were hoping her 28th Birthday would mark the ending of one life and the beginning of another for Sadie. They wanted it to be tasteful, but exciting too.

"Her favorite color is red, so I think we should try to find some pretty red balloons and streamers," Sawyer told him. "I think we have some soft yellow tablecloths in the storage room that have adorable little red roses on them, too, so I'll grab those out and wash them before the party."

She was so excited to see Sadie's face when she saw how much she was cared about by all those around her. She'd been through so much, and Sawyer knew she had missed a lot of it. She wanted to make up for the last 5 years of birthdays, one way or another.

"Say, Ryder, have you heard anything from Carson about Luke? I know it's only been a day, but I was really hoping he'd find something out by now," she said with worry in her voice. She could tell that Ryder was a bit preoccupied too.

"No, nothing. I know he's working on it, though, and he's good for his word."

"Yeah, I know. I am just worried"

"I'm just glad we found Cliff. The look on their faces when I brought him home was priceless, Sawyer." It had killed him to see Sadie and Hazel so unhappy. He had never realized how protective he could feel towards anyone until he fell in love with those two. He felt like he'd do anything to take away their hurt and see them both happy and smiling again.

They continued planning the party, figuring out which

games Sadie would enjoy the most, who to invite, and when and where to have the party.

"I really think we should do it at Quinn's. It is the perfect size, and they aren't terribly busy on Tuesday nights. What do you think?" she asked Ryder.

Ryder thought for a moment. He could tell that Sawyer had something up her sleeve, and he trusted that she would know if Quinn's was the perfect place to pull it off at or not. After all, she had planned *way* more events than he had, that was for sure.

"Sounds good to me," he said.

They talked about Sadie's favorite foods and her favorite desserts. They wanted to plan every little detail so she would know how special she was to them both.

They were so deeply concentrating on their planning that they didn't even hear Travis come in the front door. "Oh boy, what are you two up to now?" he asked with playful skepticism.

Travis knew from experience that when those two were up to something he was either in for a big mess or a trip to the hospital. He preferred the mess, personally. He took off his work boots and headed into the living room, plopping down heavily on the comfy sofa.

"Whatever makes you think we are up to something, darling?" Sawyer asserted, blinking her eyes as if to look innocent.

He wasn't buying it. "Any time you two are together, something is definitely up, and I don't have the energy to guess, so spill," he was too tired to figure it out on his own.

"We are simply planning a spectacular party for Sadie... It's her 28th birthday in a few weeks, and we want her to feel like a queen this year!" she announced. He knew her well enough to notice a hint of sadness in her voice, even though she did her best to hide it. He loved his wife, and he knew her heart. He knew that she had missed Sadie very much over the last 5 years, and that having her so far away had left a void that only Sadie's friendship could fill. As much as she loved him, he knew he couldn't take her place.

"Ah… I see. Well, plan away. I'm way too exhausted to help on this one, I'm afraid. Besides, you wouldn't want me helping anyway… I think we *all* remember the last party *I* tried to plan. I *definitely* learned the importance of making sure a place is open before you plan an entire party at it!" He laughed, with as much vigor as he could muster up.

Laughing, Ryder said, "No way, you can just steer clear of here!"

Sawyer got up and grabbed a glass of iced tea for her husband, kissing him gently on the lips as she handed it to him. He took a long drink, savoring the taste, clearly very thirsty. As he set the glass down, he sighed and leaned back, becoming as comfortable as he could get, happily letting the planners get back to their planning.

"Shoot, I almost forgot," he smacked himself on the forehead, "Ryder, I talked to Carson in town this afternoon. I had to run in to pick up some supplies for one of the tractors, and he happened to be in there chatting up the lady at the counter… as if that's hard to believe," he rolled his eyes, getting a similar reaction from Ryder, who was now chuckling. "Anyway, he said that he wanted me to let you know that he checked into Sadie's ex-husband. He said one of his deputies saw him at the coffee shop the other day. He apparently told him some story about wanting to check out the town because his girlfriend was looking to go away for a weekend, and he wanted to find her the perfect spot. They talked for a while and then he grabbed his coffee and left," he relayed Carson's information.

Ryder felt his stomach sink. "Well, obviously that was a lie!" Now he *was* worried. Sadie had been right in thinking that she had seen Luke the other day. If he was snooping around, then that meant he *could* be close to finding her. "Wow, he has some set of balls, that one. I can't believe he'd be that brazen! Did Carson say if he was still around or if he talked to him personally?"

"Yeah, he said that he asked at the hotel, and the lady said that there was an out-of-towner that had been staying there for a few days, but that he had checked out. He is using a different name, apparently. Carson said something about needing a warrant to get all his information, but that he was going to get on that right away. For now, he said to let you know that he appears to have left town."

Sawyer could see the anger evident in the gentle heave of Ryder's chest. She knew the feeling… She felt it too. She also knew that he was no good to Sadie if he was in jail, so he needed to cool down a bit. She gently touched his shoulder, grateful that Sadie had found someone who loved her the way Ryder did, someone who wouldn't ask any questions before jumping into the ring to fight for her and keep her safe.

"Ryder, you have to try to calm down. Sadie needs you, now more than ever, and she needs you level-headed. Believe me, I understand how you feel. Luke burned every letter I sent to Sadie, every last one of them! He had my number blocked so I couldn't call or text her, and he led her to believe that I didn't care about her anymore, that I had moved on without her. Because of that piece of crap, I almost lost my best friend. I missed having her at my wedding, chatting with me when I needed to talk, sharing my tears when I was heartbroken… all the times I needed her the most. Even though I'd like to wring his neck myself, I can't, and neither can you. He's just not worth it, Ryder."

Ryder listened to her words carefully, thankful that she seemed to understand, and that Sadie had such an amazing friend. He had never even considered the fact that she, too, was a victim to Luke's selfishness and narcissism. "You're right, Sawyer. I need to chill out a bit, it's just hard when I know that he could find a way to hurt them both if he really wanted to. It scares me, which makes me mad."

"I know. My guess is that he is looking for her because he knows she's happy here without him. He probably can't stand that thought. Most men like Luke think that they are the best person in the world, loved by all, so they can't wrap their heads around people finding happiness with anyone but themselves. He probably wants to ruin her birthday, but we won't let that happen. Now that we know he was around here, we can be on the lookout for him."

Ryder sighed, relieved that they could both identify together in the loathing of this guy. Everything Sawyer said was true, and sometimes he forgot that Sawyer had been left alone all these years. She had developed great friendships with Lily, Karen and Daisy. They were wonderful friends, but none of them had the ability to take the place of Sadie in her life. She and Sadie could practically read each other's minds, they knew one another so well. Their friendship was unique and amazing, and *definitely* one-of-a-kind.

Ryder remembered Sawyer speaking once about her best friend from 7th grade, and how much she had impacted her life. Other times, she spoke of her in a way that made it very clear that she missed her incredibly. For the past few months, everyone had mentioned, in one way or the other, how different Sawyer had become since Sadie arrived in Stone Creek. It had become clear that the calm and reflective part of her that showed up occasionally was a testament to Sadie's influence, as well as some of the things she valued. Occasionally, but not frequently, since Sadie came, she would stop something she was doing just to ask herself what her best friend would do if she was there. Then, she'd either agree with her course of action, or change it with a laugh. Although the dialog was usually in her head, sometimes she accidentally spoke it aloud. Travis lovingly teased her for it when he heard her.

Sawyer paused for a moment to think, trying to keep her own frustration down, knowing full-well that she could get angry easily when it came to Luke. The only reason she hadn't gone back to Washington to check on her friend was because Sadie's parents always told her that they were doing good. Obviously, Sadie had fooled them, either out of embarrassment or fear of Luke's reaction, because things were not okay, and now that she knew that, she was even angrier with herself for not seeing what was going on.

Sawyer let out a frustrated sigh. "She's the better half of our lifelong friendship, Ryder. And honestly, I think my biggest threat right now is you, so you better watch your back," she said jokingly. Even though she was laughing, she wasn't *really* joking, and Ryder knew it. He instantly felt bad that she felt like he was going to take her best friend away, but he was also happy that she thought that there was even a chance that he could do that.

He smiled at her and said, "Sawyer, you have nothing to

worry about. I plan to love her until she can't remember who what's-his-name even is, but *you* could *never* be replaced in her life… not even by me."

# Chapter Fourteen

"Sawyer, do you think we can find a way to keep this from her until *after* her party?" Ryder asked, worry plastered all over his face. After all the planning that had taken place to make Sadie's 28th birthday a success, he hated the thought of ruining it by telling her what he had just heard. He knew this birthday was personal for Sawyer, her first birthday celebration with her best friend in over 5 years, but it also meant a lot to him. "I'd really hate to ruin her birthday with all of this!"

"I agree, Ryder, but what if Luke gets to her before we get a chance to tell her?" Sawyer asked, concerned for her friend.

"We will all just have to make sure that doesn't happen. You and Travis, Carson and myself. We will all keep an eye out for anything suspicious and make sure she stays safe until we can tell her what is going on."

"But *how*?" Sawyer's confused face called for her husband's help. Travis joined them without a waste of time. "How are we going to keep this hidden from Sadie until after her birthday?"

Sawyer repeated her question, but this time it was directed toward Travis.

He could see the worry on his wife's face, and it killed him to see her so worked up like that. He moved quickly to her, gently wiping the tear that had escaped from her eye, placing a kiss on her forehead. Lifting her chin to look into his eyes, he smiled reassuringly.

"What'd fireman here say?" he asked, winking playfully at Ryder.

"Uh… nothing that is making me feel any better about all of this! Now… what do you think?" she rolled her eyes at him.

"Okay, I love you honey, but you are getting an attitude towards us right now, and it isn't going to help anything. You know you get that way when you are scared, which is understandable right now, by the way. Even so, you can't put this one on me, I'm just as innocent as my friend here," he slapped Ryder's chest, inciting a slap back in retaliation.

"Hey, I may be innocent, but you, my friend, are definitely not," Ryder poked back at Travis, causing some boyhood banter back and forth.

Stopping the momentary fun, Travis added, "Look, it's a small town, I would think we could get enough people to look out for him that we would know if he came back around. We can all make sure he doesn't go anywhere near Sadie. I mean, we *do* have Carson, and everyone knows the sheriff is the boyfriend, here's, best buddy, much to *my* heartbreak, but not that it matters to anyone." Travis had a fond habit of making jokes to try to lighten the mood, but his wife wasn't having any of it today.

"You two. Seriously, we need to figure this out if I'm going to agree to keep quiet about it. I don't like keeping things from my best friend unless it is *truly* what is best for her."

"Okay, okay. What are you still worried about, other than what we already covered?" Travis asked her, giving up at his attempt to lighten the room up a bit.

Sawyer looked at both, hoping one of the men could help her figure this out. "Legally, I don't think there's anything we can do to stop a father from seeing his own child. If he wants to see either one of them, he probably has a right to. Sadie never filed any type of restraining order or anything else like that against Luke, which I would assume means he is free to speak to both of them if he chooses."

Ryder thought about that for a second. He hadn't ever really considered that before. "I suppose you're right on that point, but his very presence anywhere near Sadie causes a panic attack in her- I'll talk to Carson to see if she could file a restraining order now. I know it's been months since the divorce and the hospital incident, but I would assume she could still get one after what he did to her, right?"

"Boy, if putting her in the hospital isn't a good enough reason for one, then I'm not sure *what* you'd have to do!" Travis said in agreement.

"Right, but if you ask her about it, she'll know something's up, won't she?" Sawyer asked, worried about this whole plan going south. "I mean, is there a way to get a restraining order on her behalf or something?"

Ryder thought about it, but guessed she would have to sign something, or possibly even give a statement in order to get it to go through the court system. Plus, it was in a different state, so he was a little worried that there would be a delay because of that. "I'll have to talk to Carson about it. He'll know what to do." He knew Carson would get on it right away, trusted his best friend with everything in him to help protect Sadie and Hazel.

"One thing's for sure, Ryder… If you want to keep Sadie safe from this jerk, then try not to be so obvious with your concern. She's sharp minded, she'll pick up on it." Travis planted a kiss on Sawyer's mouth, winked at Ryder and excused himself to go shower. He had put in a long day and was ready to get in some comfortable lounge clothes and snuggle with his beautiful wife on the sofa.

"I was hoping you'd do that sometime soon," Ryder said, waving his hand in front of his face. "You could peel paint with that smell you have!"

Both men laughed, and even Sawyer smiled. They loved making fun of each other, seeing who could make the other one laugh first. Both were thankful for the friendship they had in one another, and Sawyer was a bonus.

"Maybe we just need to chill a little, right?" Sawyer asked Ryder, taking a huge breath to calm herself down.

"I guess so. Her birthday is in two days, and we have everything covered it seems. Carson said one of his deputies thought he saw a man that matched Luke's description at the gas station the other day, but he wasn't positive. If it *was* Luke, we have lots of people on it, making sure he doesn't go anywhere near Sadie, right? It's only two days… we can do this."

"Oh, Ryder, you're even more worried than I am, I think! I know I don't say this often, but I couldn't be any happier knowing you are in Sadie's corner. I truly hope you remain there for life." Sawyer had known Ryder since shortly after meeting Travis, and there really was no better person she could imagine for her best friend than him, especially considering everything Sadie had been through.

"That's very sweet of you, Sawyer," he replied, giving her a hug. "Okay, enough serious stuff for a minute… I have a *very important* question for you! What do you plan on getting Sadie for her birthday?"

Sawyer laughed. Ryder was trying to change the subject to help her feel better, and she appreciated it very much. She felt like her nerves were in a bunch today, and she needed a distraction. "Well, remember how I said that owning a winery was always supposed to be our thing? She's *so* good with the customers and management, like *way* better than Trav, and please don't tell him I said that! Anyway, we've been working on these two new wine flavors together, both using recipes that she came up with. The samples have gotten amazing feedback from our tasters, and I can't wait to add them to our line."

Ryder loved watching Sawyer talk about Sadie. There was something in her voice that told him what the friendship they shared meant to her. Her mood had instantly changed from worried to excited, and he was noticing that he was calming down right with her. He also knew how much the customers at the winery loved Sadie. Whatever Sawyer had planned for her, he was sure she deserved it.

"Most importantly, though," Sawyer continued, "She loves being here, seems to love everything about this place, and I always see glimpses of my best friend, the way she was when we were teenagers and dreaming of this place, shining through when she's at the winery. Of course, I also see it when she's with you, obviously," she teased.

"Obviously," he smirked.

"Trav and I, we've done the paperwork to give Sadie equal

ownership of the winery!"

"Wow.  She's going to be so happy, Sawyer."  He felt the words catch in the back of his throat.  He couldn't wait to see the look on her face when Sawyer told her all of this at her party. Suddenly, a sly grin covered his handsome face as realization hit him. "Damn Saw, your gift is definitely going to beat mine!"

* * *

Darkness blanketed the November sky as Carson made his usual morning stop at Sammy's, the little cafe on Main Street in Stone Creek. The first snow of the season had fallen the day before, causing all kinds of chaos around town, just as it did every year. For some reason, even though people were used to snow each year, the first snowfall tended to take people by surprise, making them do things that made no sense to him. He shook the snow flurries off his coat before stepping into the cafe, heading over to his usual spot at the counter. He enjoyed visiting with whomever was at the counter as he had his usual, a cup of coffee and a breakfast sandwich, as he started his shift.

Today was no different. He sipped his coffee as he talked to Sarah Townsend, everyone's favorite waitress at the cafe. She was a single mom, sweet and kind, but willing to give as well as she got when it came to the old men at the counter that loved to give her a hard time. She was tall and slender, and packed quite a punch to the gut when she smiled at Carson. Today, though, she looked a little tired, so he figured he'd check in to make sure she was alright.

"How's the best waitress in Illinois today?" he asked, adding a little vanilla creamer to his coffee.

"Ha… you're hilarious, Carson. I'm okay. My youngest was up half the night with a cough that she can't seem to get rid of. Of course, she wanted to sleep by me, so I didn't get any sleep either," she said through her yawn.

"There's something going around here, I've heard. Too bad your kiddo caught it. I bet you are tuckered out today, for sure!"

"Yeah, don't get me wrong… I love snuggling both of my kids, and I hope it's a long time before they stop wanting to, but I worked a double yesterday to cover for Jill, and then got home and had kids to feed and bathe and get to bed. I was hoping for some sleep after that, but no such luck," she recalled, smiling but tired.

"Wow, I guess I better stop complaining when I have a late night. I just have *me* to take care of and it seems like a lot sometimes!" he laughed.

She smiled at him, thankful for his friendly conversation. "You always make me laugh, Carson. Thank you for that. Now, can I get you anything else, or are you good for now?"

"I'm perfect, thank you."

Carson spent the next few minutes eating his sandwich and enjoying the company of a couple of retired veterans who had come in after him and sat at the table right behind him. He loved getting to know the locals, but also loved learning about those who passed through this town he loved so much. Just as he was finishing his last bite, he heard the ding of the bells on the cafe's door. He glanced over to see a stranger walking through the door. Something about his walk made the hairs on the back of Carson's neck stand up. He was normally a good judge of character, so he had learned to listen to that feeling a long time prior. He watched as the man sat down in a booth near the front window, leaving his jacket on and grabbing a menu from Sarah as she stopped to welcome him to the cafe.


Luke hated this town. Everyone in it was nosy, pretending to be friendly but really just wanting to figure out who you were and what you were doing there. He had spent the last month trying to figure out a way to get in and out of it without having to deal with any of these damned annoying people. Everywhere he went, he felt people's stares on him, like he was some kind of freak or something. He couldn't wait to get Sadie and Hazel and get the hell out of here, the sooner the better. First, though, he needed to eat.

"Good morning, sir," a waitress said in a tone that made his head hurt worse. "Can I get you some coffee?

"Yes, please. I'll take a menu, too." Luke said, putting his best 'friendly' voice on.

"I don't think I've seen you in Stone Creek before, are you from around here?" she asked.

"No, just passin' through. I oversee construction companies, and I'm checking on a job in Chicago this morning. Once that's done, I'll head back to Nebraska."

"Oh, that sounds like exciting work! My son wants to be a construction worker one day like his grandpa. He loves to build things and tinker around in my dad's shed with his scraps. Do you enjoy your work?" she asked, making polite conversation.

Luke hated when people prodded. He just wanted to eat his breakfast in peace and then get the hell out of the restaurant so he could figure out his next move. "Yeah, it's work, but it's not too bad."

"My name is Sarah, by the way. I don't think I got yours…"

"Eli, it's Eli Stratton. Um, I don't mean to be rude, but is there any way you could put a rush on those pancakes? I'm kind of in a hurry today," he asked, trying to hurry this along a bit.

"Oh, yes, sorry. I love to learn all about the people who come through here. I think it makes this small-town girl feel like she's living some excitement through each person." She smiled and left the table to go place his order.

Finally, he thought. Some quiet. He looked around the quaint cafe. It screamed 'small-town charm' and he hated it. He would have made it more modern, replacing the dated windows, adding some maple trim, and replacing the old laminate countertops with granite. *These redneck people wouldn't know style if it bit them in the butt*, he thought with disgust. He glanced to the end of the counter and saw a police officer siting there. Perfect… just what he needed. He started to feel uneasy then, hoping the cop wouldn't start asking questions. He wasn't too bad at lying, but he wasn't the best actor, either.

Sarah walked back behind the counter and began to fill a coffee cup.

"Hey, Sarah, do you know that man that just came in?" Carson asked her as she filled a cup of coffee for the stranger.

"No, I've never seen him before. Do you know him?" she asked in return.

"No, I don't think so. Did he happen to tell you his name?"

"Yeah, it's Eli. He said he's passing through town on his way to Chicago for work," she said. "He apparently is overseeing a construction project in the city."

"I see," he replied with some skepticism in his voice. "Any chance you caught where he's from?"

"Yep, he said Nebraska. He stayed over in Flannigan last night and he said he has to be there in an hour or so, so he stopped here for coffee and a pancake before he heads into the big city. He seems a little rough around the edges, but nice enough," she added.

"I see," he said again, still not sure why this stranger had him feeling uneasy.

Fairly quickly, Luke's food came, along with his coffee. The waitress, Sarah, placed it in front of him and smiled as she told him to enjoy his breakfast. He ate quickly in an effort to get out of the restaurant before anybody else approached him. He needed to steer clear of people for now, until he figured out his plan to re-claim his wife and daughter and head home. He knew she was hiding in this hick town, and he had heard from some of the locals that she was seeing some firefighter. He was furious that she would even consider dating someone else so quickly. There was no way some hotshot firefighter could make her happy like he did. He needed to shake her a bit and get her head on straight. There was no way he was letting some *other* man play daddy to his daughter. No way!

"Well, I had better hit the road," he heard the cop say to Sarah. He had been so lost in thought that he had eaten most of his pancake without even realizing or tasting it. He carefully listened to the conversation at the counter while he finished eating.

"I have to head to the office for a bit before I make my rounds," the cop said, "You get some rest after your shift today if you can… you don't want to catch that bug and feel even worse for the wear." He smiled at Sarah, grabbing his hat and standing to leave.

"Thank you, Carson. I appreciate that." she said, returning his smile.

Luke watched the police officer grab his wallet from his pocket, place a ten on the counter and walk towards the door. He suddenly realized that he was coming right for him. Looking down at his phone, he tried to avoid any eye contact with the cop. He heard him say hello to a couple at a table close to him, and he swallowed hard, secretly willing the guy to just keep walking by without stopping. As he passed by Luke's table, he nodded towards Luke, and Luke nodded back. The cop looked at him kind of funny but kept walking out the door. Luke swallowed again, this time with relief. The look he got was unsettling, but he seemed to have escaped a conversation of lies for now. He knew, though, that it was only a matter of time until he'd see that cop, or another one, and he had to get this show on the road before he risked getting caught. He finished his last sip of coffee, threw his money down and left. He didn't even hear the waitress yell *goodbye* as he walked out. He was on a mission, and his mission seemed to have a time limit that was growing shorter and shorter.

As he walked out of the cafe, Carson felt that sinking feeling in his gut again, like he had just seen a ghost. The problem was, he couldn't quite put a finger on why that man gave him such an uneasy feeling. He saw hundreds of people he didn't know every day on the job, most with stories just like this man had, so why did he not believe him? He remembered Ryder giving him a description of Sadie's ex-husband, but this man couldn't have been him. Ryder had told him her ex had sandy blond hair, but this man's hair was almost black. Ryder said Sadie's ex had a truck, but this man had a motorcycle. None of it was matching up. Still, he got a weird feeling about this guy. Sure, he had seemed friendly enough, but something about him didn't sit right with Carson.

When he got in his squad car, Carson dialed Ryder's number. "Hey, Ryder? Do you happen to have a photo of Luke that I could have?"

"Uh, I don't, but I could get you one from Sadie's parents I think… why?" he asked.

"I just want to see his face, so I know who I'm looking for is all," he assured his friend.

"Oh. Sure. I'll ask Sawyer first, and if she doesn't have one then I'll call Sadie's folks. I'm sure they have something they could send my way. That way I don't have to worry Sadie by asking her. We're trying to keep this bastard from ruining her big day, remember?"

"Yep, I'm on it. I love Sadie too, Ryder! Not the way you do, of course, but like the sister I never had," he teased, laughing as he ended the call. He knew it was doubtful that this man was Luke, but he also knew that something wasn't right, and he wasn't about to let some maniac ex-husband get to Sadie, not if he could help it anyway.

# Chapter Fifteen

Quinn's Bar & Grill dawned with an air of festivity that enveloped the charming town of Stone Creek. It was a cool, crisp day, but it was warm for the middle of November. The sun's warm embrace was met with an unspoken promise of merriment. Quinn's, fairly bland on the outside, was adorned with strings of twinkling lights and vibrant decorations on the inside. Tonight, it was specially dedicated to Sadie for her 28th birthday, and her very first in Stone Creek, among new friends. Red streamers hung from the exposed roof joists, and a banner sporting the words *Happy 28th Birthday, Sadie!* hung over old photos of the town.

As people gathered inside the warmth of Quinn's walls, the atmosphere was that of laughter and camaraderie, the chatter of familiar voices creating an infectious energy that swept through the air. Long wooden tables were adorned with colorful centerpieces, while soft melodies of upbeat music created a backdrop that urged everyone to sway to the rhythm.

Sawyer, ever the social orchestrator, had taken the lead in

organizing the festivities, allowing Ryder a say, but basically taking over anyway. After all, what *man* knew much about planning a *woman's* birthday party? Her eyes sparkled with excitement as she exchanged knowing glances with the others. Sadie may know they were having a little get-together dinner for her, but she had no idea what they actually had in store for her. Sawyer knew that the true delight lay in the moments yet to unfold.

The afternoon was losing its sun and evening was quickly coming down over the town. Their laughter and conversation swelled in volume, a harmonious symphony of friendship and joy. Friends of Ryder, Travis, and Sawyer, who had recently become friends of Sadie's, were present, as well as Ryder's brother and sister. Carson, Travis, Sawyer, Karen, Landon, Charlie, Daisy, Lily, Tucker, Wyatt, and Stacy occupied various corners of the bar, their friendship evident in their playful banter and the embarrassing share of memories.

If only 28-year-old Sadie could see the sheer light and love that awaited her acceptance into her life. Everyone loved her, she just needed to open her heart and let them in.

Anticipation filled the room as they awaited the arrival of the guest of honor. Sawyer was watching out the window for them when she saw Ryder's truck pull up. She quickly hushed the room, announcing that Sadie was there.

As they opened the door to enter, Sadie's heart nearly leapt from her chest. She couldn't believe all the people that had filled the room. Ryder removed her jacket for her as a breeze of excitement rushed through the room. Sadie, her freckled face glowing with both surprise and delight, stepped closer to Ryder as he re-joined her. She looked breathtaking, dresses were hardly her style, but today was an exception, all thanks to Sawyer who got her to try something outside her comfort zone. Ryder locked the door behind them quickly and quietly, careful not to be seen. He led her gently forward with his hand on the small of her back, encouraging her to keep walking.

Everyone shouted together, "Happy Birthday, Sadie!"

A radiant smile graced Sadie's lips, her eyes twinkling out of gratitude and warmth. None of this seemed real to her, she couldn't believe this could all be for *her*. As she moved further into the bar, she found herself enveloped in a series of heartfelt embraces, her heart swelling with the tangible love that filled the room.

"Happy Birthday, Sadie! Your hair looks absolutely stunning tonight!"

"You're truly glowing today! That dress looks beautiful on you."

"Seriously, how does being a mom make you look even hotter?"

Laughter mingled with the heartfelt compliments and created an ensemble of affirmation. Sadie felt wrapped in a cozy embrace with the friendly words and the love she could feel in the room. Her cheeks flushed with a rosy hue, her heart buoyed by the outpouring of love from these inherited, yet dearest friends.

* * *

Everyone in this group seemed to love playing games, Sadie thought with amusement. She was starting to get used to it but was still a bit uncomfortable when it was her turn each time. Tonight, they were doing something she actually found fun- a talent show! She was having a blast watching each person share a hidden 'talent' they had, some definitely better than others, and some obviously just meant to be funny.

Sawyer was up. She did a little bit of gymnastics, and she was showing off some old moves while everyone cheered her on. The air buzzed with excitement, with her not realizing that every activity they were doing was setting the stage for the culmination of the evening's celebration. She was quite surprised that her friend could still do some of the moves she was demonstrating. She laughed until her belly hurt.

Ryder soon went up on stage with Tucker and showed a couple of firemen dance moves. She was glad everyone was concentrating on them, because she was suddenly quite hot, feeling her face get red as she watched the man she loved dance. The others might be seeing dance moves, but she was thinking of some very different ways to use that body than they were. She used her napkin to fan her face a bit, getting a smirk from Sawyer. She was relieved when the dance was done, and she could cool off again.

Travis, as was his custom to make everyone laugh harder than they already were, told some never-before-heard jokes, finishing off with some pretty spot-on accents, bringing everyone to a standing ovation.

Lastly, the stage was cleared and a digital keyboard from the corner was set in the center. A hush fell over the crowd as everyone sat back at their spot, trying to figure out who was next. The anticipation was thick as Sawyer, wearing a sly grin, motioned for Sadie to step forward.

"Alright, birthday girl, time for a special performance!"

Sawyer's eyes danced with mischief as she encouraged her friend to join her on the small stage. Sadie got up, shaking her head at her friend. She wasn't sure what Sawyer had in mind, but she could guess, and she was already dreading it. Sawyer reached out her hand and helped Sadie climb up the steps. Her excitement made Sadie laugh, feeling a little less worried about her friend's plans.

Sadie's nervous laughter rang out, a soft and melodic sound that made everyone join in. It infused the room with a feeling of enchantment. "Sawyer, what are you up to?"

With a flourish of dramatic flair, Sawyer produced a microphone from behind her back, holding it out towards Sadie. "You, my dear friend, are going to grace us *all* with your *incredible* singing. And please, don't even try to deny this wonderful and deserving audience the pleasure."

"I've heard you hum in the car a few times and it made me wonder what you would sound like if you sang!" Travis yelled. "I've been told it's quite enchanting. Enchant us, Sadie!"

Laughter erupted as the group urged Sadie on, their cheers and playful encouragement filling her up with confidence. Amidst the teasing, Sadie couldn't help herself from feeling the flutter of nervous excitement. With a good-natured eye roll, she took the microphone, her fingers wrapping around the cool metal as confidently as she could. Regardless of the trepidation she felt, she was determined to not dull the fun they were all having in her birthday party. It had been years since she had sung… she wasn't even sure she remembered how to, but she figured it couldn't hurt to give it her best try. She placed the microphone in the stand Sawyer had set by the piano before taking her place in front of the keyboard.

Sadie placed her hands softly on the keys, willing her fingers to remember where to go and what to do. Then, as if the world had held its breath, Sadie began to play. The melody was soft and sweet, a familiar Norah Jones tune, mesmerizing all in the room. She played the notes beautifully, as if her hands had memories of their own that they were sharing with the crowd. She took a breath, closed her eyes, and began to sing.

Her voice, ethereal and hauntingly beautiful, cut through the air like a shimmering melody, its notes intertwining with the hearts of everyone in the bar. The room fell into a spellbound silence, each person captivated by the angelic sound that emanated from Sadie's lips.

Ryder, his gaze fixed on Sadie, felt his heart swell with a newfound depth of emotion. Her voice was not anything like he'd ever heard. In that moment, he felt as though the world had faded away, leaving only Sadie and the hauntingly beautiful song she was singing. Her eyes were closed, perhaps because she was so shy, but he could feel her singing to him, even if everyone else didn't. He had a sudden urge to scoop her up and take her home so she could sing to him while he made love to her. Her voice was sensual and sexy as hell, and he wanted it, and her, all to himself.

As soon as Sadie's final note hung in the air and her hands left the keys, the room erupted into a thunderous applause and whistles, the spell broken by the sheer energy of the emotion that filled the atmosphere. Sadie stood, her heart racing, her cheeks flushed, embarrassment and exhilaration written all over her face. She handed the microphone back to Sawyer, at the same time feeling triumphant. She walked to Ryder who hugged her and whispered something to her that made her eyes gleam. Partially deaf to the applause and praises of everyone else, she kept smiling and blushing as she looked in his eyes, heat passing from one to the other, causing a temperature shift that all in the room could feel and see.

"Wow, Sadie, that was incredible!"

"You're, like, an *actual* angel!"

Ryder's voice was a soft murmur as he pulled her closer, his gaze unwavering. "You have the most beautiful voice, my love."

A shy smile played at the corners of Sadie's lips, her heart skipping a beat at Ryder's words. More than it did for every other voice in the bar. "Thank you, Ryder," she turned to the others, "Thank you, everyone. I didn't expect you to react like this, but I appreciate your kindness very much."

"Are you kidding me? You have an incredible voice, Sadie. Wow!" Travis said.

Sadie was left blushing as she moved back to sit in her chair.

"Travis may have taken the crown for funniest guy, but you're going home with everyone's heart in your hands," Sawyer told her. Ryder's phone rang, and everyone went off on him.

"All phones on silent, dude!" Wyatt, Ryder's brother said.

"I'm so sorry, everyone." He looked around, then turned to Sadie who was talking with the girls, her attention nowhere near him now. He turned to Sawyer instead, adding, "I have to take this."

Sawyer nodded, their understanding unspoken, as well as her curiosity. "Go ahead, Ryder."

With a final glance at Sadie, Ryder stepped away, his steps leading him to a quieter corner of the bar, but the atmosphere remained that of elation and laughter. Sawyer noticed that Carson was gone, too. No one else had noticed Carson's brief absence amid all the fun and laughter, perhaps because they were used to the town's sheriff running off to answer calls and offer assistance to those who needed him.

After a few minutes, Sawyer saw the pair come back into the room, concern on their faces. She snuck away quietly and went over to figure out what was going on. "I saw the look on your face just now, Ryder. Was that about Luke?" Ryder nodded at her. "Well, what's the situation then?"

Carson answered first, "A man matching the photo and description of Luke was seen at the winery tonight. We have no idea how he got past the security— in *and* out of the winery," Carson explained.

"That slimy little-" Sawyer said in exasperation. "What do we do now?"

"I just issued a warrant of arrest on the basis of stalking and assault. Had I known the man I saw the other day was him, I would have done so earlier. I just didn't recognize him without an actual photo since he changed his appearance to hide easier."

"Well, the important thing is that you know now and that-" realizing what he had just said, she paused, then added, "Wait… did you say assault?"

"Yes, one of my deputies called to report receiving a call from your winery a little bit ago. He says that Luke punched one of your staff members." Sawyer's eyes enlarged.

"What?" Her voice hushed, and suddenly conscious of where she was, she mouthed, "What the hell? Who?"

"It was Alyssa, but she's fine, Sawyer. She kind of dodged before he could land the blow, so his hand hit her, but not as hard as he wanted it to. She is on her way to the hospital now to get checked out. Chuck said he'd close the winery up for you and send the guests and workers home."

"Phew!" Ryder breathed in frustration. "That definitely could have been worse, but I still don't like the fact that he's out there somewhere, not with Sadie here and Hazel with Harriet and a sitter."

"How about I have a deputy head over there now to keep an eye on them? Sawyer, I think you'd better get to the gifts now and end this party sooner than later. I don't think he'll show his face around here with all these people, but I also don't want to take any extra chances. I'm going to head over to the station after I give Sadie my gift and start preparing for the man hunt. What do you two say we head back in?"

With that, Carson excused himself, heading towards the bathroom. They looked at each other, worry filling their faces. "Sawyer, I think we better get to the gifts part. Sadie will eventually have to know everything that's happened so far, and she's going to need that amazing gift from you to help soften the blow."

"Okay." Sawyer put on a happy face and re-joined the party that had continued as if they hadn't left it. Ryder followed. "Cakes and gifts, guys! Come on!"

Sadie was led back to the center of the room where a rather large red velvet cake with almond buttercream frosting was placed before her. She beamed with a smile as bright as the sun as she looked at the mouth-watering dessert. It was her favorite cake, and she couldn't wait to dig in, savoring each and every bite.

"You've got two wishes, Sadie," Sawyer said, "One that's just for you, and one we all get to hear."

She smiled as she remembered her friend's fun 'wish' tradition that she had wanted Sadie to do every birthday when they were teenagers. With a beaming smile, Sadie sat in front of the cake, her eyes alight with excitement as she prepared to make her wish. The room fell into a hushed anticipation, each person holding their breath as the candles flickered in the dim light.

"Make a good one, Sadie!" Travis called out, his words followed by a chorus of agreement and laughter.

Sadie closed her eyes for a brief moment, her heart swelling with gratitude and hope, making a wish in her heart, before taking a deep breath and blowing out the candles. The room erupted into cheers and applause, then they stopped and waited for her to make her second wish before the celebration reached a jubilant crescendo.

"I wish in the coming year that everyone here has more and more reasons to be truly happy, to feel loved, and to know that they always have each other to lean on, even when they feel like they are all alone."

Everyone went *aww* and *thank you, Sadie.* Daisy dabbed below her eye to catch a falling tear. She was so happy to have Sadie as a friend, so thankful she'd come to Stone Creek and decided to stay.

"That is the sweetest birthday wish ever," Sawyer said, then asked her to cut the cake. Since Sadie's mouth had been watering ever since they had brought her cake out, she was ever so happy to do the honors.

She carefully sliced a piece of cake for each guest, saving a corner for Hazel to have tomorrow when they were together. Sawyer put the leftover pieces in a box for Sadie to bring home with her, and then sat down to enjoy her cake with her best friend.

Before long, everyone was finished with their cake and talking amongst themselves again. As much as she wanted to let them all visit together, she knew they needed to keep things moving along, so she stood and announced that the moment had arrived for the exchange of gifts.

"Sadie, we have a very special tradition here in Stone Creek. Each person gets to bring their gift to you, and with it, offer a birthday wish."

"Oh, I love that!" Sadie exclaimed.

"Okay everyone, who wants to go first?" Sawyer asked the group. When everyone raised their hands, she addressed them with a laugh, "Well, as usual, I'll just have to pick. Stacy, you can go first, and then we'll go clockwise around the room."

One by one, the group approached Sadie, their faces alight with genuine love as they presented their offerings.

Stacy began by presenting Sadie with a set of wine glasses, each one hand-painted with flowers on them. "I want you to always know that I'm here for you if you need a friend." Stacy hugged Sadie, adding that her wish to her was that she would find laughter in every day, no matter if it was a good one or a tough one.

Carson was next, handing her a beautifully wrapped box, a mischievous glint in his eye. "Happy Birthday, Sadie. I hope you like this even more than whatever *this* guy got you," he teased, giving Ryder a thump on the back.

Sadie laughed as she unwrapped the box, revealing a set of personalized detective novels. She loved to read, and these looked like excellent books. Her eyes wide with excitement, she hugged him, "Carson, these are amazing! Thank you!"

"Sadie, you deserve nothing but the best! My wish for you is that you *never* feel alone, that you always know that you have an army of friends surrounding you." He hugged her and then politely excused himself, saying he had some work to attend to. He got some razzing from the group, but eventually they let him leave.

Lily and Tucker joined in, presenting Sadie with a charming collection of children's books that they knew Hazel would adore. "We got Hazel some cute books," Lily said with a warm smile.

"She didn't let me help decide what to get you," Tucker said. "And seeing what she picked makes me think maybe *I* should have done the gift buying!" Everyone laughed as Lily slapped his head playfully.

"She loves to read with Hazel, you nut! I thought maybe she'd enjoy some new books to enjoy with her daughter," she argued playfully with her husband while everyone in the room chose sides to add to the comedy of the show.

"She's right, Tucker. Lily, it was a very thoughtful gift, thank you," Sadie said as the laughter began to subside.

"You're welcome," Lily responded, adding "And our wish for you is that you sing as often as you can so that you can share that beautiful voice of yours with everyone around you, like you were obviously born to do."

Sadie blushed, not quite sure how to take all these kind words. She had spent so many years feeling badly about herself, like she was worthless and had little purpose in the world, other than being Hazel's mom. All the compliments were confusing, yet wonderful.

Daisy, with her love of arts, handed her a hand-painted canvas that depicted a serene lakeside scene. "Happy Birthday, Sadie. Since I can't build a lake for you to sit by and find calm, I figured I'd bring the lake to you!" she smiled, adding, "And, I wish for you to find a hobby this year that is only for you. One that makes you happy and helps you to feel the stress of everyday life melt away."

"Thank you, Daisy. I love it! And I will definitely try to do that," Sadie said, completely loving the serenity of the photo, and in awe of Daisy's talent.

Karen, who had baked the cake, gifted Sadie a basket of freshly baked pastries and desserts, each one a delectable masterpiece. "By the way, if you're wondering why this cake tastes so much like your favorite aunt's, it's because it *is* hers! I called your mom, who got me in touch with your aunt, who sent me the recipe! I mean, Sawyer helped, of course, but I hope you love it!" Sadie was so happy she hugged a little longer, tears forming up at the corners of her eyes. It meant *so* much to her that Karen had went to so much work to get her aunt's recipe for her. She missed her aunt terribly, and it was wonderful to have a piece of her here with them.

"I do love it, thank you very much!" she said through her tears.

The gifts continued to come in, every gift reflecting the unique bond she had achieved with each gift giver, as well as shared memories that had woven the group together. The birthday wishes each friend shared were a testament to the friendship that had developed in such a short time with these wonderful people. Laughter and cheers filled the air as Sadie opened each present, her heart swelling more and more with gratitude for the friendships that had enriched her life in a very short time.

When Sawyer and Ryder were the only two left to present their gifts, Sawyer pushed Ryder ahead, telling him to go first. The air around Sadie hummed with anticipation as Ryder stepped forward, followed closely by Sawyer, both almost tripping over Travis, who happened to be sitting in front of them. Their laughter and expressions suggested that they had probably planned something mischievous. Sadie chuckled.

"Hey Ryder, do we all need to leave the room for this, or is it G-rated?" someone asked loudly from the back corner, causing another eruption of laughter.

Ryder laughed but ignored the banter. As he got up to Sadie, he cleared his throat, a sheepish grin playing at the corners of his lips. He sat next to her, taking her hand in his, saying, "Sadie, I hope you are having the most amazing birthday yet. We are all so thankful that you are here with us, and we wanted to show you how much you mean to us all." He kissed her softly on the cheek, getting a few *'get a room!'* comments from the guys and some *'aww!'* comments from the ladies. He rolled his eyes at all of them, adding, "I hope you like this." He handed her a rather tiny gift, wrapped in a cute little box.

Sadie opened it, revealing a set of car keys, dangling from a beautiful sparkling key chain, yellow with red hearts. Sadie's eyes widened in surprise, her heart skipping a beat as she took in the sight of the keys. Everyone gasped.

"Ryder?" she called softly, confused.

"I remember the one evening when we had gone to supper in town that you saw that restored Ford truck over in the parking lot, and you said you wanted one like it one day," Ryder explained, his voice was as tender as it was enthusiastic. "I did some checking online and found one that's the same year and model and in great shape, and…well…now it's yours." He stumbled through it with a serious lack of smoothness, which had him wishing he hadn't done this in front of everyone. What if she hated it? Why wasn't she saying anything?

Sadie was rendered momentarily speechless, her eyes misting with disbelief and overwhelming joy. Had he really bought her a truck?  She blinked away the fog in her brain as he mumbled on, "It's not brand new, but I know you have been wanting a vehicle of your own, so I thought maybe you-"

"Ryder, you got me a truck?" she interrupted, finally finding her voice. She remembered the one he was talking about- it looked nice, not too fancy, but more than anything, it had reminded her of the one her grandpa had driven when she was a young girl. She had thought it would be perfect for her and Hazel, a way to remember him and share a piece of him with her daughter.

Ryder nodded, both suddenly aware that the room had fallen into a silence, with the only sounds heard being Sadie's soft appreciative sighs. "Oh Ryder, that is the most thoughtful gift anyone has ever given me! Thank you!" She stood and hugged him, and forgetting that everyone was watching, she laid a hot and heavy kiss on him. When she heard the hoots and hollers that followed, she stopped, suddenly remembering they were not alone, and feeling embarrassed and shy. Ryder was looking at her with so much love, and she wished they were alone so she could thank him the way she wanted to. Feeling flush from the thought, she sat back down, afraid her legs wouldn't hold her.

"Um, wow, OK. You're welcome, and Happy Birthday," Ryder said, wondering who had turned the heat so high in the room. Turning to Sawyer with a naughty grin, he added, "Unfortunately, even though my gift is pretty good, it's not the biggest gift you're getting tonight."

Sadie was confused at first, then suddenly looked at him and asked, "What are you talking about, Ryder?"

"Well, you know Sawyer, always having to one-up everyone. I'm pretty sure you'll be blown away when you see Sawyer's gi—

ouch!" Sawyer pinched him before he could finish and pushed him aside, enticing even more laughter from the group.

Sadie's heart, still swelled with a depth of emotion that words could hardly capture, was so full. This was *definitely* the best birthday she had ever had. She couldn't believe the amount of thought everyone had put into her gifts, or even more how much effort Sawyer and Ryder had put into planning this wonderful night in her honor. She was so lucky to have them, as well as all her new friends, in her life.

Sawyer stepped forward, eyeing Ryder for almost ruining her moment. "Sadie," she said, taking her hand in hers as she sat with her. "My gift to you is a little unconventional, but it's a gift I've wanted to give you for a long time, and I hope you'll love it."

She handed Sadie a beautiful box, one that looked like it could fit a tablet of paper. The weight of it felt light like a feather, and Sadie's curiosity piqued as she lifted the top off, finding a large envelope inside. She opened the envelope, slipping the papers out so she could read them. Her eyes widened in astonishment as she read the words on the page. Once again, the room had grown silent, as everyone waited to hear what was in the envelope. Drops of tears rolled down her cheeks, her lips trembling, and her chest going up and down with every deep breath she took, trying hard to contain her emotions.

"It's legal paperwork," Sawyer explained, her voice steady and sincere. "You are now a co-founder and co-owner of this winery. In addition, the form is included that would rename and rebrand the winery, allowing you to help Travis and I come up with a name together, one that we are all a part of creating."

Sadie was speechless. She had quit trying to hide the tears as they were now freely falling down her cheeks. She couldn't believe this was happening, that Sawyer wanted to share this with her after all these years. Sawyer added, "The deal isn't done unless you sign those papers, so it's your choice, of course, but Travis and I are excited to welcome you to the Cranberry Creek Farms team if you would like to partner with us."

Tears welled in Sawyer's eyes as she looked at Sadie, her heart overflowing with an abundance of concern and gratitude for another chance at doing life with her best friend.

Disbelief and gratitude overwhelmed Sadie. "Sawyer, this is... I don't even know what to say."

Sawyer's smile was soft and genuine. "Sadie, this winery isn't the same without you, and wouldn't be here without your part in the dreaming process back when we were girls. You've been here with me through it all, so this just makes it official. This is also a celebration of your strength, Sadie, and a reminder that you have a family here who love you, and who will go out of their way to fight for you no matter what."

"I know, and I am so thankful for all of you and your kindness," Sadie said, addressing the whole group.

"Well, what do you say, will you join us?" Sawyer asked hopefully.

"Yes, I'd be honored to." Sadie said, causing the group to erupt in cheers and claps. Sadie and Sawyer hugged each other tightly, their bond unbreakable and undeniable. The room was filled with happiness and excitement at the promise of a new partnership and many new friendships as they made a silent vow – that no matter what trials and tribulations awaited them, this group of friends would always stand by each other's side.

While the party went on, the atmosphere was electric and exhilarating. Games were played, stories were shared, and laughter rang through the walls of the restaurant. And, as the night progressed, Sadie found herself snuggling with Ryder, becoming more apparent to her that she could be in a room full of people and not feel funny about showing her affections towards him. Still, she couldn't wait to spend some time with him later, *properly* thanking him.

As the night came towards an end, Sadie stood and asked Sawyer for the mic she had used earlier. She needed to thank everyone, and she hoped the right words would find her so she could help them to see what this had all meant to her.

"I don't know what the biggest highlight is for me today," Sadie started to say, "because there are way too many to count. I want you all to know how blessed I feel right now, and how grateful I am to be a part of this amazing group of friends. If I had to choose my favorite gift today, it would be all of you, together here, celebrating with me. Thank you, from the bottom of my heart, for accepting me into your lives, and for making me feel so cared about. It truly means more than I could ever find the words to say."

Sadie always knew what to say, she was always good with words. Even so, the last few years hadn't proven that to be the case with her at all. Nothing she had said had been good enough for Luke. Here though, among these people, she felt it again. Without her even knowing it was happening, her heart was mending, and her confidence was returning.

"If you hadn't said that," Sawyer whispered to her a few moments after her speech of gratitude, "There might have been an uproar over whose gift was the best!" They both laughed. Sadie hugged her best friend, knowing she was probably right.

* * *

Ryder drove Sadie home after the party. He occasionally stole glances her way, loving the sheer elation he was seeing on her face. He was so thankful that the party had been a hit, that he had been able to keep her safe so far. He had a sick feeling in his gut, realizing he was going to have to end that happiness soon, that he would have to tell her all about the things he had heard lately. He hoped she wouldn't hate him for keeping it from her.

"I hope you had fun tonight," he said, breaking the silence.

"Oh Ryder, thank you so much for everything you and Sawyer did for me tonight! This was seriously the best birthday I've ever had!" she told him, excitement in her voice.

"I'm glad to hear that. Look, there's something I need to tell you, and I'm not quite sure how to-"

Ryder's phone interrupted him, pausing the conversation for a moment. He grabbed it from the console of his truck, answering when he saw it was the fire station.

"This is Ryder," he answered.

"Ryder, we have a barn fire on Hwy T, just north of town." Ryder instantly recognized Lou's voice. Lou was the shift leader for nights. "We are short guys right now... can you come in and help out?"

"Yeah, I just need to drop Sadie off quick and then I'll meet you guys there. Shoot me the address quick."

Hanging up the phone, he picked up speed, throwing his lights and siren on, lighting the darkness around them with red. "I'm sorry, Sadie, but I have to head to a fire. I promise I'll head your way as soon as I get done. We need to finish this conversation."

"Your sister said she was going to run Hazel home quick when she left earlier, so I'll just enjoy some snuggle time with my daughter and get some much-needed sleep. Can we have that talk tomorrow instead?" she asked, yawning as the high of the night started to crash.

"Sure, that's fine. I'm sorry about this," he told her, feeling badly about the ditch-n-go. As he reached her house, he leaned over to give her a kiss before she jumped out and headed for the house. He looked around the yard, making sure it looked safe, and didn't leave until he saw her shut the door behind her. He hated leaving her like this, especially with Luke on the run, but he didn't have much of a choice.

He grabbed his phone and hit the button to call Carson. If he couldn't be there with her, he was at least going to let him know to be on the lookout.

"Ryder, what's up?" Carson answered on the first ring.

"Hey, man. I just got called to a fire out on T, so I had to leave Sadie alone at the house. I saw Stacy go by me just a second ago, she was dropping Hazel off. I never got a chance to tell her about Luke, so I'm worried about leaving her there alone with no idea of the situation that has been unfolding."

"I see. I can have a deputy head that way in a little while, but right now he's over at the fire, and I'm on my way over to the winery to meet Trav and Sawyer and go over what happened tonight with them." his voice was tired, and Ryder knew his friend was doing everything he could to keep Sadie safe.

"I appreciate that, Carson. Thank you."

He hung up the phone, worried, but knowing he needed to relax a bit. He had to focus on the task at hand, and make sure that he and his firefighters were safe. Then, he'd go back and check on Sadie and Hazel himself. He'd sit there all night if he had to, at least until that sicko was locked up. As he pulled onto Hwy T, the blaze lit the sky like fireworks, a constant stream of red and orange, mixed with heavy black smoke that seemed to billow into the night sky as far as the eye could see. He could smell the smoke, and it made his pulse begin to race. Fires were scary, no matter how much gear you had on. Still, it was nothing compared to the fire in his gut when he thought of the danger the woman he loved unknowingly faced.

# Chapter Sixteen

Sadie slept peacefully, dreams filling the infinite space between sleep and awake. In her dream, she was walking in the valley, looking into the beautiful summer sky, smelling the growing fruit around her. She could feel the sand beneath her feet, still wet with morning dew's kiss. She turned as she heard soft footsteps behind her, smiling as she saw Ryder approach. The soft chiseled features of his face appeared to glow as the golden sun shone on him. Her breath seemed to catch in her throat as she gazed lovingly at his masculine beauty.

Her thoughts were broken as he continued to walk towards her, his strides long and smooth. She smiled as her heart leapt in her chest. She couldn't seem to control her heart rate when it came to this man. As he got within reach, she closed the gap and flung herself into his arms. She could smell his cologne as she pressed into his firm chest, feeling all the worries of the world melt away. She knew he would keep her safe, felt it deep within her heart. He bent his head to kiss her softly, emotion flowing through them both.

"Sadie, I love you more than I ever thought I could love another person," Ryder told her.

"I love you too, Ryder," she said.

The two turned, moving hand in hand down the freshly groomed path, picking wildflowers as they walked. They talked and laughed, enjoying one another's company as the time passed. Sadie felt as though she couldn't possibly be happier, as though the dreams she had dreamed as a little girl were finally coming true. Ryder handed her the flowers he had collected, combining them with hers, creating a mystical bouquet of beauty, a mixture of green, purple and yellow, with a touch of white. She lifted the flowers towards her face, breathing in deeply to smell their fragrance. As the flowers reached her nose, she realized something wasn't right… they didn't have the scent of flowers, but rather… smoke? That didn't make sense… she turned to find Ryder, but he was nowhere to be found. Instead, she saw smoke rising from the ground, the smell all around her, causing her to feel like she couldn't breathe. Looking around frantically, she finally saw Ryder walking towards her. She tried to scream for Ryder, but her voice seemed to be gone, "Ryder…" she cried, barely able to speak. As the smoke started to clear, she realized it was Luke! She turned, trying to run, but her feet were stuck to the ground, and she fell, unable to move or breathe.

Sadie awoke suddenly to the choking smell of smoke, rubbing the back of her hand against her eyes, trying desperately to wake herself up completely. As she started to wake further, trying to make sense of what was dream and what was reality, smoke began to creep under her bedroom door, a frightening jolt to her senses. She jumped out of bed and ran to her door, feeling the knob. It wasn't hot, so she opened it carefully, seeing smoke coming from the kitchen. She peeked at Hazel quickly, seeing that she lay peacefully asleep and cuddled up to her large teddy bear. She closed her door gently, laying a rolled-up blanket at the bottom to keep the smoke from entering her room a little longer.

Sadie knew she had a fire extinguisher near the fireplace in the living room, so she hoped she could run and grab it and put the fire out before it got any worse. Running down the hallway, she stopped dead in her tracks, realizing the fire had filled the kitchen and was starting to move into the living room and entry to the house. Panic struck as she realized there was no way out! Sadie ran back to her bedroom, grabbing her cell phone and hitting the button to call Ryder. He didn't pick up. She tried Sawyer, but it was the middle of the night so she must have been sound asleep, not hearing her phone.

Sadie ran back out to the hallway, checking on the smoke again. Seeing that it was getting worse, she kept Hazel's door shut, not wanting to wake her up until she figured out what to do, and not wanting the smoke to fill her room. She dialed Ryder again, and again, and again, but he didn't pick up. He usually picked up no matter what the time was, so why wasn't he picking up? Sadie ran to her bedroom window, trying to get it open, looking desperately for a way out. It was jammed somehow. She put all her weight into it, trying to open it but it wouldn't budge. She'd have to try Hazel's window. As she quickly moved back towards Hazel's room through her own, she glanced down the hallway, choking on the smoke. The air was getting harder to breathe in, and she was terrified that they weren't going to find a way out.

All of a sudden, she heard a loud noise from the burning rooms. She stopped by the doorway to her bedroom, looking towards the noise, and that was when she caught sight of him, breaking through the kitchen door from the back and quite literally walking through the fire towards her. She suddenly felt her legs give way and she fell to the floor, trying desperately to catch her breath, smoke filling her lungs with every gasp.

Ryder stopped at Sadie, picking her up and moving her to her bed. "Sadie, look at me!" he said, panic filling his voice as he carefully shook her. When she looked up at him, her eyes bloodshot and dazed, he let the breath he was holding out, thankful that she was still alive. "Wait here, I'm going to get Hazel!" He ran across the hall and into Hazel's room. He knew Sadie would have told him to get her first if she could have spoken, so he scooped her up, still sleeping, and carried her to her mother. "Sadie... I need you to stay with me, Hazel needs you!" he said, shaking her again to clear the fog from her brain.

Sadie looked up at him, fear engulfing her. "Hold her," he said gently. "Okay?" He laid Hazel down next to her mother as she started to wake up, crying as she coughed, the smoke beginning to fill her little lungs as well. Sadie held her close, telling her it would be okay through her own coughs, as Ryder ran out the door and into the fire. She did her best to hold Hazel so that her face was away from the open air. *What was Ryder doing,* she wondered. She was so confused... how had this happened? Was this just a dream? Was she imagining she had seen him? She could feel her breath getting shallow, and knew she needed fresh air soon or she was going to pass out. She prayed silently, trying not to scare her sweet little girl any more than she already was. *This is not how we are going to die,* she told herself, willing herself to breathe through the soot that was filling her lungs with every breath she took. The pain in her chest was getting unbearable. She watched the door, waiting for Ryder to return.

Ryder ran back down the hallway, dropping to his knees when he hit the living room, feeling his way to the fire extinguisher. He finally felt it in his fingers and grabbed it, turning to feel his way back to the smoke-filled hallway, coughing from the smoke as it threatened his lungs. He wished he had kept his turnout gear with him after the barn fire, but he had insisted they take it back to the station for him. He knew from experience that they only had a small window of time before the fire would completely engulf their pathway to the door, and the window was closing quickly. When he got to the bedroom doorway, he stood and crossed to the bed, seeing the two people he loved most in the world lying there, struggling to get air.

"Sadie, I need you to get up, can you do that?" he asked her, picking Hazel up in his arms and covering her with a blanket from Sadie's bed. He found a glass of water by her bedside and poured it over the blanket, covering as much of it as he could, gently reassuring the crying child that all would be okay. He did his best to sound calm, trying to assure her instead of scaring her any more than she was already. "I need you to help me, Sadie, please!" he begged her, praying she'd have the strength to make the run they had to make to get out.

He didn't think there was any way he could carry them both safely, especially with the burn he was feeling in his lungs from that last bout of smoke inhalation, yet he wasn't about to leave either one behind either. If they didn't hurry, he'd be forced to break the window, but with the fire moving closer to the bedroom, he was afraid the fresh air coming in would cause bigger problems than they already had. The best route was out the front, and he had to find a way to get them there.

"Ryder? Just take Hazel and go!" Sadie said, tears falling down her cheeks, marked by a path of black left behind by the smoke.

Ryder reached down and shook her again as she struggled to stay awake. "Please, Sadie, please! I need you to walk!" She wasn't responding to him. He knew he didn't have time to think, so he laid Hazel in her arms and pulled the tab on the fire extinguisher. Then, he picked them both up off the bed together. The load felt heavy in his arms, and he begged God to help him make it out the door, his lungs screaming at him with every breath he took. He shifted them so he could still operate the fire extinguisher with his hands, then headed out the door.

When he hit the living room, he began to spray, seeing fire creeping through the room, almost completely covering the wall between the entry and the kitchen. He sprayed a pathway to the door, kicking it open as he got to it. They got outside and he gasped for fresh air, doing his best not to fall as he left the porch and got the two as far from the house as he could.

As carefully as he could, he laid the two down on the grass by his truck, opening the passenger door so he could put them inside. He put Sadie in first, laying her carefully into the back seat. She was breathing, but each breath was labored and shallow. He had to get her to the hospital, and he needed to do it fast. He could hear Hazel crying behind him, scared as she saw the blazing fire behind her. She was screaming something, but he couldn't make out what, so he picked her up quickly and hugged her close to his chest, trying to calm her down. That's when he saw him. Cliff, Hazel's precious best friend, was lying on the grass by the truck he had given Sadie, lifeless. He turned her away so she couldn't see him anymore and placed her on the floor so she could be by her mother.

"Cliff!" Hazel was crying.

"Hazel, sweetie, I need you to listen to me, okay?" he told the distraught child. "I need you to snuggle up with mommy right now while I drive you both to the hospital to get help, okay?" he pleaded with her.

She looked at him, tears falling rapidly down her soot-stained cheeks. Nodding, she turned and lay her head on her mamma's chest. She was coughing, but not as much as they were, so he was thankful for that. He knew, though, that he needed to get them all to someone who could help them quickly, or things may turn for the worse rapidly. Ryder jumped into the driver's seat and took off down the driveway, lights and siren blazing. His heart was petrified for Sadie. She had taken in a lot of smoke, and he was scared to death that she wasn't going to make it. He looked back at the two, forcing a smile as Hazel looked up at him.

"It's going to be okay, sweetie," he tried to assure her, "I'm going to get mommy help as fast as I can."

Sadie started to cough then, and gasp. Her eyes remained closed, but her body was fighting furiously for air. He was just pulling into the hospital, honking loudly to get the attention of the ER staff. He saw people running out, obviously checking to see what was going on, and seeing who it was, running back in and coming out with a gurney. They met him at his truck as soon as he stopped by the emergency department's ambulance bay. He looked behind him at Sadie, who was still gasping for air, and instantly felt his heart sink. There, on her face near her mouth and nose, he saw something that scared him more than he had ever been scared in his entire life, blood. Sadie was coughing up blood.

"Mommy... mommy, please wake up!" Hazel was screaming between sobs.

"It's okay, sweetheart, we are going to help your mommy, but we need you to come with us so we can help you too, okay?" a nurse was saying, trying to pry Hazel from her mamma's side, "It's okay." The nurse pried the screaming little girl off her mamma and placed her on a stretcher, another nurse coming to her aid to help keep Hazel safe and steady so they could get to her mother.

Tears filled his eyes as he stumbled down from his truck, running around to the passenger side. As he reached the other side, they were quickly placing Sadie on a 2nd stretcher, wheeling her inside with haste. He felt like his whole world was ending... his usually calm demeanor was now replaced with panic. He couldn't lose her!

"You can follow us, Ryder, but you need to stay out of the way so we can work, okay?" someone said, Ryder unable to make out the person's face. He shook his head, but the face remained a blur. Ryder could feel his heart beating in his ears as he turned to follow them, his feet suddenly heavy, as though the concrete below him had opened and was pulling him in. In the distance, he could hear someone asking him if he was okay, but they were moving farther and farther away from him it seemed. He grabbed at his chest, feeling as though the air had suddenly vacated his lungs, leaving only dust to breathe. He fell to the ground, darkness slowly swallowing him until all that was left was a black void.

"Dr. Louis, we need another gurney, stat!" Allie, a nurse at the Stone Creek Medical Center, yelled as she watched Ryder fall to the cement. "It's Ryder, he collapsed!"

As quick as lightening, Dr. Louis, the doctor on call in the ER that evening, summoned a stretcher and another team of nurses to run to the ambulance bay and grab Ryder. There was chaos all around them as they put each of them into a room, nurses, CNA's, and doctors running around each patient, frantically assessing the damage each one had sustained from the fire and the smoke. Stone Creek was a small town, and they had a small hospital to match. They had every able hand in the hospital down to the ER in a matter of minutes, lending help where it was needed.

"Someone had better call Carson right away! He needs to get down here and figure out what happened to these three!" Dr. Louis told the woman at the desk.

"Yes, Sir. Do you want me to call Ryder's mother too?"

"Yes," he responded, "I think you better do that too. Maybe she will know how to get in contact with the family of the mother and daughter he brought in as well."

The woman quickly went to work, contacting Carson first. After only one ring, he picked up, accustomed to calls from the ER in the middle of the night.

*This is Carson...*

"Hello, this is Nancy Roland at the hospital. We have a situation here that we need you to come assist with. Ryder Mack is here. He brought in an adult female and a female child and then collapsed after he arrived." she told him.

*Holy shit, are they okay?*

The female child is doing well, but the female passenger and Ryder are in bad shape. They appear to have been in or near a fire." she explained, as thoroughly as was possible without direct knowledge of what had happened.

*I just heard my pager go off for a structure fire, so I'm guessing that has something to do with this. I'll be right there!*

The line went dead before Nancy could ask about the woman and child he had brought in with him, so Nancy hung up the phone. She figured she'd just have to ask about them when Carson arrived at the hospital. She looked at her computer screen, dreading the next call. Talking to the family members of a patient that was brought in like this was never easy, and it was the worst part of her job. She looked on Ryder's medical record to find his next of kin. Locating his mother's number, she dialed, waiting for her to pick up.

*Hello?*

"Hello, is this Annie Mack?"

*Yes, that's me.*

"Annie, my name is Nancy Roland, and I am calling you from Stone Creek Medical Center. Ma'am, your son, Ryder, arrived here a few minutes ago. He had a woman and child in the back seat that appear to have been involved in some sort of accident involving a possible fire."

*Oh, my goodness! Are they all okay?* Nancy could hear the panic in the mother's voice.

"Your son collapsed after getting them all here, ma'am, and he is in with the doctors now. Dr. Louis is the doctor on call, and he asked me to contact you in case you'd like to come down to the hospital. As soon as we have more news, I can let you know."

*Um... oh my... yes, I'll call Sawyer, Sadie's best friend. She'll want to know, and she can bring me there,* Annie said, stumbling through her words as her thoughts ran wild in her mind, fearing the very worst and hoping for the very best, all at once.

"Ma'am, is the woman that Ryder brought in's name Sadie?"

*Yes, it is. And the little girl is Hazel. Oh my... are they okay?*

"I can't share any details with you, ma'am, as that would be a privacy violation, but I can tell you that the doctors are working on assessing each patient now, attending to their individual needs."

*OK, I appreciate the call. I'll get a hold of Sawyer and be there as soon as I can. Please tell the doctors that that's my baby on the table, so they had better make sure he's okay, or they'll be answering to me!*

Nancy hung up the phone as the line went dead. She liked this woman already, and she hadn't even met her yet. She knew she'd feel the same way if that was any one of her children in those rooms.

* * *

Sawyer awoke, startled by the sound of pounding on her front door. Travis woke at the same time, jumping up out of bed to run to the front entrance. She could swear she heard sirens in the distance, but was confused about what was going on. As Travis passed the living room window, she heard him yell for her, "Sawyer, come quick! The cottage is on fire!"

Sawyer jumped out of bed, racing to the window. There, in the distance, she could see the blaze, topped off with thick smoke that seemed to stretch to the stars in the night sky. "Oh my God! Sadie and Hazel are in there!" She could see red lights flashing as they approached the cottage driveway. She threw on some jeans and a sweatshirt, grabbing her cell phone and heading to the front door. It was a neighbor, waking them to let them know about the fire and that they had called 9-1-1. "We have to get over there, Trav!" she screamed, telling him to get dressed fast so they could get to the cottage.

Sawyer ran out and jumped in Travis' truck, waiting for him to get out the door so they could go. Just as she saw him come out, her phone started ringing. She grabbed it from her pocket, guessing it was Carson or Ryder calling to tell her about the fire. Instead, she saw that it was Annie, Ryder's mom. Confusion filled her mind as she answered it, wondering why Annie would call her now, of all times.

"Hello Annie… is something wrong?" she asked, worry filling her now throaty voice.

*Sawyer! I need you to come pick me up! The hospital called and said that Ryder, Sadie and Hazel were in some sort of accident, maybe even a fire, and they are in bad shape! Please, I need to get down there, and quick!*

Sawyer blinked a few times, trying to make sense of all that she was seeing and hearing at one time, all jumbled up in her brain like an intricate puzzle. As Travis jumped into the driver's seat, he heard her saying, "We'll be there in 10 minutes to get you!"

"What the hell was that about?" he asked, sharing in the same confusion she had faced only moments before. When she didn't answer, he prodded, "Sawyer, what's going on?"

Pale, feeling as though she may throw up at any moment, Sawyer relayed the message that Annie had just told her. Travis reached over to take her hand. "Sawyer, I'm sure everything will be okay, we just have to stay positive for all of them, and especially for Annie." Although Sawyer's voice seemed to be lost, he accepted her nod and stepped on the gas, racing as quickly, yet safely, as he could to get to Annie. As he passed by the road that led towards the cottage, he had to stop for more fire engines to fly past, obviously aware of the blaze now and ready to fight it until it was out. Seeing them gave him some comfort since he knew his wife and Ryder's mom both needed to get to the hospital in case things went south.

"Sawyer, do you think we should call Sadie's folks now, or wait until we get there and know what's going on?" he asked her, squeezing her hand to pull her from the daze she was in.

"Um, I think we better wait so we know what she and Hazel's conditions are, so we can give them better information than we have now." she said, feeling the tears falling down her cheeks. How had this happened? They had made sure everything was up to code when they bought the cottage, and Ryder had checked it all over again before Sadie moved in… it couldn't have been anything like that. Sadie was the least careless person she knew, so she highly doubted she had left anything unattended or left the fireplace burning wood while she slept. That couldn't be the case, she just knew it. So, what could it be?

As they rounded the corner leading to Ryder's childhood home, they could see Annie standing in wait on the porch. Travis jumped out and helped her into the front seat, Sawyer moving to the back to give the older woman space. She looked so pale, worry covering every corner of her beautiful ageless face. Sawyer reached up, gently squeezing Annie's shoulder, assuring her that everything was going to be okay, that it *had* to be okay.

Travis, Sawyer, and Annie reached the hospital in record time, seeing Ryder's truck in the parking lot, obviously moved there by someone at the hospital. They also saw Carson's squad car by the emergency entrance. Sawyer jumped out, helping Annie as she stepped down from the truck. Travis went to park it out of the way while they walked quickly in the doors. As they looked around, they saw an urgency in all the ER staff that made them even more nervous about what was happening. Sawyer could feel the chaos in the emergency room, it seemingly matching the marching band of soldiers running crazy in her head at that very moment. She scanned the room for the information desk area, and led Annie there, finding a woman with a concerned smile on her face.

"Hello, my name is Sawyer, and this is Annie Mack. We were told Ryder, Sadie & Hazel are being treated here. Can you tell us where we can get more information, please?" she asked, trying not to let the panic in her voice be detected.

"Yes, I can find someone to update you. My name is Nancy, and I'm the one who spoke with you earlier, Ms. Mack. If you could all just have a seat over in the waiting area, I'll have them come find you there," Nancy told them, pointing towards a small room to the left of the ER with vinyl-covered sofas and chairs scattered about. They met Travis by the doors, telling him to come with them. Sawyer was trying hard to swallow back the incredible urge she had to puke. This all seemed to be a nightmare, and she begged God to wake her up so it could be over. Unfortunately, there wasn't a chance that this was going away.

After what felt like an eternity, a doctor, sheathed in a white coat and dress pants, appeared in the doorway of the waiting room. Sawyer nudged Travis, who had fallen asleep next to her, laying his head on her shoulder with his hand in hers. He jumped, obviously in the middle of dreamland.

Annie spoke first, eager to know the condition of her son and the two people he loved most, besides her, of course, "Are they okay? Please tell me they're all okay!" she pleaded, tears filling her eyes for what felt like the millionth time since she had received the terrible news earlier.

"Ms. Mack, my name is Dr. King, and I've been treating Ryder since he arrived here in the night. He suffered a great deal of smoke inhalation, as well as a couple of minor burns on his hands and arms, but he is currently in stable condition. Respiratory therapy spent about an hour with him, giving him steroid treatments and oxygen, which helped him to clear his lungs of the smoke so they could fill back up with good, clean air. He will need to stay here for a day or two for observation, but he should be okay. He was very lucky, ma'am." he relayed in a serious, yet kind tone.

Sawyer gave Annie a hug, thankful that Ryder was going to be okay. Annie was trembling as tears flooded her eyes and made a path down her already moist cheeks. She worried about Ryder all the time, being a firefighter and all, but this was different. She wasn't sure what had happened tonight, but she knew she was going to be thanking God every day for a very long time that her boy had made it through this okay.

Suddenly, the happy tears were replaced by new worry as Sawyer asked, "Doc, what about Sadie and Hazel? Are they okay too?"

"Sawyer, you were listed as Sadie's emergency contact, along with her parents. We were able to get a hold of them a little bit ago to notify them of the incident, as well as update them on her progress. We do have permission to speak with you, as well, so I am happy to update you on their condition as well."

Sawyer held Annie's hand in one of hers, and Travis' in the other. She was petrified, if she was being honest. She was so thankful that Ryder was okay, but what about the other two? Were they okay too? She couldn't lose her best friend, not again! And Hazel, that sweet little girl, what if she wasn't okay either? Her mind was racing, dizziness threatening to envelop her body. She tried to blink it away, willing it to subside.

The doctor continued, "I'm happy to report that Hazel is doing wonderfully. She is on the 2nd floor, in the pediatrics area, where she can be monitored for the next 24 hours. It appears that Ryder and Sadie were able to keep the smoke away from her for the most part, which is a miracle. She is coughing some, but the nurses in peds will give her nebulizer treatments as needed, and continue to watch her for any late symptoms that may arise." He paused for a moment, giving them a second or two to catch up with him. "I'm going to go on in and swap out with Dr. Louis now, as he is the doctor who is working with Sadie. He'll be able to give you a much clearer picture of her condition. If you'll please excuse me," he said, turning to leave the waiting room.

The room was quiet, except for the soft sob that occasionally fell from Annie's mouth. She was so thankful for Hazel and Ryder's good news, but also feeling the heavy weight upon her heart as she awaited the news about Sadie. Her son had finally found a woman he loved with his whole heart, the same way that her precious husband had loved her. She was devastated at the thought that he may lose his beloved now, so early in their budding relationship. So much had happened, and she was exhausted from worry. As the second doctor approached, she wiped her tears and took a deep breath, willing herself to be strong for Sawyer and for Ryder, who was in another room fighting a battle of his own. If she knew her son, and she did, it was probably taking several nurses just to keep him in his own room instead of rushing to Sadie's bedside to be with her. *For now*, Annie thought, *I'll be strong for everyone.*

As the doctor approached, Travis looked at his wife who seemed to be in shock. Seeing that she was in no shape to ask what needed to be asked, he spoke for her. "Dr. Louis, my name is Travis, and this is my wife, Sawyer. We are all very worried about Sadie, and we hear you are the one who knows her condition best. Can you please update us on how she's doing?" he asked, doing his best to keep his voice cool and collected, for his wife's sake.

He put his arm around Sawyer, trying to replace her fading strength with his own, there to support her in case the news the doctor was about to reveal was not good. He closed his eyes for a second, blinking back tears, as he heard the doctor speak, "Yes, I am the one who has been treating Sadie since she arrived. It appears that Sadie was breathing in smoke for quite some time. What we have learned from speaking to Ryder is that she made sure her daughter was okay and tried to call for help, which was good, but unfortunately, she couldn't care for herself and her daughter at the same time. She is-"

"Oh, God," Sawyer interrupted, turning to fall into Travis' arms, sobbing uncontrollably. The doctor quickly moved forward, touching her shoulder, assuring her, "It's okay, ma'am. I was about to say that she is about the luckiest patient I think I've ever seen!" he finished, a smile on his face.

"Wait, what?" Sawyer asked, visibly confused and not sure she was hearing him right. "What did you say?" she repeated.

"Your friend is one tough cookie! She suffered some burns

to her lungs and is still having a hard time getting her breathing under control, and her blood pressure is fluctuating a little more than we would like it to, but I truly believe she will pull through this. She is going to need to be in the ICU for a couple of days, followed by a few days in a transitional room, but she should recover fully from this." he said, smiling at the three in front of him.

"See," Travis said, cupping Sawyer's chin in his hand and placing a tender kiss on her lips, "I told you it would be okay."

"She will *definitely* have a long road ahead of her while her lungs heal, so she is going to need to rest, as she'll tire easily. If she doesn't, she'll end up right back here, so between the three of you, her parents, and Mr. Mack, you will need to help assure that happens," Dr. Louis said, seriousness taking over his previously calm tone.

"Oh, you better believe we will do that!" Sawyer said, jumping up and hugging the unsuspecting doctor. He smiled and stepped back when she released him, apologizing for her excitement. "It's okay, I understand, and I know you've all been through a lot in the last few hours. I think maybe you should all go home and get some rest. Neither Ryder nor Sadie will be able to have a visitor for several hours yet. I promise to have the nurse call if there are any changes."

With that, he turned and walked away, a deep sigh escaping his body. It had been a scary and exhausting night for the staff at Stone Creek Medical Center too, Annie thought. "I think the doctor is right. Sawyer, maybe you should head on up and see how Hazel is doing. I bet she is quite scared right now. Travis, do you think you could run me back home? I'd like to take a nap and then make some goodies to bring back to these kind people who have taken such good care of my Ryder and his love."

Travis smiled, "I think that's a great idea! Sawyer, does that sound good to you?" At her nod, he added, "How about you give me a call when you are ready to come home, and I'll come pick you up? I want to get a couple of hours of sleep and then I need to go figure out what happened at the cottage and what I need to do next." He pulled her into his body and hugged her, showing her that he had her back, no matter what.

Sawyer smiled up at her husband, kissing him softly, and then turned towards the elevator, bound for the second floor. Travis was right, Hazel was probably scared, and she was the only one that would be able to calm her down right now. Plus, she needed the distraction from racking her brain over how such an awful accident could have almost taken her very best friend in the whole world from her, all in the blink of an eye.

# Chapter Seventeen

A fresh blanket of snow was falling, covering the earth in a sparkle of white fluff. The sky was gray, and the air was crisp. Ryder sat in the chair next to Sadie's bed, watching the winter scene unfold outside the window. An elderly man was helping his wife out of their car, placing a hand around her waist as he helped support her. He turned, sliding a wheelchair behind her so she could sit on it. She looked up at him, warmth and love in her eyes. He turned and pushed her towards the entrance of the hospital, leaving his running car behind him, the exhaust blowing puffs of gray into the clean air around it. Just behind them, a van waited to drop its passenger at the door next. Winter in Illinois was cold, the air biting at your face when you walked into it, and he didn't blame people for wanting to get indoors quickly.

He turned his gaze to the beautiful woman sleeping in the bed in front of him. He couldn't believe how close he had come to losing her. She and Hazel had grown to mean everything to him- he wasn't sure he could go on without them. He had seen so many people lose loved ones over the years as a firefighter, and he had thought that he was next. One thing was for sure, he would never look at a fire the same way again after yesterday. Coughing, he covered his mouth, doing his best to slow his breathing. He took a drink and then sat it back on the table next to him. As he looked up, he saw the most beautiful sight he'd ever seen; Sadie was waking up. She looked at him, then around the room, clearly trying to figure out where she was, worry filling her face.

Wanting to help her understand, he sat on the bed next to her, holding her hand in his. "Sweetheart, it's okay. You are at the hospital. Hazel is upstairs with Sawyer so they can keep an eye on her, but she's doing amazing. I'm right here with you, so don't be afraid." He leaned in and kissed her forehead. "You sure did give me a scare," he said, gazing into her eyes as he spoke.

"What happened, Ryder? I remember smoke everywhere, and I didn't know what to do. I couldn't breathe!" she said, panic rising in her voice. Something on the monitor began to beep, telling him he needed to calm her down, quickly. She started to cough, grabbing her chest as the pain felt almost unbearable. She tried to stop the coughing, trying to find air to fill her hurt lungs.

"It's okay. Everything is going to be fine. You are safe now, and so is Hazel, okay?" he assured her, rubbing her cheek as she pressed into his hand, her cough finally subsiding.

As the beeping stopped, he continued to try to explain, the words seeming to be hard to find, "Sadie, Carson stopped by while you were still sleeping, and we talked. He said that he went out to the cottage after the fire was out, and he was able to grab the cameras I had installed a couple of days ago."

"What? Why did you put cameras at my house?" she asked, confused.

"Because I knew Luke had been seen in town, and I needed to try to protect you and Hazel from him. He is clearly obsessed with you, and you don't want to know what an obsessed man can do when they lose it!" he said.

"Ryder, how would you know what obsessed men are like?"

Ryder felt a surge of anger and fear. How could Luke do such a thing? How could he be so evil? "Because, unfortunately this isn't the first fire I've witnessed that was set by an obsessed or angry ex."

"Wait, what are you saying, Ryder? Are you seriously implying that Luke set the fire?" Sadie once again became agitated, causing her heart rate alarm to ring loudly in his ear. Ryder told her to calm down. He was worried that he was telling her too much, but also knew Sadie well enough at this point to know that if he *didn't* tell her, it would be even worse.

"Sadie, you need to take some slow deep breaths and calm down or you're going to start coughing again. Maybe I should wait until you are feeling a little better to tell you all of this," he said, concern in his voice.

"No, it's okay, Ryder. I will try to stay calm, I promise. I just need to know what happened or I'll never be able to control my mind from guessing," she countered.

"Like I told you before, you are safe now." he told her, giving her time to relax again. "As I was saying, I put cameras up at your house, as well as a fire monitor. I was trying to do everything I could think of to keep you two safe. Carson says that the camera's weren't damaged in the fire, so he went to his office to watch the footage and he saw Luke there at your cottage when we got back from the party. He was hiding in the bushes." Giving her a second to take that in, he continued, "Then, after seeing me kiss you and drop you off, he turned and disappeared into the thicket."

"Well, if he left, then why is it that you think he started the fire? I just can't believe he would try to hurt his own daughter, Ryder. He had to have known she was there too." she said, struggling to wrap her mind around what Ryder was telling her.

"Carson said that after you and Hazel were asleep, Luke came back. Apparently, he tried to enter the house, but Cliff stopped him."

"Oh, God, Cliff! Where is Cliff, Ryder?" she asked, instant fear turning her eyes to glass.

"Sadie, Luke killed him. I'm so sorry. He hit him in the head with a rock when he chased him off the porch. He was probably scared that Cliff would wake you up, so he had no choice but to shut him up." Ryder reached over, wiping the freshly fallen tears from her cheeks. It killed him to see her like this, so broken and defeated.

"Please don't cry, sweetie. I'm so sorry I couldn't stop him before he got to you. If I had just said no when they called me to the fire earlier, I would have been there with you, there to protect you both. Then, none of this would have happened, and Cliff would still be here," he said, tears falling down his cheeks in a steady stream of regrets.

Sadie reached up and touched Ryder's face, so much in love with him, and so thankful that he had saved them from the fire.

"It's okay, Ryder. You got there when we needed you the most, and that's what counts," she assured him.

Ryder sat on the chair again, this time laying his head on her bed with her hands in his, forming a pillow beneath his auburn curls. They sat there together, just trying to make sense of how this had all happened but needing each other's company to continue on. After a few minutes had passed, he took a deep breath, causing his lungs to argue, the coughing becoming difficult to stop. Hearing the coughing, the nurse came in to check on them, putting Ryder's oxygen mask back over his face, telling him to leave it there for a little bit. He rolled his eyes but didn't move the mask.

Sadie tried to laugh, but it felt as though her entire body was filled with a thick tar, making it hard to laugh or breathe deep without coughing until her stomach muscles threatened to burst. Instead, she smiled. Then, she said, "You can tell me the rest later, if you'd like. I think you need some rest too."

"I'm okay, really. I need to finish so you know everything that has been going on. It's eating me up inside, Sadie." he said, earning him a bewildered look from her. "Carson said that Luke grabbed a can of gasoline from the bush, dumping it on the back porch by the kitchen."

"Oh, Ryder, I knew he hated me, but Hazel? What did she ever do to deserve a father like that?" she cried in disbelief. She knew she had chosen poorly when it came to Luke, but how could she have ever thought that he would be safe for Hazel to be around? She had messed up even more than she realized. "What have I done?" she asked, sobbing uncontrollably.

Hugging her close, he did his best to console her, putting his own anger away for the moment so he could help her make sense of the circus of emotions colliding in her mind right now. Her body shook in his, all the fear and sadness transferring from her body and into his. She would wretch occasionally with coughing, leaving her injured lungs gasping for air, until he would help her breathe calmly again.

A nurse came in to give her additional oxygen, a steroid injection, and at one point added a mild sedative to her IV to calm her down. As her sobbing subsided, the medication doing its job, she lay down and slowly closed her eyes, drifting off to asleep after exhausting herself until there was nothing left to sustain her.

Ryder sat back on the chair, laying his head next to her on her bed, holding her hand in his. As he lay there, he succumbed to the sorrow he was feeling and cried, the tears wetting the bed where his face lay. He knew he had more to tell her, but he couldn't stand watching her suffer like that. Why couldn't he have just gotten there sooner? Why didn't he take her more seriously when she first told him she thought she had seen Luke? He should have made her get a restraining order then, not waiting until the threat was right in his face! He would never forgive himself for any of this… he told her he'd keep her safe, but he hadn't. When she woke up, he was going to make sure he told her how sorry he truly was. One way or another, he needed her to know that he was here, and that he'd never let anything happen to her again.

* * *

Sadie's eyelids fluttered open, as the blinding winter sun stretched its arms out and touched her cheeks with warmth. She rubbed her eyes, trying to make everything come into focus. She could hear a familiar sound near her bed, one that had her thinking she had been here once before. Confused, she turned to her left, everything finally coming into focus. She smiled as she found herself looking into the face of a very cute little girl.

Upon seeing her mommy's eyes open, Hazel cried, "Mommy! Mommy, you're awake!".

Sadie's smile widened as she reached out to touch Hazel's face, running her fingers through her curls, secretly thanking God for watching over her little princess. "Well, hello there," she said, "What's your name, little princess, and what are you doing in my room?" she teased, eliciting a goofy face from her daughter.

"Mommy, you're silly." Hazel said, giggling. Hearing her daughter giggle, Sadie started to laugh, only stopping to cough. She looked at her water, asking, "Sweetheart, could hand mommy her water, please?"

As Hazel turned, Sadie heard a voice that seemed to come from nowhere, saying, "Here, let me get that for you." Sadie's eyes filled with tears as she realized whose voice it was… her mom. She took the water from her mother, sipping slowly and breathing in the air from her mask, trying to calm the coughs down. Her mother had a concerned look on her face, and Hazel was looking at her with fear in her eyes.

"Mommy… are you okay?" she asked her.

"Yes, sweetie, I just have a cough, kind of like you did last spring when you got a cold, remember?" she assured her. Hazel nodded, seeming to be satisfied for the moment.

Sadie's father, also hiding in the corner apparently, stepped up behind Hazel and scooped her up in his arms, causing another round of giggles to come from the adorable little bundle of laughter. Sadie felt so much better knowing her parents were there with her, there to take care of Hazel and keep her safe.

"When did you two get here?" she asked them after the coughing finally subsided.

"We got here about an hour ago. When the hospital called us, we hopped on the first flight to Chicago, grabbed a rental car, and headed right to the hospital. We had to make sure our best girls were okay, right Mamma?" he asked, directing the question at his wife, who was smiling back at him.

"Absolutely," she said, "Every girl needs her mom when she's sick or hurt, so here I am to help wherever I can." Leaning over, she kissed Sadie on the forehead, feeling for a fever like she had always done when Sadie was a little girl. Sadie grinned, "I love you, Mom. And you too, of course," she said, looking at her father.

"Well, the doctor has given little miss Hazel, here, a clean bill of health, so we are going to go ahead and take her back to Sawyer's house. We are staying there until you get back on your feet, so we can help wherever we are needed," her father told her in a tone that told her there'd be no point in arguing. "Anyway, I think maybe we should head over there and get situated, that way we can come back later and visit when you've had some more time to rest. Does that work for you?" he asked her, with more of a statement than a question in his voice.

"Yes, Daddy. I'm pretty tired still. Whatever they gave me is making it kind of hard to keep my eyes open. Working so hard to breathe isn't helping either, especially if I get too worked up. I think I'll just take a little nap if that's okay." Sadie said, her eyes feeling heavy.

"Sounds good, sweetie," her mom said, kissing her forehead

again and then waving as she walked out the door with her husband and Hazel.

"I love you, sweet pea!" she called out to Hazel.

"I love you too, Mommy!" Hazel responded, already waving at the nurses who were telling her goodbye.

*  *  *

Ryder walked into the hospital for the fifth time in as many days. He was getting a little sick of the smells around him and the confines of the brick walls. He had nearly jumped out of his seat when he'd gotten the call from Sadie's dad saying that she was being released and asking him if he'd like to go pick her up. He couldn't wait to bust her out of this place, and he planned to convince her to bring Hazel and come live with him. He needed to be close to her so he could keep an eye on her. He wasn't making the mistake of leaving her alone again anytime soon, that was for certain.

"Hey, Ryder!" he heard a voice calling behind him. He recognized Carson's voice immediately, turning to greet his friend with a hug. "Boy, you're a hard fella to try to find, you know that?" Carson teased.

"Well, you found me now, didn't you? What's up?" Ryder asked, laughing.

"I heard you were picking Sadie up... I'm so relieved to hear she gets to go home... well, to get out of here anyway.' He said, not quite sure of the right words. "Anyway, I wanted to catch you quick before you go in so I can give you an update on the Luke situation."

Ryder's demeanor instantly changed. His face hardened with anger, his fists automatically responding by tightening. "Did you find that bastard?" he asked. "Don't forget, you owe me one, and I want to cash in by spending a few minutes alone in a room with him, cameras off!" he said, Carson worried that steam would literally start coming out Ryder's ears soon if he didn't calm down.

"Yeah, yeah. I know. Unfortunately, we haven't located Luke yet, but we are getting closer. It seems that Leo Baker, the old guy that lives out on Birch Avenue, about 20 minutes east of town over there," Carson said, pointing east, "noticed something the other day that he thought was fishy. He said there was smoke coming from the fireplace at that rickety old shack that's out in the field just past his horse pasture." He paused a second to make sure Ryder was following, and that he knew where he was talking about. Nodding, he continued, "Anyways, I just got off the phone with him, and I decided to head over there to check it out myself. If it's Luke, and my gut tells me it is, I'll find him. My guess is that the sick bastard stuck around to make sure the job was done, and, if he realized they survived, he may have stuck around to finish it." he said, concern in his face.

"Well, he's not going to get the chance, I'm not letting her out of my sight until he's found and in jail, Carson." Ryder told his friend, assuring him he'd handle it if Luke tried to come anywhere near Sadie or Hazel again.

Carson patted his friend on the back, smiling a knowing smile. "I know you'll protect them, man. Just be careful, please. Call me right away if you see him… Sadie and Hazel need you to be there for them, not in jail."

With that, Carson left him and headed back to his squad car.

Opening his door, he turned to Ryder and added, "Hey… we're going to find him. That's not a promise, Ryder, it's a fact." he said with conviction. Ryder had never known his friend to lie, so he nodded, turned, and went to find the love of his life so he could bust her out of this 'prison'.

On the ride home, Ryder noticed that Sadie hadn't said more than two words, that she was gazing out his truck window, seemingly deep in thought. He couldn't even imagine all the things that were going through her head. He wanted to wave a magic want and have the events of the last few days disappear, allowing them to start over on the day of her birthday party. Unfortunately, that's not how it worked, and he knew that.

He reached over, taking her hand in his, breaking the silence as she turned to look at him. "A penny for your thoughts?" he said, smiling at her.

"Ryder," she began, "there's something about all the stuff you told me the other day that is really bothering me, and I can't seem to make sense of it."

He looked out the front window, keeping his eyes on the road as he swallowed hard, knowing what was probably coming next. "You can ask me anything, Sadie." he said, waiting for her to address the elephant that had been standing between them for days.

"Well, you told me that you put cameras up because you knew Luke was in town, but you never said anything to me about him being around," she said. "When was he in town? And how did *you* know, but not *me*?"

There it was. The question he'd been dreading ever since he and Sawyer had decided to keep Luke's presence in town from Sadie. Sighing, he looked over at her briefly, confusion and hurt in her eyes.

"I found out that Luke had been seen in town 2 days before your birthday, sweetheart. Carson told me, and I decided not to tell you until after your birthday party, because I didn't want to let him ruin another special moment for you." he confessed, feeling the heavy weight of guilt pressing down on his shoulders. He looked over at her, reaching for her hand, but seeing her pull away as if his touch would burn hers. He closed his eyes for a second, feeling her hurt piercing through him like a dagger to the gut. He had promised to never hurt her, and here he was, doing just the opposite.

"How could you *keep* that from me?" she said, tears welling in her eyes.

"I'm sorry, Sadie! I was just trying to protect you! I thought that if I put cameras up and watched you and Hazel closely, that I could keep you safe until after the party. Then, I was going to tell you right away." he tried to explain, falling short.

"I can't believe you'd lie to me like that! You know how I feel about people being dishonest with me, Ryder! Look what your lies did!" she shouted back, clearly very hurt and angry.

Ryder flinched, her words hitting him with the force of a fist. She blamed him, and rightfully so. Because of him, she was badly hurt, and her little girl could have been too. To make matters worse, they had lost everything in the fire. His thoughts were broken by her final comment before going silent again, "How can I ever trust you again?"

Ryder followed the freshly-plowed roads through the valley, past the winery and into the long and winding driveway leading to Travis and Sawyer's house. He felt as though he'd been punched in the stomach, and he didn't know how to make it right. He pulled the truck up next to the rental car her parents were using, putting it in park.

"Sadie, I-"

"Ryder, please don't," she interrupted through tears. Sadie opened her door and slid down to the ground gingerly. She shut the truck door behind her and walked up the steps and into the front door, never looking back.

"Dammit!" Ryder yelled, slamming his door. He hit his fist on the side of his truck, hard enough to hurt, but not hard enough to leave a dent.

"Hey… You okay?" he heard from the house.

Seeing Travis walk down the steps, he took a breath and walked around the truck, trying to hide his frustration. "Yeah, sorry. I'm not feeling the best, so I think I'm gonna have to head for my place to get some sleep," he said, doing his best to sound tired and not angry.

"I bet you are wiped. Are you sure you don't want to say hi to Sadie's folks? They're right inside, helping Sawyer with lunch. I'm sure they'd love to meet you…" Travis walked to Ryder, patting him on the shoulder.

"Can you please tell them I said I'd stop by tomorrow sometime to say hi? I need a little time to work through all this shit." he said, getting an understanding nod from Travis.

"I got ya, brother. I'm sure they'll understand. Get some sleep and let me know if you need anything, okay?"

Travis backed away from Ryder's truck as he jumped in and left the driveway. He knew the look he had seen on his friend's face, and it wasn't from being tired. Something was wrong, and he was pretty sure it had to do with Sadie. Shaking his head, he walked back to the house, getting ready to hear all the complaints he was going to get about letting Ryder leave without saying hello. With a sigh that he seemed to pull from his toes, he opened the door and entered the gauntlet.

* * *

Carson pulled up to the driveway that led to the deserted shed, thankful that the snow wasn't too heavy for him to drive up the old driveway when he was ready to. According to Leo, this place hadn't had any occupants in over 10 years, so there was no reason for smoke to be coming from the chimney, yet it was. "Someone must be in there," the man had told the sheriff. Carson had a feeling that he knew who was in there, and he wasn't about to go in alone. Luke Benson was a dangerous man, one who needed to be apprehended. He had radioed for two deputies to meet him at the house, all stopping at the entrance to the farmstead where Carson sat.

"Listen, this man is wanted for assault, arson, stalking, and attempted murder of a woman and her child. He is extremely dangerous, and we need to do this quickly and strategically so he doesn't get away from us again." he told the deputies.

"He has a motorcycle, so if he's still here, I'm guessing it will be somewhere near the shed." he informed them, each listening intently to the plan. "I'll go in from the front while you two cover the back corners. This is our best chance to take him in peacefully, so let's not blow it." he finished.

"Sounds good, Carson. Let's get this done with so these families can rest knowing he's off the streets and done terrorizing them." said one the of the deputies, earning a nod of agreement from the other.

The three officers got back in their cars and, turning their lights to low, headed down the moonlit drive that led to the small shed tucked into the trees. As they got closer, they could see fresh motorcycle tracks leading away from the entrance to the dilapidated building. Carson pulled off the path as he got about 100 yards from the building. Both officers followed suit, exiting their vehicles to flank the shack on foot so they wouldn't risk being seen or heard as easily.

When Carson saw that the officers were in place, he slowly approached the entrance to the building. Gun in hand, he felt the creaky steps beneath his feet as he crept up each one, slowly and purposefully.

"This is the Stone Creek Sheriff's Department. Anyone inside needs to come out with their hands up," he shouted, loudly enough for anyone inside to hear clearly. He stopped at the top step, listening for footsteps or noises inside the shack, clues to tell him someone was inside. Nothing moved, nothing sounded.

*"Come on, where are you?"* he whispered to himself, feeling his blood thicken as his senses were on high alert.

When he got to the door, he glanced at each deputy, exchanging nods, silently warning them that he was going to enter. Glancing in a broken window by the doorway, he added, "Luke Benson, this is the police… we know you are here, and you are surrounded. Come out slowly…"

Still nothing. With a deep breath, he kicked the door in, his gun-filled hands leading the way as he moved into the unfamiliar space.

He looked around the room, and realizing it was empty, he dropped his gun to his holster, frustration filling his body. He turned, walking back out the door, yelling for his deputies to stand down. Joining him on the deck of the rickety old building, they stared at Carson curiously.

"What's going on, Carson?" one asked, "Is he gone already?"

"Yeah, it looks like he left a little while ago," he told the officers. "The logs in the fireplace are still smoldering, so I'm guessing he hasn't been gone long. He had to have left on the cycle, so we better call-in backup to find him."

With that, he left the steps and walked over to his car. He radioed for backup to head out to the property. Returning to the other officers, he led them back into the building. They needed to try to find any clues they could to tell them where he was going, as well as confirm it was Luke that had been hiding there.

The three entered the shack again, looking for clues into the mystery unfolding in front of them. He was becoming increasingly frustrated with this whole thing. He had grown to care very much about Sadie and Hazel, and he wanted to make sure they would be safe. With Luke running around out there free, nobody could sleep for fear of what he would do, or try to do, next.

"Hey Carson, you better come look at this," his youngest deputy, Marcus, said from the small table in the corner.

Carson walked over to the deputy, grabbing a handwritten note from him. He read the note, sighing as he realized what had happened in the deserted place they stood.

*That bitch doesn't deserve to live. If she thinks she can just leave town and take my daughter, telling her that some firefighter is her new daddy, then she is in for a surprise. I gave them everything, and they gave me nothing in return. Now, they'll see what happens when they go against me. **If I can't have them, nobody will.***

# Chapter Eighteen

After sleeping for an hour or so, Ryder headed for the kitchen to heat himself up some leftovers his mother had put in his fridge for him while he was in the hospital. He smiled as he opened the lid and found his favorite potato soup inside. His mother made the best potato soup in the country, as far as he was concerned. After several days of hospital food, this was really going to hit the spot. He tossed it into the microwave, closing the door and hitting the buttons. He looked out the kitchen window while he waited for it to finish heating. He'd tried to sleep, but he kept seeing Sadie's devastated face as he told her about not telling her Luke was in town. She was never going to trust him again, and he had worked *so* hard to earn her trust over the last 5 months that she had been here. How had everything gotten so screwed up in such a short amount of time?

Hearing the 'ding' of the timer, he opened the microwave and grabbed his soup, the aroma filling the air with the smell of potatoes and ham, and sat at the table to enjoy his mother's creation. As he spooned the delicious soup into his mouth, he thought about everything that had happened over the last 3 weeks, all the decisions that had been made, and the consequences of each. He had done what he thought was best, and she couldn't see that right now, but maybe, with a little sleep and some thought of her own, she'd come around. He figured a guy could at least hope.

He finished his soup, considering licking the bowl clean so as not to waste any of the incredible soup, but he decided against it, placing it in the dishwasher to be washed when it got full. She was angry at him now, but there had to be a way to convince her that he had only had her best interest in mind when he had made the decision not to tell her until after the party.

He decided he would never forgive himself if he didn't try, so he threw a jacket on and headed out the door, hell bent to give it everything he had. He had to convince her, one way or another, that he would never lie to her again, and that he loved her and could not live without her. *Here goes nothing,* he thought as he started the truck and made his way towards Sawyer's place. He wasn't going to leave until she said she'd give him another chance. This had to work.

* * *

Sawyer went to the door to see who had knocked and was happy when she saw that it was Ryder. He usually just walked in, so she gave him a curious look as she opened the door for him to move past her. As soon as he crossed the threshold,

260

he saw Hazel's face light up from the kitchen table where she was coloring with her grandma.

"Ryder!" Hazel exclaimed as she ran towards him.

Ryder knelt and hugged her.

"Hey, princess," he said. "How are you?"

"I'm fine, now," she said, "and so is mommy! She came home to Sawyer's house just like me!"

"I'm so happy to hear that," Ryder said. "Did you give her a big hug when she got here?"

"Yes," Hazel said, turning to Sadie, who was sitting in the living room next to her father. "I love you, Mommy!"

"I love you too, honey," Sadie said, her eyes kept away from Ryder.

Ryder got up and walked into the living room to the sofa Sadie was resting on. He nodded at her father before turning his attention to her. "Um, Sadie, would it be okay if we talked for a minute... alone?" he asked, hoping they could go someplace private for a little bit, away from all the ears in the room around them.

The room suddenly became very quiet as Sadie refused to make eye contact with him. The pain of betrayal was written all over her face, and he couldn't stand the thought that this was all his fault. He glanced towards Sawyer, his eyes pleading her to help him out.

Taking Ryder's cue, Sawyer addressed the room that was filled with curious onlookers. "What do you say we all take a ride down to the winery for that tour we've been talking about all week? Hazel, would you be my tour guide assistant?" she asked, earning an excited "Yes!" from the little girl in question. They all bundled up and headed out to Sawyer's vehicle. In the warm months they would have walked, but it was way too chilly out today for that.

Once the coast was clear, Ryder moved around the sofa and sat near Sadie's feet. He had to fight the urge to take them in his hands and place them on his lap, the need to touch her as strong as his need to breathe. Instead, he put his hands on his knees, trying to find the words he'd been searching for all day.

"Sadie, I love you," he said. "I love you more than anything in the world. You and Hazel mean everything to me, and I am so very sorry for upsetting you. That was the last thing I ever wanted to do, and I realize now that I was wrong to keep things from you, no matter what my intentions in doing so were."

She sat, staring at the fireplace, feeling it's warmth against her face. She wanted to forgive him, wanted to feel his arms around her, but how could she trust him again after he lied to her?

"Ryder," she said quietly, "I told you how hard it was for me to trust anyone, especially you. Even so, you still lied to me. How could you have kept something so important from me?"

"I was trying to keep him from ruining your birthday, but more importantly, I wanted to keep him from causing any more of that feeling of fear inside you all the time, from always wondering when he would show up to ruin your happiness! I couldn't stand the thought of that, Sadie."

"I understand that. I just need you to understand that because you didn't tell me he had been seen around, I wasn't prepared for him, and because of that, we almost died, Ryder!" she said, panic in her voice.

"I know, and, believe me, I will never forgive myself for that. All I wanted to do was protect you, and instead, I did the very opposite. I don't blame you for hating me, and I'm sorry that

I messed everything up."

Ryder looked deep into the fire, wishing with all his heart that he could go back in time and handle this whole thing differently. He loved Sadie with everything inside of him, and he didn't know how to fix what he had broken. After a minute of silence, Sadie sat up, sliding her body down the sofa until she was next to Ryder. She reached over and gently turned his face towards hers, both looking into tear-stained eyes. "I'm so sorry, Sadie," Ryder said, tears falling freely down his chiseled jaw.

"Ryder, I'm sorry too. The truth is I shouldn't have put what happened on you. It wasn't your fault… It was Luke's. I was just scared, and I needed someone to blame. I'm sorry for doing that to you. I love you very much, and I know you were just trying to protect me."

She placed a soft kiss on his lips, and then curled up in his arms as he hugged her. They sat on the sofa together, in one another's arms, for what felt like an eternity, before he pulled her face to his with a deep kiss. He loved this woman with his whole heart, and he was never going to let her feel anything less than safe in his arms again. He had to make sure she knew that he wasn't going anywhere, and that he would love her forever.

"Sadie," he said, looking into her eyes, her hands in his, "I know this may not be the best timing or the way I would have done this had the fire not happened, but I would love if you and Hazel would move into my house with me. I want to go to sleep next to you every night, and I want to wake up to your beautiful face every morning. I love you both, and I want us to live together, if you will accept my offer."

Sadie looked at him, feeling a surge of emotion. She loved

him too. She loved him more than she could express. He was kind, gentle, brave, and handsome. He was everything she had ever dreamed of. Everything she wanted in Luke, everything she thought she saw in Luke, but Luke had turned out to be this monster who would set his own child on fire just because things didn't end up the way he planned.

Ryder may be a good man, but he was also a reminder of what she had lost five years of her life chasing after. He was a reminder of what Luke had done to her, and of the danger that lurked around the corner if you didn't give a man exactly what he wanted.

She felt a wave of panic wash over her. She couldn't do this! She couldn't put herself or Hazel at risk. Instead, she said the first thing she could think of, "Ryder, I have been through a lot, and I am super tired. Would it be okay if we talked about this tomorrow? I'd like some time to think about it before I answer."

"I understand that.  I'm sure you're wiped out," he said, tucking her back in so she could rest before everyone got back. "I'm just going to hang out for a little bit, and when they get back. I'll head out. I have a shift tonight at the station, so I need to head on over there soon anyway. I love you," he said, kissing her on the forehead.

"I love you, too, Ryder." she said in return, drifting off to sleep. Even now, days after the fire, she couldn't stay awake for more than a couple of hours.

Even in sleep, Ryder could tell that her breathing was difficult, and she seemed to wear her out easily. He hoped a little rest would help her to decide about moving in with him. He wasn't quite sure what he would do if she didn't say yes. He wanted a life with Sadie and Hazel, and he prayed that they wanted one with him, too.

** * **

The winter sun shone in through the window as Sadie woke up. She had slept poorly, having a difficult time turning her brain off long enough to get any decent amount of sleep. She knew what she wanted, but she also knew what she needed, and they were not agreeing at all. She wanted to run to Ryder, move in with him, and form a family with him, finally finding her happily ever after. The problem was, she had to protect her heart, and more importantly, Hazel's, so she knew she had to be logical about this.

Before heading to bed last night, she had decided it was time that she and Hazel move back home with her parents. She needed to put some space between herself and Ryder so that she could think a little bit, and this was the only way she knew how to do that. She had spoken with her parents, and they had agreed to take the train back to Seattle with Sadie and Hazel first thing in the morning. They didn't have much left after the fire, so she didn't have to pack. They would have some breakfast and then head for the train station. Although her heart was breaking, she needed to go home. It was the only place she could *truly* feel safe while she figured out what to do next. She didn't want to go, but she had to. She had no tears left, had cried them all out in the night, so she sighed, deciding she might as well get on with the inevitable. She went to the bathroom, patting some cold water on her face, hoping to lessen the swelling in her face from all the crying in the night.

Sadie got dressed and headed for the kitchen, the smell of her mother's pancakes filling the air. She could hear Hazel's giggles all the way down the hallway. As she got to the kitchen, she stopped in the doorway, smiling as she took in the sight of Sawyer, her mom, and Hazel all working together to make the delectable breakfast treat. Seeing her, Hazel smiled, "Good morning, Mommy!"

"Good morning, sweetie pie. Boy, that sure smells good!"

"It's Grandma's pancakes! They are so yummy!" she said, giving her a hug.

They all sat down together and had breakfast, a sense of sadness in the air as they knew that goodbyes were going to be coming soon. Sadie knew that it would be hard to leave Sawyer again, but she also knew that they were both old enough to know it wasn't forever. Sadie just needed some time to figure things out. She had assured her that she'd be back, in time. Until then, she'd told Sawyer to please hold onto the paperwork they had drawn up that would give her co-ownership of the winery. Sawyer had been happy to oblige.

As they finished up their breakfast, Sadie heard a loud knock at the door. She was surprised, as she hadn't even heard anyone pull up. As Sawyer got up to go answer the door, Sadie's heart dropped- what if it was Ryder? *He should still be on shift*, she thought, but she had wanted to slip out without him knowing. When she heard the voice on the other side of the door, she relaxed. It was Carson.

"Uncle Carson!" Hazel yelled, running over to give him a hug.

"Well, if it isn't the brightest little sunshine in town!" he said, giving her a little poke on the nose. "My day just got a whole lot better after seeing your cute face!"

"We're having pancakes! My grandma makes the best ones ever." she said, hopping down and running back to the table to finish her breakfast.

"I wish I had time to try those… they look delicious!" he said, nodding to the rest of the room. "Um, Sadie, would it be okay if we had a quick word in the other room?" he asked.

"Sure Carson, that's fine. We can go in the office if that works," she replied, standing to lead him to the home office.

Sadie wasn't sure what was going on, but Carson had a look on his face that had her worried. She knew they hadn't found Luke yet, and she was hoping this wasn't more bad news about him being around here or hurting anyone else. From the sounds of things, he had gone completely crazy, and she knew that he wasn't done yet, his letter had said as much. She wrapped a throw around her shoulders, suddenly feeling cold, as she waited patiently for Carson to tell her what he was there for.

"Sadie, I have some news for you. Is it okay if we sit down. It's been a long night, and I'm a bit tuckered," he said, the seriousness in his voice making her nervous.

Sadie sat in a chair across from Carson and waited for him to continue. "I got a call this morning from Captain Stearns of the Illinois State Patrol's office. He was calling me about Luke. He stated that they got a tip last night that Luke was at a truck stop about 70 miles from here, and when two of his officers approached him, he got on his motorcycle and sped off. They apparently got into a high-speed chase with him trying to arrest him. Captain Stearns said with the darkness and high speed, Luke took a curve too fast and went over an embankment. The officers tried to help him, but his injuries were too extensive. Sadie," Carson said, reaching over to take her shaking hand, "Luke died as a result of the crash."

Sadie sat, unable to move. A tear fell down her cheek as she tried to process what she had just heard. How could this be happening? She wanted him to pay for what he had done, but she'd never wish for anyone to lose their life, especially not her daughter's father. Had she driven him to this? She suddenly didn't feel too good.

Sensing her fragility, Carson moved closer and asked if she was okay. Not hearing a response, he walked to the doorway, getting Sawyer's attention and summoning her to the room. He quickly relayed the message to her, and then she said she'd take it from there. He left the two friends together in the room.

"Sadie... Are you okay?" Sawyer asked, worried that she hadn't spoken yet.

"Um... I ... Oh my... Sawyer, what do I do now?" she asked, sobbing into her friend's arms. Sawyer sat with her, letting her cry until the tears ran dry and her body was exhausted. She helped Sadie curl up in the comfy chair, covering her with a blanket. Once she was sure Sadie was asleep, she quietly left the room, closing the door halfway behind her.

"Is she okay?" Henry asked her as she walked back towards the kitchen.

"She's asleep, finally. She is pretty numb right now, I think."

"Carson told me what happened. It's an awful lot for her to process, on top of everything else that is going on."

"Yeah, but she's tough. She needs all the love she can get from all of you and she will make it through this."

Deciding to let her rest, they all spent the next hour getting everything ready to go for Sadie and Hazel, knowing they needed to hurry in order to get to the train station on time.

"As much as I want to help her through this, I know she is in good hands with both of you," Sawyer said to Henry.

"She will be okay, Sawyer. Thank you for everything you've done for them both. I think she just needs some time to heal and work through a few things, and then I'm sure she'll be back here in no time. She's been through a lot lately, and she needs to figure out what comes next. As much as we want to take the pain from her, we can't. She has to learn how to do that for herself, and I don't think she can truly love Ryder until she learns to trust and love herself."

After everything was packed up, Henry woke Sadie and helped her into the car. They headed to the train station in Chicago, hugging Sawyer and saying their tearful goodbyes. After boarding the train and finding their seats, Sadie still felt numb. How would she ever explain to her daughter that her father had died? Worse yet, how could she explain what he had tried to do to them just days before? Did she even have to? She didn't want Hazel to grow up with the same issues that Luke had caused in her… she wanted her to trust her mother, and if that meant sharing things that hurt, then so be it. She had to be honest with her, when she was old enough to hear those things. For now, she just wanted to sleep, so that is what she did.

* * *

Ryder was dog tired. His shift had been busy, and he'd gotten very little sleep. He couldn't wait for a shower and his own bed. He pulled his truck into the driveway and shut it off, considering just sleeping right there for a while, but opening the door and hopping out instead. The winter air was crisp and cold, taking his breath away for a moment. He slammed the door shut and trudged through the snow to his porch. He really needed to shovel his path, but that would have to wait. First, he needed a long, hot shower and a nap. Then, he'd shovel.

As he got to his door, Ryder noticed an envelope was stuck to it with a magnet. He grabbed the envelope and went inside, stripping off his jacket, hat & gloves, and putting his boots on the warmer. He walked over to the fireplace and put a few logs on, lighting it so it would fill his home with the kind of warmth only wood could produce. Sitting in his comfortable old recliner, he opened the envelope, instantly recognizing the writing inside as Sadie's. He unfolded the letter and slowly read it.

*Dear Ryder,*

*I'm not quite sure where to start, but I need to try to help you understand. This morning, Hazel and I left with my parents. I need some time to think everything through. So much has happened, and I'm having a hard time figuring out what comes next for us. Please understand that I need to protect her at all costs, even if it means that I put my happiness aside for hers. I know you are a good man, and I know that you aren't Luke, but I also know that he made lots of promises to me once too. I want so badly to trust you and to believe you, myself, and Hazel could be a family and could have a chance at happiness, but there's a part of me that just can't seem to let go of the fear that something will happen. I love you, and I know that Hazel does too. I just can't move in with*

*you, and I can't be with you, at least not now. I have to find a path for Hazel and myself, and as much as I want it to, that can't include you right now, or at least until I am sure it is what is best for Hazel and I. I hope you can forgive me, and I'm sorry from the bottom of my heart if this causes you more pain.*
*With All My Love,*
*Sadie*

# Chapter Nineteen

December in Seattle was often wet and gray.  It was the month that got the most rain, and very little snow, on average. This year, though, it was different.  This year had been dry, compared with most, and promised the possibility of some fluffy white flurries. Christmas Eve had seemed to come so quickly, and as Sadie looked out the window at her parent's home, she imagined the beautiful white wonderland that Sawyer and Travis must be looking at out their own window. She had been looking forward to that this year, and now, everything was messed up.  Nothing had gone as she had planned, yet again. She missed her friends so much, and she was looking forward to a call with Sawyer before they headed to church later.

Christmas Eve with her parents was a cozy and festive type of evening, with a delicious dinner, a warm fireplace, and a beautiful Christmas tree, filled with brightly-colored ornaments and handmade creations.  The fireplace in the family room was adorned with hand-quilted stockings her mother had made, one for each of them. There was garland hanging around the room, and little singing stuffed animals on the coffee table. Rose loved Christmas, and so did Sadie. It was a magical time, and she had missed the joy of Christmas over the last 5 years.

This year, she was excited to experience the magic of her family's Christmas with Hazel. Still, even being in this space, with her parents and her daughter, something was missing. If she was honest with herself, she could probably find the answer to what that was quite easily. She looked across the room, over to a table where Hazel was playing every game possible with Grandpa Henry. Their laughter warmed her heart. She was *so* thankful that her daughter was spending time with her grandparents, something Luke hadn't allowed when they were together. In the kitchen, her mother was making dinner, and Sadie's mouth was already watering just smelling the wonderful creations her mother was known for baking.

Seeing his daughter's forlorn face, Henry brought Hazel in to help her grandma with the baking so he could have a word with Sadie. He sat next to her, smiling his most comforting dad-smile. "What's on that beautiful mind, Sadester?" he asked, hoping she'd share with him.

"Nothing, Dad. I'm just thinking is all." she said, dismissing his concern.

"Sadie, I know you better than you think, so spill." he said, laughing softly.

"I am so happy to be here this year with you and Mom. I've missed this *so* much. It's just, something feels off, like something is missing I guess, you know?" she asked.

"Well, I am guessing you're thinking about Ryder, am I

right?" he asked, knowing her better than she realized.

Sadie nodded, "Yeah, I suppose you're right. I miss him so much, Dad. I hoped it would go away, but it is just getting worse," she said, sadness filling her face.

"Then why is it you are still here instead of there, with Ryder?" he asked.

"Dad, you know why! He lied to me. I want to trust him, and I understand why he did it, but what if he does it again? I don't think I can go through all of that again!" she said.

"Sweetheart, I love you with my whole heart, but I want you to listen to me. You are putting *way* too much pressure on that man. He is a man, plain and simple. He is going to mess up… we all do! I have hurt your mom more times than I wish to admit, but she's still here, and she still loves me. She has hurt me, too, and I've always forgiven her, and vice versa."

"I know that, but I need to protect Hazel."

"Sadie, he's not Luke. He never has been and never will be. You have to stop comparing him to Luke. That's not fair. If you keep doing that, you will never have a chance at a normal, fulfilling relationship, and that would break your mother and I's hearts. You deserve happiness, and Hazel deserves to see what happiness looks like." he said, hugging her close.

Sadie's eyes filled with tears, knowing her father was right, but not sure how to tell her brain and her heart to both believe it. "Oh, Daddy, I messed things up. I doubt he even wants me anymore. He asked me and Hazel to move in with him the night before we left. I never told you that, but he did. He told me how much he loved us both and that he wanted us to be together, and I just left, with nothing but a note. I didn't even say goodbye! I'm not sure if he could ever forgive me for hurting him like that," she cried, hugging her father close.

Henry gave her a squeeze and then put his hand to her chin, lifting her soaked eyes to his, "Little girl, that man loves you. He loves your happy and your crazy alike! He knows what you've been through. He's more patient than I am, that's for sure!" he laughed as she rolled her eyes.

"Very funny," she said, laughing softly.

"Sadie, you need to think very carefully about what you do next. You are the only one who has the power to forgive Luke for what he did to you and Hazel so that you can move on with your life. Your little girl deserves a mother who is happy and healthy, one who teaches her how to love and be loved. She needs you, and you deserve to forgive yourself, too. Until you do that, you won't ever be truly happy with Ryder." he said lovingly.

"I love you, dad," Sadie said, kissing her father on the cheek.

"I love you too, kiddo," he said back. "Now, how about we go eat some of that amazing food your mother has been working so hard all day to make us?" he said, grabbing Sadie's hand and leading her to the kitchen.

* * *

"Mommy, Mommy, wake up!" Sadie heard as she rubbed her eyes, trying to figure out if she was dreaming or awake. "Mommy, please get up! Santa came!"

Hazel came running to Sadie's bed, scaling the whole thing in one pounce. Sadie looked into her bright, excited eyes and smiled. "Merry Christmas, my sweet little girl!" she said, hugging Hazel.

"Merry Christmas, Mommy!" Hazel responded, "Can we please go open presents now? There are lots, Mommy!" she said.

"Yes, let's go brush our teeth in the bathroom first, and maybe make some sense of that mop you have on your head, and then we'll go check out that tree!" she said, leading Hazel to the bathroom. They both brushed their teeth and Sadie brushed and braided Hazel's hair quickly. Hazel was so excited that she could hardly sit still.

"Mommy, I got you a… oops, Grandma Rose told me it's secret!" she said, giggling.

"You and your grandmother sure do have a lot of little secrets!" she said, giving Hazel a little tap on the nose as she smiled mischievously.

Sadie laughed, giving Hazel a tickle before letting her down from the sink to grab her hand and lead her to the living room. She could hear her parents in the kitchen and could smell her mom's special Christmas cocoa heating on the stove. The smell reminded her of her childhood, and the familiarity of it made her feel safe and happy. She and Hazel joined them, each one making their cocoa the way they liked it, Sadie with whipped cream and shaved candy cane, and Hazel with whipped cream and marshmallows. She gave her mother a smirk as she added some sprinkles on top.

"Just to make it pretty, of course," Rose said as she winked at Hazel.

She was looking forward to calling Ryder later, after opening presents, so she could talk to him about everything that had happened, and hopefully about moving back there after the holidays. She had thought a lot about it after church last night, and she had made peace with many things. During church, the pastor had spoken about forgiveness and sacrifice, and she had felt he was speaking directly to her. She decided that it wasn't up to her to carry the weight of Luke's abuse any longer, that it was time she allows herself to move on and find happiness, for both her sake *and* Hazel's. She only hoped that Ryder would agree, and that he could forgive her, too.

"Mommy, look what Santa brought me! It's a new bike!" Hazel said from the living room, bouncing up and down with excitement.

"Wow! That is a very pretty bike! It's even yellow!" Sadie said, mirroring her little girl's excitement and awe. "And look, Hazel, it even has a spot for your doll to ride with you!"

"Tilly will love it! Ooh… Mommy… It has training wheels, too!" Hazel added. She'd been wanting a bike for months, and Sadie was elated that she loved it so much.

"Well, that Santa sure is a smart fella', huh?" Henry said, laughing as he walked into the room and saw his granddaughter's happy face. He began looking around the room, under pillows, behind the furniture, and under the blankets. His bewildered look peaked the little girl's curiosity.

"Grandpa, what are you looking for?" she asked.

"Well, I was just trying to find my matching bike! Where do you think Santa could have left it, anyway?" he asked, a playful grin on his face.

"Grandpa! Don't be silly, big people like you don't get yellow bikes! And Santa can't fit bikes big enough for you in his sack, either!" Hazel said, her innocence shining in her beautiful blue eyes as she took her grandfather seriously.

"Oh, well, I suppose that's true, cutie pie." he said as they all laughed while he pretended to think about it. "In that case, maybe we should see what else is under that tree!"

For the next hour, Hazel, Henry, Rose and Sadie opened their gifts from one another. For the first time since the fire, Sadie relaxed and felt truly happy. Her heart felt full, and she was so thankful for her parents and their loving embrace. They had always been there for her to fall back on anytime she'd slipped in life. She knew in her heart that they always would be, no matter how old she got. She also knew that she would be that sense of stability for her daughter, and she finally knew that the only way to do that for her was to be healthy and happy herself as well. Now, she only hoped that Ryder would be willing to give her another chance, because she loved him and wanted to spend the rest of her life with him.

"Mommy, did you hear me?" Hazel asked, pulling Sadie from her thoughts.

"Oh, I'm sorry sweetie, I didn't. Can you tell me again?"

"Yes," she giggled, "Grandma and Grandpa made me save the best present for last. It's for both of us! Can I open it, Mommy? Please??" she pleaded with her mother.

"Well, I would think you sure could! Where is it?" Sadie asked her excited little girl.

"Grandma, can I open it, please?" Hazel pleaded.

"Actually, this is one you and your mamma get to open at the same time, okay?" Rose asked, smiling at them both. "This gift is actually not from us, it's from Sawyer! She sent it and asked us to give it to you on Christmas morning."

Sadie should have guessed that Sawyer would do something sweet like that for them. She missed her so much. She couldn't wait to call her later and tell her all about their special Christmas morning here in Seattle, and about the peace she had made last night with the demons of her past. She knew

Sawyer would be stoked to hear that she was planning to come back to help her run the winery. This time, she was going there to stay.

Handing her a red envelope addressed to her and sealed with an adorable Rudolph sticker, Rose gave Sadie a hug, relaying Sawyer's message to her, "Sawyer made me promise to hand deliver this to you, the last gift of Christmas morning, and to make sure that I gave you a big hug too. So, here you go!" she said, giving her daughter a big hug.

Sadie sat in the rocking chair by the fireplace and carefully opened the envelope, finding a beautiful Christmas card inside. It had a photo of a log cabin tucked in the woods, with snow all around it. The sky in the photo was blue, with the moon lighting the snow and treetops. There was a tiny touch of glitter on the top of the cabin's snow-covered roof. Above it was a cute little poem about the peace found only at Christmastime. She smiled as she opened the card to find a handwritten message from Sawyer inside.

My Dearest Sadie-
I hope you are having an amazing Christmas with your family. I remember how special this holiday was to your mom, and I am sure it is just what you needed to help find your center again. I want you to know that we all hope you choose to return soon, we miss you terribly here! I sent a special package to your mom so she could give it to you and Hazel on Christmas morning. I hope you like it, and I hope it makes you both happy! You deserve every wonderful thing this world has to offer you, Sadie! I love and miss you! Merry Christmas!
Love,

## Sawyer

Sadie's eyes filled with tears; They were happy tears mixed with the sad tears you shed when you miss your best friend dearly. She wished she was here so she could give her a big hug. For now, though, a phone call and a promise of a hug in person soon would have to do.

She carefully folded the letter and placed it in the card. Standing, she set both on the table, and looked at Hazel, eagerly awaiting the present that was apparently waiting in the other room. She smiled at her, saying "Okay, we can go see what Sawyer sent to us now! You lead the way!"

Hazel didn't need to be told twice... she hopped up and ran into the other room, followed closely by her mother. Henry and Rose stayed behind a bit, allowing them to find their gift together. She heard Hazel squeal as she saw a large wooden dollhouse sitting in the middle of the room. It was beautiful, white with little yellow curtains on the windows and adorable mini furniture all about. There were even mini dolls for her to let her imagination run free with. She was ecstatic. Sadie laughed as she watched Hazel jump up and down and twirl around. She had never seen her so happy, and it warmed her heart for sure. Sawyer sure knew her way to Hazel's precious heart, that was for sure! As she watched her little girl playing with her gift, she felt her dad put his arm around her shoulder.

"Sweetie, that is the part of the gift that Sawyer sent for Hazel. Your half is in the front entryway. We'll keep Hazel occupied if you want to go grab it quick," he said, giving her a loving squeeze and a kiss on the forehead.

Sadie figured they wouldn't have to work too hard keeping Hazel occupied as she didn't seem to know anybody else in the world existed at that moment, so she agreed and sneaked out of the room quietly to go find her gift. She wondered what Sawyer could have possibly sent her. It was probably some of her favorite wine or something… she sure had missed her fruity blend of yumminess! As she turned the corner into the entry, she stopped, unable to move her feet one step farther. There, right in front of her, was Ryder. He was even handsomer than she had remembered, and she could smell his cologne from across the small space. He was smiling at her, and he had a stunning bouquet of roses in his hand, as well as a small gift.

"Merry Christmas, Sadie," he said, smiling with that mischievous grin, the one that she loved so much, covering his face.

She couldn't seem to form a word in response. She just stared at him, tears instantly filling her eyes. She couldn't believe he was there! Had Sawyer done this? Her parents? Was he *really* there, or was she just dreaming he was? If she could make her hand move, she'd pinch herself, but it didn't seem to want to function at the moment.

"I hope it's okay that I'm here… I don't want to-"

"Oh, Ryder!" she interrupted, her words finally finding their way to her mouth. Somehow, she willed her feet to move, and she closed the gap between them swiftly, flinging herself into his arms. She held on so tightly, she was afraid she'd hurt him. She felt his arms wrap around her as he set the flowers on the small stand near the door. Ryder's arms were warm and filled with love, giving her a sense of safety and calm. He cupped her chin with his hand, lifting her eyes to his, and placed a tender kiss on her lips. "Hello, my love," he said, need written all over his face.

"I'm so sorry, Ryder," Sadie said, hoping his presence here meant that he would forgive her for running off without talking to him first. "I acted so childish when I left. I was scared, and your offer was so sweet and made out of love for Hazel and I, but I panicked instead of receiving it the way I should have. All I can say is that I had been through so much, and my mind just wasn't at a place that could see things as they truly were quite yet."

Softly touching her cheek, wiping the tears that were slowly falling, he smiled. "Sweetheart, you have nothing to be sorry about. I should have known better than to spring it on you like that. I've reprimanded myself a good plenty since then, and I hopefully have learned a lesson in patience."

"Ryder, you are literally the most patient person I've ever met in my whole life!" she said, an awkward laugh escaping her throat.

"Well, I wasn't patient *then*! Especially since that was when you needed me to be the most patient! I'm sorry that I acted like that. You and Hazel are the best thing to every happen to me, and I can't imagine my life without you both in it. I love you, Sadie."

Ryder leaned into her then, pulling her into a kiss that made her knees feel like noodles under her. She reached her hands to run them through his soft curls, pulling them ever so softly to press his mouth into hers with urgency and need. When he broke the kiss, she could feel her breath getting heavy, her eyes looking deeply into his in a way that made his gut clench and his groin swell. He knew he had to stop before they did something very inappropriate in her parents' entryway.

"Uh, we had better leave it at that for now or we are going to have a predicament on our hands in front of your parents," he laughed. "I'd rather not have to answer to that one just yet, seeing how I just met them and all."

Sadie laughed, feeling the happiness rise from her toes, going all the way through her before escaping from her mouth. She had felt happy with Ryder before, but this was different. She was free now… free from blaming herself for everything. Sure, it would rear its ugly head now and again, and she supposed that was normal, but she knew how to calm those fears now, and she had this amazing man to thank for that. Whether he knew it or not, he was healing something inside of her, and she knew that with time, the fears and the self-blame would lessen, and the thought of that made her feel as though the vulnerability she had felt before was slowly leaving her. She was free to love this man with her whole heart, and she planned to do just that.

"I suppose we had better go in the other room and show Hazel what, I mean *who*, Sawyer sent us for Christmas. She's having a blast with that dollhouse, but somehow I think she'll like *this* gift even more. She's missed you very much, Ryder."

"I've missed her, too. I love that little girl like she's my own, Sadie. I hope you both know that." Ryder took Sadie's hand and followed her to the other room.

As they rounded the corner, Sadie saw the smile on her parents faces, and she returned the gesture. Those sneaky little devils… they knew all about this, and they had kept it from both she and Hazel all morning. She wasn't sure why it surprised her, but it still made her laugh that they were able to pull it off. Her father was notorious for letting things slip and not being able to keep secrets.

Sadie turned her attention to her little girl, who was still playing intently with her dollhouse. "Hazel, look what Sawyer sent us from Stone Creek…" she said, earning a sideways glance from Hazel.

"Ryder!" Hazel shouted, getting up from the floor and running into his arms. Ryder picked the little girl up and swung her in a circle, pulling her in close for a big hug. He closed his eyes, wanting to bottle this moment and keep it in his heart forever. "I missed you so much!" she said, clinging to him in a way that Sadie could totally understand, seeing how she had just done the same thing in the hallway.

"I sure missed you too, munchkin," he said, giving her a kiss on the forehead and pulling her out from him to look her over. "Boy oh boy, I think you grew a foot since I saw you last! What did your mom feed you, alfalfa?" he said, laughing.

"Nope!" Hazel said, laughing, "just pancakes, chicken nuggets, and basketti!" she said. "Oh, and chocolate milk too. Grandpa says it makes my bones strong."

"Well, your grandpa is a pretty smart guy!"

With that, he set Hazel down, telling her she could go back to playing with her dollhouse. He walked over to Rose, giving her a hug and telling her "Merry Christmas, and thank you for helping me to pull this off. I *definitely* owe you."

"Honey, you don't owe us a thing. Just make our little girl happy, that's all we ask," she said, hugging him. Behind his back, she gestured a thumbs up to Sadie, earning a loud laugh from her and a "Hey, I saw that!" from her dad.

The rest of the morning was a happy blur of joy that could only be made perfect by the magic of Christmas. They opened gifts from Ryder, as well as some others he had brought from many of their friends in Stone Creek. She sat by him on the sofa, holding his hand in hers and stealing glances his way whenever possible. She was so in love, a type of love she'd never felt before, and she couldn't believe how her life turned out. Only 6 short months ago, she was in a hospital bed after being beaten, and, other than to her daughter, had felt worthless to everyone. Now, she felt safe and loved, and she knew that this man would love both herself and Hazel the way they both deserved to be loved. She felt so very blessed.

"Oh Ryder, this is beautiful. Thank you!" Rose told him, giving him a hug after opening her gift from him. Smiling from ear to ear, she showed Sadie the beautiful bracelet he had gotten her. It was silver, with a little charm that said mom, and another that said grandma.

"You're welcome. I tried to find a *basketti* charm for it too, but there apparently isn't a big need for those, so I had to settle on the heart one that's next to the others," he said, laughing.

"Huh, who would have guessed there wasn't a big calling for that?" Rose replied, mirroring his laughter.

Hazel was next, elated as she opened a stuffed monkey that was bigger than she was. Of course, he had found a yellow dress with sparkles all over it to put on the monkey. The fact that she was pretty sure he had dressed it himself made Sadie laugh. When he saw her laugh, he leaned in and asked, "What's that for, ma'am?"

She whispered, trying to stop the laughter, "I just can't stop picturing you dressing that big monkey in a dress! How do you know it's a girl?" She couldn't help herself, she let the laughter roll, causing her parents to join in.

"Wow, you try to do a nice thing for someone, and this is what you get?" he asked, laughing playfully.

After the laughter settled, Ryder asked Hazel if she wanted help carrying the monkey to her bedroom. He picked it up and followed her, holding her tiny hand in his as she led him towards her room. While they were gone, Henry, Rose, and Sadie picked up the wrapping paper and ribbon that was thrown around the room.

"Sweetheart, you look so happy," Rose told her, stuffing a wad of paper into the garbage bag her father was holding for them. "We are sorry we didn't tell you about Ryder coming, but we really wanted it to be a surprise. I hope that was okay…"

"Yes, Mom, it's more than okay! Thank you to both of you for knowing my heart and knowing what I needed, as always," she said, pulling them both in for a hug. "Before all of this, I was actually planning to let you both know that I made a decision last night. Hazel and I are going to go back to Stone Creek. We are going to stay with Ryder, if he will still have us. I love him very much, and I know he loves both of us, too. It's time for me to leave my past in my past and chase my dreams again. I know it's a long way from home here in Seattle, but we'll visit often, I promise. I just have to do this for us, do you understand?" she asked hesitantly.

To her surprise, her dad's response was simple, "It's about time!" he said. "Honey, we knew you needed to do this on your own terms, and we couldn't be happier that you are deciding to move forward. Luke is gone, and what he did to both of you was wrong and so devastating. You can't keep thinking about that, though. You have to let that go, and I'm so glad to see that you are truly doing your best to do that."

"I love you guys so much," she said, tears threatening her eyes again. She wiped at them, adding, "Ah… you'd think I'd be out of these things soon!"

"We love you both dearly," her mother said, hugging her again before excusing herself to check on the tasty meal she was working on for lunch. Her father headed out the back door to throw the garbage into the dumpster they had behind their home.

Realizing that they had been gone for a while now, she headed towards Hazel's bedroom to see what she and Ryder were up to. Halfway there, she met them in the hallway, both of them wearing a grin that made her very suspicious of what they were up to.

"Sadie… Hazel and I have something we'd like to talk to you about, if that's okay?" Ryder asked, causing her to be even more curious of their motive.

"Okay… what's up?" she asked speculatively.

"Let's go in the living room so we can all get comfortable," he said, grabbing her hand and leading her to the rocking chair. As she sat, she saw Hazel looking at Ryder, giggling like a little schoolgirl who was up to something. She smiled, loving the look of her daughter interacting with Ryder. He was such a natural with her, like he had been in her life since the start, and that was one of the things she loved most about him.

"What are you two up to, anyway?" she asked, giving them both an investigative eye.

"Um… nothing…" Hazel said, giggling again and looking at Ryder, her hand over her mouth to keep whatever she wanted to say inside.

Reaching out to hold her hand, but keeping an arm around Hazel as well, Ryder spoke gently. "Sadie, I love you," he said. He turned to Hazel and added, "And Hazel, I love you, too, little bug." He gave her a loving squeeze, making her lay her head on his arm. The tenderness between the two was touching, and she felt her heart swell watching the interaction. "We love you, too, Ryder."

"To say I've missed you both would be an understatement.

I've spent the last month wondering what I was going to do if you didn't come back, and then I realized that I had to come here to convince you that we need each other. I want to spend *every* Christmas with you and Hazel. I want a life with you and Hazel in it, *each* and *every* day. I promise to do my best to always make you both feel safe and loved, and to make a home and a family with you."

Sadie smiled. Ryder had forgiven her, without her even having to ask. *This man is full of surprises*, she thought.

"Ryder, I want that too. I've done a lot of thinking, too, and I would like to move back to Stone Creek, and, if you'll still have us, we'd like to come live with you," she said, reaching out to run a hand down his cheek.

"Hazel and I just had a little conversation in the other room about that very thing!" he told her, smiling back at Hazel.

"Yes, can we please move back with Ryder, Mommy? Please?" Hazel begged.

"Yes, of course we can, sweetie," Sadie told her, giving her a hug when she jumped into her arms. Turning Hazel to sit on her lap, she looked at Ryder, amazed at how handsome he was, thankful that he had chosen her to love.

As she looked in his eyes, she realized something seemed different. Ryder was usually quite calm and cool, but right now he looked a little jumpy, like he was worried about something.

"Is that okay with you, Ryder?" she asked, tilting her head in curiosity over his sudden change in affect.

"Yes, I'd love nothing more than to have you two come back and live with me," he said, moving closer to her. "But I have to confess that I had something a little more than that in mind."

"What do you mean?" she asked, confused.

"Hazel, can you give mommy that gift I gave you in the other room?" he asked her, nodding his approval.

Hazel smiled at Sadie, pulling out a little box from a pocket in her pajamas. Handing it to Sadie, she sweetly asked, "Mommy, can we marry Ryder?"

Sadie sat for a moment, staring at the little box her daughter had handed her, trying to let the words Hazel had just asked process in her brain. She looked at Ryder, tears filling her eyes, and noticed that his were full as well.

"Sadie, would you please consider making me the happiest man on this planet by marrying me?" he asked her, holding her knees with his hands as he looked into her eyes.

"Please, Mommy?" Hazel added, begging in an innocent way that only a child can.

She looked back at the little box in her hand. It was small and wrapped in a golden foil wrapping paper, with a ribbon tied on top. She slowly opened the box, as if whatever was inside may jump out at her. Her heart caught in her chest as her eyes landed on the ring inside. It was stunning. It had a beautiful diamond in the middle, with small diamonds all around it, forming a circle. She looked at Ryder again, allowing the tears to fall.

She took a deep breath, trying to find the words that would show him exactly how she felt at this very moment. All she could find were, "I want nothing in this world more than I want to marry you, Ryder."

Amidst the cheers coming from Hazel, as well as Rose and Henry who had apparently peeked in to see what was going on, Ryder placed the ring on Sadie's finger, picking her up and spinning her in his arms, kissing her on the lips in front of everyone. She could get lost in this man's kiss, and she couldn't wait for a lifetime of this feeling. In that moment, she realized that she had found home, and now that she had found peace inside herself, she was able to see that, in Ryder's arms, she felt truly safe. She could feel his heart beating in sync with hers, a surge of love filling her heart and telling her that everything was going to be okay.

Sadie turned and picked Hazel up, giving her a hug and a kiss and telling her how much she loved her. She couldn't wait to call Sawyer, to tell her that she was coming back to Stone Creek, and that she was going to marry Ryder. Her life was spiraling, but this time it was from happiness, not fear. If she was lucky, it would never end.

Turning towards Ryder again, she kissed him, eliciting a giggle from the little girl in her arms. Looking in his eyes, she knew they were going to be okay. She couldn't wait to start her life with the man she had grown to love.

For the first time in her life, she was pushing out the fear, and instead, she was *trusting her heart.*